Rafferty Lincoln Loves...

Emily Williams

There is nothing so good for the inside of a man as the outside of a horse. — John Lubbock, 1894

RAFFERTY LINCOLN LOVES…

First published in Great Britain in 2018 by
Lutino Publications

Paperback ISBN 978-0995742116

Lutino Publications
lutinopublications@yahoo.com

Rafferty Lincoln Loves...

A note on the author

Emily Williams lives by the seaside in West Sussex with her family and a large menagerie of small pets. After graduating from Sussex University with a BA in Psychology, Emily trained as a primary school teacher and teaches in a local school. **Rafferty Lincoln Loves...** is her second novel. Her debut novel Letters to Eloise was published earlier in the year to great success.

For more information about Emily and her upcoming novels, please follow her on Twitter @EmilyRMWilliams. Please leave a review for **Rafferty Lincoln Loves...** The author loves to hear your thoughts and views.

Foreword

It is fantastic to see a contemporary novel for young adults embracing passion and love for horses, as well as advocating for their welfare. I remember a childhood spent dreaming of horses so it was fascinating to be back with a teenage perspective again. The novel, therefore, appeals to both the young and not-so-young adults alike.

As the ambassador for the British Thoroughbred Retraining Centre (BTRC), I am delighted that the novel, *Rafferty Lincoln Loves…* will support this dedicated charity for the welfare of retired racehorses.

With a successful career in racing spanning many years, I have been extremely fortunate to work with the most magnificent of Thoroughbred horses, including the lovely bay stallion, Authorized. This remarkable horse helped me to succeed in my first win at one of Britain's most prestigious races, the Epsom Derby.

Thanks to the tireless work of the BTRC, retired racehorses can excel in many other fulfilling careers such as show jumping, polo and dressage.

Author Emily Williams, a horse owner herself, expertly weaves her love and knowledge of equines throughout this poignant novel, which centres on four disparate teenagers and the missing racehorse, Profits Red Ridge. Emily's fast-paced novel not only explores the relationship and incredible bond between horse and rider but also delves into darker aspects relevant to today's challenging world of growing up.

The novel took me straight back to my horse loving teenage years and now, with teenage children myself, I can certainly be sympathetic to the humorous dilemmas of the lead character, Rafferty Lincoln. I remember the days spent riding Sylvia, my childhood palomino pony, with great fondness. I was lucky to have more talent than Rafferty when astride my pony, despite us coming last in our first ever pony race. The laugh-out-loud moments in this novel ease you through a turbulent but beautifully written tale of love and loss.

A special thanks to Emily for writing this accomplished novel for a charity dear to my heart. *Rafferty Lincoln Loves...* deserves to be celebrated for bringing an important cause to the forefront of today's young adults.

**Frankie Dettori MBE, Ambassador for the
British Thoroughbred Retraining Centre**

The British Thoroughbred Retraining Centre

'For the Welfare, Rehabilitation, Retraining and Rehoming of Retired Racehorses'

The proceeds from the novel 'Rafferty Lincoln Loves…' will be donated to **The British Thoroughbred Retraining Centre.**

BTRC is dedicated to improving and promoting the welfare of retired racehorses through education, retraining and suitable rehoming in order to ensure that our Thoroughbreds have a rewarding and valuable life after their racing careers have ended.

Each year thousands of horses leave racing, some because they reach the natural end of their career and others through injury or lack of ability. Established in 1991, The British Thoroughbred Retraining Centre was the UK's first charity dedicated to ex-racehorse welfare, retraining, rehoming and protection for life.

'I am thrilled to have written this novel for the BTRC and to be donating the proceeds to such an important and dedicated charity for the welfare of retired racehorses.' **Emily Williams**

For Dad —
who, inadvertently, can be blamed for
my love of horses

Prologue

Champion Racehorse missing after fatal car accident on the A5 from Shropshire

A motorist has been killed and another critically injured in a head-on crash between a car and a horsebox.

A horse was also killed and champion racehorse Profits Red Ridge, who was travelling in the trailer with two other horses, is missing.

Police are investigating how the accident occurred, but witnesses said that the car veered across the road into the horsebox, causing it to overturn.

The driver of the car was pronounced dead at the scene.

Witnesses also said they saw two of the horses escape the wreckage, but sadly the third died from strangulation at the scene.

Locals found one of the horses and are keeping him safe until his owners can be with him.

However the thirteen-times winner Profits Red Ridge's whereabouts are currently unknown, but police have started a search for the missing racehorse.

The police have issued a statement asking the public for any information on the missing horse, which has been described as a '16.3hh Red Bay Gelding, with three white socks, and a star, strip and snip marking'.

If you have any information about how this accident happened, or the location of Profits Red Ridge, you can contact the West Mercia police or your local station.

The investigation continues.

Chapter One

The endless, head splitting pips from the alarm clock rang out, piercing into my fuddled sleeping brain. It was far too early in the morning. Four pips in a row, over and over again until, with a foggy mind and clenched first, I leant over and slammed the clock into silence. The little square of plastic jumped off the bedside table, split in two, and disappeared beneath the heaped clothes on the floor. Clothes piled ready for mum to wash hopefully.

I groaned and rubbed my reddening fist with the palm of my other hand, then swung my legs out of the bed. A bed barely contained my growing and somewhat lanky frame.

5 a.m.

I sat for a few seconds, head wrapped in my hands and ruffling my messy hair. I tried to clear the usual morning haze from my skull, before shaking some sense into my head, and leaping into action. Within minutes, I had thrown on a pair of shorts and a T-shirt and headed out the door, grabbing my faded and slightly rusty BMX from the garage. Dad had promised me a new, bigger one for my last birthday, but his promises didn't mean much most of the time.

I shivered as goose bumps raised the hairs on my arms. The mornings were still cool, only being April, as summer hasn't properly arrived. But like most others, I refuse to believe it hadn't come and the winter clothes have all gone. It had been so nice recently I had begun to tan already.

Looking back, I always wondered who saw whom first. Did the horse already know I was approaching from the rhythmic whirring of my wheels as I free-glided down the hill, or did I see the horse first, grazing on the grass verge down the dip in the narrow country lane?

Either way, as I skidded up onto the embankment, the horse snorted, threw back his head, and backed into the road blocking my path. The huge brown arse and flying hooves skittered about on the gravel. The pebbles sprayed up, pelting at the bike's metal frame and pitting the paintwork. I threw the bike down onto the grass and stepped towards the horse, hands out wide, like a cowboy. It didn't appreciate my effort.

This wasn't what I had bargained for. I hadn't even made the first house. I chucked my bag over towards my crumpled bike, the newspapers spilling out and flapping in the breeze and tried again. The horse snorted and tossed its head into the air, eyes rolling and showing white.

Him, her, I wasn't sure yet. I couldn't see any evidence to show either way, nothing swinging under there. I tried to get another glance under the horse's belly but it gave a little whine, its front legs rising a little off the road. Its nose was huge and pulsating like a vein.

We stared at each other. Two pairs of eyes waiting for the first move. I don't know how long we stood frozen, but the horse's huge black eyes glanced away first, behind me, before I noticed another bike approach from behind.

'What's going on?' a boy, possibly a couple of years younger than me, hollered. The horse danced on the spot and then backed up the lane at his voice. 'I need to get through. That your horse?'

'Does it look like my horse?' I shook my head at him and narrowed my eyes. He, too, eyed me up and down, his eyes squinting at me through the low sun on the horizon.

'No, it doesn't,' he grinned, showing crooked teeth. I recognised him, mainly through the rumours whirling around the canteen at school, rather than from an actual encounter. His hair ruffled wildly around his face as though he'd just woken up. 'But I do need to get past.'

'So do I,' I nodded at his newspaper bag and over at mine, with the flyaway pages strewn on the wet morning grass. 'We'll both get our heads bitten off if we go back without this lot delivered. Presume you deliver from Bill's shop, too.'

'Yeah. Any ideas then?' he asked. The horse, bored by our conversations, had returned to graze by the side of the narrow lane, keep a large beady eye on us as it snatched hungrily at the damp grass. The hawthorn hedges were high, trapping us in. 'Can't we sneak past it?'

'Tried that,' I told him. 'Spooks easy, that one.'

'Then scare it off?'

'You go first then.'

'You're the oldest and biggest,' he grinned again, sliding down off the bike and throwing it roughly to the ground. 'You go first.'

I don't think I had ever seen him smile at school. Usually, he would shuffle into the canteen with his head down, alone, collect his food from the counter, and disappear. Most days, he wouldn't appear at all; then the whispers would start. He was small for his age, skinny even, with dirty blond hair needing a good trim and always covering his eyes. Come to that, I don't think I'd even heard him speak before. Just whimpers and squeals when the sixth formers had cornered him. We all turned our backs. I shook off the shame beginning to creep over me.

We stared in silence at the horse grazing. Its lips twisted as it bared its large teeth and tugged at the long blades. A black heap of hair ran down through its ears. I blew air through my mouth up into my nose making a puffing sound and shuffled my feet, scraping at the gravel. Dad hates me doing that, acting like a bored teenager, which I am usually.

I debated turning home, time was getting on and the bus came through the village at half seven. If I missed it, the hour walk over the hills would give me a slightly red, sweaty, and frustrating start to the day, which I have had many an experience of. Worse still, I'd be late for register and then have to join the riff raff of detention kids after school. Most of whom were there for bad language or fights in class.

'Come on,' the boy said, at last, turning his bike back up towards the hill. 'Let's ditch the newspapers somewhere and go. The horse isn't moving.'

I frowned, 'We can't do that.'

'Watch me,' he answered matter-of-factly over his shoulder as he pushed the bike back up the steep hill. I shook my head but followed, pushing the wet and probably ruined papers back into my bag and yanked the bike up. The horse pricked up its ears with interest as we turned our backs on it and plodded up the incline. It wasn't worth the energy cycling.

'It's following us,' he remarked. I glanced behind at the crunch of hooves following our bikes and footsteps. Every time we turned, the horse immediately stopped, backed up a few steps, and looked at us wide-eyed. As we walked on again, it would lower its head almost nodding, and then follow. It became a game, until near the top, finally the boy grew irritated and tired, and turned to charge at the horse yelling, more angrily than needed, 'Piss off, will you?'

With surprise, the horse threw back its head, raised up off its front legs and charged back down the hill, kicking out its long back legs and rocking like a bronco from the fairground.

'Problem solved,' he said, solemnly, and turned back again.

I stood and watched the horse, which stood quivering all over at the bottom of the hill, ears pricked and staring back up at us. It didn't feel right, just leaving it there, but I knew nothing, I mean nothing, about horses. I am not sure I even like them, big hard hooves and teeth tearing holes in your arm.

No thanks.

Bikes, basketball, and computer games for me, and sometimes girls if I am lucky. Not that I am, but there is always a chance my luck could change. There was nothing I could do so, resigned, I turned back up the hill again. The boy had disappeared ahead. I puffed my way alone to the top.

By the time the hill flattened out, with fences and farmers' crop fields on either side, the sun had swung up into the sky and morning was in full force, burning the mist from the valleys away. I glanced at my watch.

Oh, complete bollocks.

Time had passed quickly and usually by now, I would be looping my way home back along another track, having reached the two furthest houses on my round. I don't remember any other houses this way, or any other rounds from Bill's shop for that matter, so I had no idea where the boy had been heading.

'Here he is.'

I turned to the voices coming up ahead of me. The boy cycling side by side with another, much closer to my age than the other, were coming back towards me.

'What's going on?' I asked.

'Will was coming this way too,' the boy nodded at Will, who eyed me from beneath his glasses. He seemed smaller up close. Maybe not as similar in age as I thought. 'But I told him not to bother. He wanted to see for himself. So see, down there. There it is. A horse. Now we can all go.'

'I know you,' I said, screwing my eyes up, then looking at Will and pointing a finger.

'I… I… don't think so,' replied Will. He looked nervous, not meeting my eye, unlike the other boy, who didn't seem to care, even though he was the one usually taking a battering from the other kids at school. He had an aura about himself away from school. Will just looked shit-scared.

'What's your name?' I asked.

'Will,' he stuttered.

'No,' I slammed my palm into my forehead. 'Not your first name, your surname.'

'Wilbur Ashburn.'

'Ah,' I said.

'Liberty,' the boy and I breathed in unison, my voice floaty and soft and his, harsh with scorn attached. I smiled at him, ignoring the tone, and resisted the urge to jinx. Even in these circumstances, school social standing stood. I am surprised he hadn't acknowledged the school situation or shown some slight reservation towards me.

But he hadn't; not one bit.

'My sister?' Will asked, puzzled.

'Your sister,' I sighed, loudly. There was nothing else to say. His sister was Liberty Ashburn.

My idol.

'She's at home,' he said, even more confused. 'Is that your horse?'

'No, why does everyone think it's my horse?'

'Just asking,' Will replied. 'Bumped into… Dexter, wasn't it? Bumped into Dexter on my way home from my paper round and he said you were here with a horse.'

'Is this your way home?' I asked, knowing full well this wasn't the way to Liberty Ashburn's house.

We all knew the way to her house. Had stood outside looking up trying to guess which one was her window; trying to picture her bedroom with its soft silk sheets. We all wanted an invite to her summer barbeque in the garden. I'd had an invite last year with the basketball team but, still only fifteen at the time, Mum wouldn't let me go. I made up some excuse about ball practise. Liberty and her group of friends hadn't acknowledged me since. I had been relegated to less than the friend zone. The non-existent zone.

'Where are you going? This is the wrong way to get to school.'

'Short cut home,' replied Will. 'There's a footpath up the other side of the dip, takes me back along behind the estate. It's too narrow to cycle though, so I have to push the bike. Knee deep in nettles now, so no use for you,' he nodded at my shorts and bare, becoming slightly hairy, legs. 'And you're not from my estate, though, are you?'

'Hate to break this up,' said Dexter, 'but it's nearly seven already. We'll not be making our bus. Not that I care.'

I don't remember Dexter ever being on the bus. In fact, I don't remember him being around school much at all recently.

'What about the horse?' asked Will. 'Shouldn't we get someone? It looks lost.'

The horse had recovered from the shock of Dexter's chasing and had plodded up the hill towards us.

'Leave it,' said Dexter.

'Maybe we should get someone,' I said, doubtfully.

'I could get my sister,' Will said, shrugging his shoulders in defeat. 'But our house is a couple of miles back. Can't get past the horse to get to the short cut so it'll take a while. We'll be late for school.'

'Liberty,' I breathed.

'Yes, Liberty,' said Will, pushing his glasses further back onto his nose. 'She goes horse riding and everything. Well she used to, she'll know what to do.'

'Let's go,' I said, jumping onto my bike and following behind Will. I called over my shoulder, 'Bye, Dexter, see you around school…maybe.'

'Bye?' Dexter asked. 'Don't be a dick, I'm coming, too.'

Chapter Two

Liberty.

I couldn't believe I was standing in Liberty Ashburn's house. And there she was. Wet black hair, scraped up high with some kind of clip, and her body freshly washed from the shower. The peachy smell and everything, all wrapped in a white towelling dressing gown.

Liberty is the girl at school everyone wants to be friends with. The one everyone is nice to, in case, one day, she will acknowledge their existence. And as far as I know, or imagine, she's nice, too, unlike some of the other popular but more mean girls. Don't get me wrong, I'm not unpopular and have my fair share of girls trying to get my attention, just nothing in Liberty's league. I sound shallow, but that's what school is like. It's all a league thing.

She wasn't quite as enthusiastic to see us.

'Get out my way,' she barked at Will. She stopped and stared at Dexter. 'What's he doing here?' Then, she swooped across the landing from the bathroom, on those long legs glistening with water, and slammed her bedroom door behind her. 'And stop your gawping.' A wet trail followed behind her from the bathroom.

'Are you okay?' asked Dexter. 'You look like you've pissed yourself. Or worse.'

I turned and punched him on the arm, slightly harder than I intended. He looked wounded for a second, before bouncing back. He glanced back at his watch, which had thin plastic straps, looked cheap, and probably was a hand-me down. He seemed nervous about time-keeping. 'Come on, Romeo, let's get going. Waste of time, this.'

'No,' urged Will, blocking our path. He held out his hand towards us, willing us not to leave; pleading up at us both. 'She will help. Promise. She's just a bit cool in the mornings.'

'Cool? She's practically an ice cube,' I muttered. 'I thought she was nice, too. I was wrong.'

'Libby,' Will knocked on the door gently. 'Libby, please can I talk to you? It's important.'

'Fuck off,' came her sharp reply. 'To both you, and your friends. I'm getting dressed. Go to school and leave me alone.'

'Please Lib, we're… desperate. Really, really desperate.'

'Desperate,' Liberty poked her head around the door curiously. 'Desperate for what? If it's drink or drugs or anything like that, boys, you're wasting *your* time. You know Mum and Dad will kill me if I corrupt you with my wayward behaviour. Anyway, Will, you are far too young and boring. Rafferty on the other hand,' she paused, looked me up and down and smiled. I blushed annoyingly, red creeping onto my cheeks. She bit her lip and winked. 'Rafferty Lincoln, I've heard all sorts of rumours about you.'

I tried to wink back. 'Call me Raff.' My reply came out a little too quickly, and too rehearsed. 'The rumours are all true.' I tried to keep my voice light and steady but failed miserably.

'Hmmm, Raff,' she replied softly, 'I doubt that.' She closed the door on us, clearly bored already. I slouched in defeat. I'd come across like a moron. I may get all the attention at school, but when it matters, I always get it wrong.

'Come on,' I said, pulling at Dexter's scrawny arms. 'You were right, she is a waste of time. The bloody horse can do one and find its own way home.'

'Horse?' The door opened again. She had taken off her dressing gown and stood peering around in her bra and school leggings. I didn't know where to look. My head began to swirl excitedly. I could make out the black rose pattern on the fabric. I clenched my buttocks, not sure why, but it helped.

Stay calm, I told myself. Any false move and one big fat rumour would make it around the school and ruin my social life forever. No girl would look twice again. People would snigger as I passed. Rather like what happens to Dexter on a daily basis whenever he turns up to school.

'Yes a horse,' said Dexter, butting in. 'Big, stupid brown fucker down Petersfield Lane.'

I winced at his words. I can swear, you know I can swear, but somehow it felt crass in her presence. I don't swear at home, mum would kill me, so when I slip a word or two into the conversation it's either with complete anger, or forced and deliberate to appear cool. I will make an effort not to anymore. I needn't have worried, Liberty ignored Dexter's words anyway and turned to me.

'In a field?' she asked. 'I don't know of any horses down Petersfield Lane, or anywhere in the area.'

'No, it's blocking the lane. I couldn't do my paper round.' I felt properly stupid and about thirteen, not sixteen, well, nearly seventeen, as the words came out. Who still does a paper round at sixteen? I just like the freedom of having a job which doesn't involve talking to anyone. So I can daydream. Mainly about Liberty, but I won't mention that.

'A horse,' she said again, slowly. I could see her eyes light up at this, blue and twinkly. 'You've found a horse?'

'It's lost,' said Will, waving his arms, excited his sister was finally engaging in our news. His glasses lurched precariously off his nose and he steadied them with a finger. 'Scary horse though, wouldn't move out of our way. But it followed us up the lane for a bit.'

'Until Dexter scared if off,' I said. Dexter looked up at me and shrugged.

Liberty grabbed my arm tightly and my heart fluttered with happiness.

'Show me.'

School attendance now abandoned, we set off back through the village towards the country lanes. Towards Petersfield lane. Liberty had flung a black top and pale grey hoodie over her bra — the gorgeous patterned bra.

We arrived at the top of the hill and looked down into the dip, now cleared of the early morning mist. The valley lay empty bar the sound of birds.

'Where's the horse?' asked Liberty.

'Gone,' we said.

'That's obvious,' she replied. 'Where was it?'

'There,' we pointed to the empty road ahead.

I couldn't help but feel the disappointment flood through my body. Not because the horse had gone, but because the adventure maybe over already. The chance to spend a few more minutes with Liberty slipping slowly from my grasp before it had even started. The first and only time she'd ever touch me. I had already fast forwarded to our first kiss on her soft lips, but the giant bubble of dreams popped with a loud resounding bang.

'Well, great, this was a giant waste of time,' she spat at us angrily. 'And now I'll get a detention for being late for school, and so will you lot, which means, even more trouble from the parents for me. Fabulous.' Liberty shook her head, her black mane in the ponytail whipping around her shoulders. She turned to leave, pulling her mountain bike around in a circle and glancing back at us. 'Pathetic, childish trick, boys. Hope you're proud.'

We stared down the valley in silence, as her wheels crunched through along the lane behind us. Dexter looked up at me, raising his shoulders up in a shrug. Will stared ahead, his sharp face grim and determined. He continued to stare, eyes becoming round and wide.

'What's up?' I asked.

'Shhh,' he whispered back. 'Listen.'

I strained my ears but heard nothing. Maybe the odd tweet of a bird in the bushes around us, and some birds dotted about in the high hedgerow lining the lane. A cow mooing… maybe. I dunno. I'm not the country type.

'Listen,' he urged, leaning forward on his bike. 'Over there.' He pointed down to the other side of the dip. The lane rose back up again and disappeared into dense woodland.

I could hear a faint whine.

'It's the horse,' Dexter joined in, excitedly. 'It's still there!'

I thought for a second about my priorities. At this point, I couldn't care less about horses but there was one thing I cared about. 'Well don't stand there,' I urged. 'Go back and get your sister. NOW!'

My booming voice startled him and he hurriedly spun his bike around and pelted back down the road towards the distant figure of Liberty.

A pert bottom and head of black hair pedalling off into the distance.

Chapter Three

Liberty leapt to action at once. We watched in awe as she barked orders, and we raced around like worker ants to fulfil them. There didn't seem to be an agreed plan, except Liberty was in charge, and we were to follow her every command. It was as if her life-long pony-owning ambition had come true.

Hoarded equipment, unused lead ropes, head collars, (she named the equipment for me) and brushes, lovingly stored in plastic boxes, were dragged out and spread over her bed. Along with dozens and dozens of backdated pony magazines and hordes of horse-related books. All of this sprung out of her small wardrobe.

Will was left behind at the top of the lane in charge of watching the horse. He looked frightened at the idea, with his eyes huge behind his glasses and knees trembling. He tugged at the grass from the verge and flung it at the horse, who snorted, ignored his offerings completely, and tore at its own grass.

'Just don't let him move,' Liberty told Will. 'Keep him in this valley.'

'Him?' I asked.

'Yes, him,' Liberty scoffed. 'Didn't you know it was a him?'

'No.' There wasn't much else I could say. My ignorance in horse matters was obvious.

Her room now gleamed like a horse shop cavern. Beside the red lipstick marks on the Justin Beiber posters, and the make-up table cluttered with what I thought were lipstick tubes and perfume bottles, there was subtle evidence of her pony-mad days. I picked up a little horse ornament off the window ledge and turned it over in my hand, cool, hard and smooth.

'Don't touch,' she said, and frowned.

I was startled by her sudden voice, the brass horse nearly slipping from my grip. I gave her a wry grin and steadied the horse in my hand. With exaggerated carefulness, I returned it to its position on the ledge. I tapped the little horse on its back.

'Cute,' I remarked, and moved away.

I've never been in a girl's room. That may shock you. I know I come across as confident but it is an image I portray to survive school. It's not the actual truth. I've NEVER been in a girl's room. Except for my little sister's room and she doesn't count. She's a child. It's like a treasure trove in Liberty's room. I want to touch and sniff everything. Okay, maybe not sniff — actually, yes — but you probably don't want to hear that.

Her room is so the total opposite of mine. It's neatly organised with books piled on her desk and an array of pink frilly things all around, like a sweet shop of delights to see and touch. I kept my hands firmly in my pockets to avoid the risk of touching something I shouldn't, again. My palms sweated slightly.

Liberty had finished delving into the back of her wardrobe. An entire wardrobe dedicated to horse-related items had tumbled out, including tight riding clothes for Liberty to wear — I forced myself not to picture her in them — and a shiny patterned riding hat. Everything shone new.

There were no horsehairs on the brushes, or mud on the clothes, or a speck of anything.

'It's all new,' I remarked, stating the obvious.

'Yes,' she answered shrugging, and didn't elaborate.

'Why's it not been used?' I probed.

'Didn't have a pony.'

'And you didn't get one?'

'Nope. None of us did.'

'Why not?'

'We all thought someday our parents would give in to the desperate pleas and see us girls were knowledgeable and responsible enough to own a horse. But they never did.'

'Why?'

'Guess they didn't have the thousands in the bank we all thought. So all the equipment collected was stored away. Think Tilly managed to use some of her stuff at the stables she worked at for a bit. I had riding lessons for a couple of years, but that was all. Learnt most of it from reading.' She gestured at all the books littering the bed.

'Sucks,' I said, and whistled. I screwed up my eyes, trying to picture her friend Tilly. The girl always hanging around in Liberty's shadow. Shorter, mousier maybe and that's about all I could picture. She faded in comparison to her friend. I smiled as I pictured Liberty, hair loose on her shoulders as she sat on top of the canteen table, talking animatedly to her gathered friends.

Like bees around honey.

Liberty looked at me sharply as I pondered. 'It's not funny.'

'I didn't say it was,' I said. 'Just thinking how dedicated you all were. And it was for nothing. Feel sad for you all.'

Good comeback, I praised myself.

'It's the same for about a million girls. Some were lucky enough to actually get near a horse, and others weren't. I wasn't. I can only imagine the thousands spent on horse brushes, buckets, lead-ropes and hay nets, never to get used.'

'Shed loads,' I laughed.

'Probably. Someone should collect them all up for horse charities. I bet there is endless pony stuff in girls rooms around the country and less than a handful of it will ever get near a horse.'

'Well, this is your chance then. To get your shiny new equipment near a horse.'

'Yep,' she replied, nodding at me eagerly. 'As long as we don't fuck this up. So you boys need to do what I say.' She flung the last of the bits into her backpack, determinedly, grabbed a half-opened packet of spearmints off the bedside table, and headed towards the door. 'Coming?'

I nodded and scrambled after her.

Liberty took a while to calm Will down. He spoke too fast, stuttering as he tried to tell us what had happened.

'Slow down,' she squatted down to his height, with both hands on his shoulders and shook him hard. 'What happened?'

'It wasn't my fault,' he wailed, lowering his head. Floppy, brown, curly hair fell down over his glasses.

'Get a grip idiot,' Dexter barked. 'Just tell us.'

'Don't shout at him,' Liberty's voice was stern and commanding. For once Dexter listened and was silent. 'Go on, Will, tell us.'

'The horse was eating the grass nicely for a while. I got bored so I sat on the grass whilst it grazed.'

'He,' Liberty corrected. I frowned at her and gestured for Will to continue.

'Then *he* spooked at something. Thought he was going to run me over. He came really fast, but then he skidded on his legs and turned back towards the other side of the valley. That's when I heard it.'

'What?' I asked.

'A tractor was coming.'

'Oh shit,' Liberty whispered, her dreams evaporating along with, although different ones, mine also. 'Did the driver see the horse?'

'No, the tractor hadn't come over the top of the hill, but the noise was horrible. I didn't know tractors were so loud and grindy. Metal scraped along the gravel.' He shuddered.

'Where's the horse?'

'I panicked,' Will sobbed, his shoulders heaving. 'When the horse saw the top of the tractor, he came running back at me. I didn't want him getting past me and along the lane to the village, so I tried to scare him.'

'How?' Dexter asked.

'I flung my bike in the way. So he turned back towards the tractor and panicked even more. The horse then turned sideways and jumped the bloody hedge. Right up and over it. The hedge is taller than you, Rafferty. Like this big,' he gestured with his arm trying to stretch up as tall as he could. 'How did he do that?'

Chapter Four

The sun had already slid down behind the horizon as, dirty and bedraggled, we set back off towards home.

To face the music.

Liberty had successfully managed to text an excuse home earlier in the day, something about homework club and picking up Will from a friend on the way back. Other friends had covered for them in class. They were both off the hook.

I knew I hadn't been as lucky. I never take my mobile on my paper round. Too worried it would slip out of my pocket.

A rookie error I won't make again.

I hadn't been home since I left for my paper round in the morning. Dexter seemed unconcerned about the consequences. As we reached the crossroads and said our goodbyes, Liberty swore us to secrecy. No Facebook posts, internet searches, no messages, emails or texts, anywhere mentioning even a whiff of horse. Spoken in fierce whispers with a few threats thrown in, we all nodded at her. Too tired to argue, we shook hands in agreement, waved, and went our separate ways.

I listened half-heartedly to the earful from Dad as I slid down onto the top step on the staircase, leant my head on the banister, and waited it out for him to finish. He was clearly reading from a script Mum had designed. The conversation was far too calm to be his own words.

Then, agreeing to whatever consequences they'd given me, I pulled myself upstairs and still fully dressed I slid into bed, relieved.

The horse tracks had been easy to follow. After we'd lifted each other over the slightly flattened hedge, the trail across the long dewy grass led into a woodland at the far end. We tucked our bikes into the hedge, hidden on the other side from the road, and set off with our backpacks. Dexter followed each footprint with exaggerated steps.

'He must have been running,' he said touching the flattened shafts of grass.

'Cantering or galloping,' Liberty corrected.

'Whatever,' Dexter replied, and danced over to the next print, his hair whipping around in the wind. He touched the print and sniffed his fingers. Clearly, he watched too much Bear Grylls.

'Where to next, Mr Grylls?' I asked him. He looked up at me with a blank expression on his face and then continued his dance, squatting and waving his hands over the tops of the grass.

'Don't waste your time on him,' Liberty said.

'He's alright,' I replied, feeling slightly protective of the odd kid whose life must suck at school.

'Don't get too close,' she warned. 'He's not very popular.'

'Why?' I asked curiously.

'He's odd.'

'Yeah so am I,' I grinned at her, and it made my heart lurch when she grinned back too.

'Yes you are,' she smiled. 'Very odd.'

'Being odd is no excuse. I have friends.'

'You're different,' she said slowly. 'You're popular because you're different.'

'Different how?'

'Different,' she smiled. 'But you still do the normal stuff like your basketball and playing games with the others online. Saves you from complete oddness. I don't think he does any of that.'

'But that's not enough.'

'Enough?'

'Enough to deserve the beating he gets.'

'Guess he's unlucky.'

'I don't buy it,' I said. 'There's got to be more.'

'Just leave it alone,' she warned. 'It's not worth getting yourself into trouble for someone like him.'

'Someone like him?'

'Leave it,' she repeated, tucking her hair behind her ears, clearly flustered. I didn't press her further. After all, did I care about Dexter and his issues? No. So I left it and changed the subject. Well, ended the subject. I flicked her shoulder playfully, and raced off after Will and Dexter, who were entering the woodland ahead.

After another three hours of travelling around in circles, just as we began to despair, we heard a high-pitched whine again and turned our path towards it. The thick woodland spanned about three square miles of dense, uncurling bracken, brambles tearing at my bare legs, and larger gaps where grass managed to push its way through.

The horse stood in a clearing, head down grazing, as we approached. Liberty put her fingers to her lips and motioned for us to remain behind her. We did as we were told and slumped to the ground, reaching for the water bottle in Will's backpack to slurp thirstily. Will handed us around a mint but Liberty snatched the packet off us before it was my turn. Dexter crunched hungrily on three at once and grinned at me apologetically, with a mouth full of white bits.

She put one in the palm of her open hand and walked towards the horse.

'Shouldn't we work out what to do first?' I asked, trying to whisper loudly enough for her to hear me.

Liberty turned to glare at me. 'Shhhh,' she hissed.

'Say the horse eats the mint, then what? It might run off again and then all this has been to waste. What's our actual plan?'

'Raff's got a point,' Will stood up to face his sister, who towered above his small body. 'What are we going to do with it?'

'Shouldn't we have thought about this long ago, before walking all this way?' asked Dexter.

'You didn't have to come,' snapped Liberty. 'You weren't invited.' But she returned to where we were sitting and sat down. The horse regarded the four of us coolly, but carried on grazing.

'You brought something to catch it, didn't you?' I asked her.

'Yup, a head collar and lead rope, it should fit, though the horse is bigger up close than I thought. A lot bigger actually. Most of my stuff is for a pony.'

'The pony that never was,' I said, wistfully.

Liberty frowned at me, clearly not remembering our bond in her bedroom. Unless I had imagined the bond. She rummaged in her backpack and brought out a twisted stretch of mauve rope and a heap of metal, buckles, and purple material. She unbuckled and re-buckled parts of the metal until she held it up, satisfied. 'There, it should fit now.'

'Then what?' asked Will. 'If you manage to catch the thing, what do we do with it?'

Liberty went quiet. She had never actually thought through her plan this far. Finding the horse had become the priority.

'Shouldn't we tell Mum and Dad?' asked Will.

'NO,' we all shouted back at him.

'Okay,' said Will, sitting up on his knees and facing all of us. For the youngest one in the group, he certainly had his head in the right place. 'Let's make a plan then. Liberty, you need to catch the horse. Then, we all need to think of somewhere to keep it.'

'Anyone's parents mind a horse grazing in the garden?' I laughed, shaking my head at Will. 'This is silly.'

'I don't know anywhere we can afford to keep a horse,' Liberty said sadly. 'I've lost touch with everyone from the stables. And Tilly would talk at school. She wouldn't be able to help herself.'

'I know somewhere,' Dexter looked at us. Liberty looked back at him, her blue eyes shining hopefully. 'Somewhere a bit isolated. No one will ever know he's there.'

'Are we allowed to keep him there?'

'Don't care,' said Dexter. 'No one will ever know, so what's the harm?'

'Is it suitable for a horse, though?' Liberty asked. 'You can't just keep one anywhere.'

'It's got grass. Lots of grass. And water. And a place inside if it rains. Do horses need anything else?'

'That's pretty much it,' Liberty's eyes lit up. 'Where is this place?'

'It's back by the valley dip where we found it. Up the other side where the tractor was coming and along a few miles.'

'So ages away,' groaned Will.

'Know anywhere else then?' Dexter yawned, and lay back on the woodland floor, stretching out with his hands behind his head.

'No,' replied Will, poking Dexter. 'Come on then. Let's get started.'

We all looked at Liberty.

'Oh,' she said. 'My turn then.'

Liberty was right. The horse did like mints but it took the rest of the packet before she managed to get near enough to slip the rope around his neck before he panicked again, running away from her. Now the horse stood, head down, nostrils wide, breathing at us, with the tied rope trailing on the ground. Liberty looked hot and defeated with dirt splashed across her forehead. She'd flung her hoodie over a low tree trunk and stood panting in her black vest top, eyeing up the horse.

'I give up,' she breathed, screwing up her lips. 'Someone else's turn.'

'No way,' replied Will, backing away.

'Raff?' she asked, winking at me. I would have loved to say yes, to be the knight in shining armour and step up. And the horse to swoop into my arms and then Liberty, but alas that clearly wouldn't happen. I shook my head at her sadly.

'No way sorry,' I said. 'Horse's and I don't mix. Ever.'

'I will,' said Dexter.

'No,' said Liberty.

'Whatever,' shrugged Dexter, bored. 'Let's get going home.'

'Have we another choice?' I asked Liberty holding my palms wide, and shrugging. 'Give him a chance.'

'Fine,' she said. 'But once you've got him, Dexter, pass him to me.'

'Who says this horse wants to be caught?' mused Will.

We ignored him.

Dexter got back into his Bear Grylls mode and sunk to his knees, creeping forward and whispering to the horse. I fully expected the horse to give another whine and rise onto its back legs before pelting it out of there, but he didn't. The horse lowered its nose further to the ground and took a step towards Dexter. He continued talking to the horse and crawling forwards until the horse's nose touched his. The horse sniffed at his lowered shoulders and brushed his nose through Dexter's rough hair.

Dexter's hand had already reached amongst the leaves lining the woodland floor for the trailing rope and his other hand brushed through the horse's thick fringe and along his neck. He slowly rose to his feet, head nuzzled into the horse's neck as his hands rubbed down the horse's body. Then he turned, made a click from his mouth, and the horse followed him over to us.

'Easy,' he grinned at Liberty. 'Where's the head collar?' Silently, she picked it off the floor and handed it over. Dexter slipped it over the horse's nose and buckled it around the horse's ears. He untied the rope wrapped around the horse's neck and clipped the rope onto the head collar. He then passed the end of the rope over to Liberty.

She took the rope gingerly, looked at it for a second or two, and then passed it back to Dexter. 'The horse seems to like you,' she said. 'You lead him.'

'You know about horses, don't you?' I asked him.

'A little,' he admitted, and patting the horse's neck, he led the way out of the woodland back towards the lane. Will and I picked up the backpacks and scurried behind.

'More than a little,' Liberty muttered, following behind us.

Chapter Five

'This is your plan? Are you seriously kidding me.' Liberty's voice raised an octave and she spun around accusingly, pointing a manicured finger. 'Aaaargh.'

I am beginning to love it when she's angry. Her cheekbones appear higher and a flush appears on her nose. She is so feisty and pretty when cross.

I must admit, the plan did seem a little far-fetched. Dexter had the good grace to colour slightly too, but the usual shrug and indifference bounced back.

'Are you a complete idiot?' she accused.

We had been walking for a good few hours. Out of the woodland, across the meadow and back past our bikes, which I wished we could jump onto. Then onwards down the lane we previously couldn't pass. The horse walked meekly next to Dexter, without a single peep. Dexter's arm rested lightly on its neck. Will struggled to catch up, his legs much shorter than mine and with clearly no stamina. I'm not greatly athletic but with the basketball and an occasional run, I keep my legs toned enough to not be suffering yet.

Will on the other hand, puffed behind us.

The lane led up away from our village and towards the canal. We crossed over a bridge, one behind another, and down the narrow hill to the towpath running along one side of the canal. We had been lucky enough not pass a single soul on our way. The lane didn't lead anywhere so there was no real through traffic.

Once on the towpath we followed the windy, nettle-filled path for a couple of miles until Dexter stopped and pointed ahead. We all stared in disbelief.

'Waste of time, this,' mumbled Will, shaking his head.

'Let's call it a day,' I agreed. 'Take the bloody horse to the nearest farmer, dump it, and go home.'

'Let's not be hasty,' Liberty said slowly, wiping the sweat from her forehead, before shaking her head. 'It isn't all bad. But where is the grass you spoke about Dexter? And the water?'

Dexter pointed up the bank beside the towpath to a steep meadow on the side of a valley, with knee-high grass and purple thistles, then back down at the murky brown waters of the canal.

'He's not drinking that,' Liberty said and wrinkled up her nose at the smell from the canal.

'There isn't anything else.'

'We'll sort it,' she replied. 'And the meadow, does it have a fence? A gate, or a way in?'

'Around there,' Dexter pointed to the side of the towpath, to a rickety stile covered partly with brambles. 'We can get over there, but there's an overgrown gate somewhere up the side for the horse to get in. It's padlocked, though, and I don't know which way to take the horse around to get to it. The fence runs all the way up the valley around the corner to those trees and back. The field narrows at the top corner, then opens up to a big bit behind those trees out of sight. It's not huge but there's tons of grass, bit steep though. I'm sure he won't mind.'

'And that,' I pointed at the thing we had all managed to avoid looking at. 'Is that the shelter you talked of? Are you mad?'

We all looked down at the source of our initial horror. The boat was faded beyond any colour than, well, wood. It didn't bob in the water like boats should; it was well and truly grounded to the murky bottom, which was probably a good thing.

Built to imitate a canal barge, the boat was longer than a normal fishing boat, but had a tall wooden cabin running along the entire body. Tall enough, Dexter must have thought, to house a horse.

'Is it safe?' asked Will sceptically.

'Only one way to find out,' I replied and swung myself onto the front decking. It groaned under my weight, but held. There wasn't a door to the boat, just an opening into a large open cabin, slightly sunken down a couple of steps into the bottom of the boat

'We'd need to build a stable door,' Liberty pondered, leaning over the side and looking down at me. 'And board up most of those windows, especially the ones lining the towpath. Just in case.'

'Its big enough,' I nodded at her. 'More than big enough, but how will we get the horse onto it?'

'Build a ramp?' suggested Will, climbing up to join me.

'Who owns this?' Liberty asked suspiciously.

'No one,' replied Dexter.

'No one?' I frowned at him. 'How do you know?' I looked around the inside, which was around four metres long and three wide. A couple of broken tables were piled in the corner, perfect for our building project, and then a blanket and pile of clothes. I looked sharply out at Dexter. 'Have you been here before?'

'In passing. Biked past the boat for years, no one has come and gone in a long, long time. Really, it's completely hidden here. The canal is barely used and I've never met anyone on the towpath. Barges don't come this way with all the low bridges. Since the lock was put in they use the other canal. Anyway, what's strange about a horse grazing in the abandoned field? No one will bat an eyelid.'

'We need water,' said Liberty. 'Lots of it.'

'We can fill up our bucket,' suggested Will. 'There must be a field around here with a self-filling trough and water pipe. Then try, somehow, to find something large enough to be more permanent. I've seen bath tubs used sometimes.'

'I'll look for one of those,' offered Dexter.

'Where on earth will you find a bath tub?' laughed Liberty.

'The skip,' replied Dexter, nonchalantly.

'Okay,' Liberty turned back to her ordering around mode. I eagerly anticipated her directions. 'First we need to open up the field gate, break the padlock or something, and find a way for the horse to get in. Then we need to fill up the bucket, at least short term for the horse tonight. Then we can fix up the boat as a stable.'

'What about hay?' Dexter asked. 'It's the wrong time of year for hay cutting.'

'We'll think about getting some,' replied Liberty. 'Must be some farmer with last year's bales we can bribe with free newspapers or something. There's plenty of grass anyway, he shouldn't need much hay yet.'

'Won't he get lonely?' asked Will.

'We'll get him a companion,' suggested Dexter.

'One thing at a time,' laughed Liberty, blue eyes shining happily. 'There's still so much more we need to do. Anyway, we're his companions.'

Inspection done, we turned to leave the boat. The horse still grazed quietly by its side with the lead rope looped over a hook. Dexter untied him. I took one final glance around the boat, then back down at the clothes piled in the corner and at a plastic tub of food hidden under the table. Fresh food: bread, cheese, crackers, and eggs lying unspoilt in the container.

Someone had used this boat before, recently, and I had my suspicions.

Chapter Six

It wasn't until three days later we heard the news. The news changing everything, but nothing at all.

By then the horse, which we had nicknamed Spearmint (Minty for short), had settled into his field. Dexter had successfully scavenged a large metal tub from the skip and had siphoned off water from the farmer's field to fill it up each day. He used an old tangled hose I'd found in Dad's garage. A slight wave of guilt went over us for the stolen items and water, but this quickly vanished.

In return for a few hours labour mucking out stinky cow barns, a farmer had offered us twenty bales of hay. For my sister's rabbits, I had told him. The farmer narrowed his furrowed eyes at me, but remained silent.

We balanced the hay bales on the back of my bike and rode them one by one to the deck of the boat, where Will stacked and threw a tarpaulin over them. The inside of the boat and makeshift door were beginning to take shape with a few pinched screws and tools here and there. The towpath-side windows were boarded up.

Minty was yet to be tempted inside, but the weather had been too nice to bother anyway.

Dad frowned whenever he came across me rummaging in the shed for tools or lying worn out in the lounge. I began to think he was onto us, but then he would turn back to his paper or soap opera and I'd be forgotten. Only my little sister began to notice my longer absences.

Dad sat at the kitchen table, as usual sipping on a steaming morning coffee with the local paper open. He looked rough, unshaven with shirt open and bloodshot eyes. His head bent close to the paper, straining to read without his glasses. He delighted in using a rival paper shop to deliver our weekly papers instead of Bill's. I held my tongue and added it to the list of reasons to dislike him.

I happened to glance down at the headline as I scooted around him to reach for the toast.

My eyes widened.

'Remember,' he was saying, large stained thumbs ready to turn the page. I strained to read the last words before he flicked the page over. 'You're still far from being off the hook, young man, so straight home after school.'

'I've detention first,' I replied, distracted.

'Well straight home afterwards.'

'Okay,' I mumbled. I caught the last few words before the page was flicked. I straightened up. 'No problem Dad. If I miss the last bus, I will be an hour or two walking, though. See you later.'

'Ride your bike, you lazy...'

I grabbed another slice of toast to take with me and bending down to grab my bag, I gave my sister a quick kiss on her head. Abby squirmed and giggled. I gave her a mini wave and rushed outside.

By break-time, my whole body felt jittery. My knees knocked and my ankles danced on the spot. I needed to see Liberty. The lesson before lunch dragged.

'Mr Lincoln. Mr Lincoln.'

I looked up at the voice. 'Er…yes. Sorry.' I turned back to my history book, unable to concentrate on the words swimming beneath my eyes.

'Mr Lincoln?'

'Yes?' Obviously looking at the textbook wasn't what I was supposed to be doing. A murmur of laughter spread through the classroom.

'The answer please.'

'And the question was?' I tried to flash my best grin up at the teacher. Cheeky grins always work don't they? The response was deadpan. Maybe not with grumpy, old teachers then.

He gave an exasperated sigh, 'I'll see you at three o'clock.' The classroom murmur turned into full on laughter. 'Anyone else like to join him?'

The class settled quickly, and the history lesson continued.

I remained frozen.

The detention excuse had been just that, an excuse. I couldn't afford the time to be actually in detention. My parents believed school had come down hard on me for my bunking off debacle, but in fact, Liberty had been an expert at forgery. Liberty's careful letter perfectly mimicked my mum's handwriting and signature. There had been no detentions. Just a fabricated misunderstanding between my parents and poor old me lying in bed sick.

Lunchtime bore no relief. I couldn't walk straight up to Liberty, could I?

School rules still applied.

Year groups were arranged into groups, or tiers. Liberty and her friends were at the top. They could sit anywhere, do anything. My friends and I were somewhere marginally below. We commanded the sports hall, pitches and fields, and basketball zone outside, but inside, we followed Liberty's group's rules. Below us were a cross section of other groups, equally as happy to do their own thing.

Sometimes I envied them.

They escaped the pressures of the need to fit in all the time. The pressure to slick their hair the correct way, to have the correct amount off the sides shaved. To always have presence on Snapchat or Facebook — or whatever social media was in fashion on the day.

Far, far at the bottom, were groups of children whose lives must be hell. Daily teasing, daily taunting. Never-ending rounds of daily torture whilst we all watched, mostly oblivious, or without doing anything.

And below this, sat Dexter.

I caught Liberty's eye and tried to gesture towards the door, but she turned her back. I felt my cheeks burn at the rejection. A sensation I'm not used to.

I found Will amongst his social crowds; he had the look of terror as I approached his table. Several of his friends looked down or disappeared as I approached. I think Will wished the ground would swallow him up, too, but he was trapped in the corner.

'Can I have a word, Will?' I asked, placing my hands on his shoulders in an act, I thought, was friendship. Clearly it came across as threatening as several friends cowered.

'Er…not now,' he stuttered.

'Now Will. It's important,' I cleared my throat and looked around the table at the other kids. Mostly small, like Will, some hastily gathering away a pack of cards spread on the table. I wished I could join in. Our group never played cards. 'It's about the basketball try-outs.'

'Basketball?' Will finally looked up, confusion across his face.

'You know, the try-outs,' I said, slowly.

'No, I don't know.'

'The try-outs,' I tried again. 'I need to talk to you urgently about them. Can I have a quick word. In private?'

Will's hands shook as he reached for his lunchbox and threw it into his backpack. 'I don't think I'll play basketball this term after all.'

His response astounded me. I almost laughed aloud. I guess for Will and whatever his crowd were into, basketball didn't impress. Every group had their own standards. I admired him for sticking to his guns.

'That's a shame, Will,' I told him. 'Coach said he saw potential in you. Great potential. Well if you ever change your mind, there is always a place for you.' I left, with the murmurs of whispers behind me, and Will's head leaning over the table towards them.

Alone again, I resolved to wait it out before I spread the news.

Dexter was nowhere to be found, as usual.

Chapter Seven

Liberty's lips looked fuller as she talked. Her hair, still damp from the shower, hung loosely around her shoulders. It had the shiny colourful quality bird feathers do. Like a raven's. I could see hints of red and green shimmering in there. I wanted to touch and caress the strands with my fingers. I'm not sure she'd appreciate my fingers near her.

'Rafferty, are you listening?'

She had the habit of twisting the stands of hair that fell in front of her eyes around in her fingers. Twirling them around and around. I'd noticed her doing that at school before; it must be a nervous habit. I'm not sure I have one. Maybe the shuffling of my feet and the weird sounds I sometimes make from my mouth.

I tried making one now.

'Rafferty?'

Her neck was almost swan-like. Long and slender and an off-white, almost creamy colour. She didn't look real. Like a corpse.

No. Bad wording.

A mannequin. Anyway, something pearly white and smooth.

'Rafferty.' She pushed me hard and I slid down off the side of the boat, where I'd been perched, watching the sunrise glistening on the murky film of water. I 'mock' collapsed to the dirt of the towpath, rolled over and looked back up at her. The sun shielded her face from me, so I held a hand up. 'Were you even listening?'

'Of course,' I grinned. I reached my arm up towards her, hoping she'd take it, but she batted it away. The perfect movie moment, rejected yet again. I hoped I looked impish and sexy lying on the ground beneath her but she carried on talking. Ignoring me.

'You're not helping. We've got a huge problem.'

The thing is, I'm not sure I cared. I cared about losing the horse because our morning and after school meet-ups would end; but caring actually about the horse, I'm not sure. My panic of earlier in the day had fizzled out now I was at the canal with Liberty. She's all I wanted to see.

'It's only a problem if we make it a problem.'

'What do you mean?' she asked.

'Well, we don't have to do anything.'

'I'm with Raff,' agreed Dexter, appearing from inside the boat, where he'd be storing yet more bales of hay. He seemed to enjoy mucking out dirty barns. We didn't even need any more hay. Minty still had yet to venture into the finished stable, and appeared happier running free in the field. Dexter swung himself up from the deck onto the side of the boat and spotted my bag. 'Ooh Raff, is that a pack of crisps?'

'Yeah,' I frowned. 'You want it?'

'Please,' he grinned, tugging it out of my backpack and pulling it open.

'And you, Will?' Liberty asked, bringing us back to the issue. 'What do you think? We all have to agree.' She emphasised the *all* to make sure we were doubly clear.

Will pondered over it for a minute or two, kicking his legs back and forth onto the boat's wooden side. Drumming a pattern. He pulled out the crumpled newspaper article from his pocket and smoothed it out onto his knee. Then he read it out aloud, for the tenth time, and we listened in silence.

'It's a dilemma,' he finally said.

'Who says it's Minty?' shrugged Dexter, licking his finger and dipping it into the bag to catch the last crumbs.

'Missing racehorse, red bay, three white socks,' Liberty gulped, looking up at the silhouette of Minty up on the hill. Her eyebrows knitted. 'Striking star, snip and strip down the face. It's got to be. Come on.'

I had no idea what she was talking about.

'No,' Dexter said. 'No, it's not got to be. He didn't look like he'd left a horsebox. No trauma from any road accident. He had nothing on him. No head collar, no travelling leg things, nothing. He has no marks on him to say he's that horse. The missing racehorse, what's it called?'

'Profits Red Ridge.'

'It's not him.'

'Why do you think they called him that?' I asked.

'What?' glared Liberty, annoyed at my interruption off topic.

'Profits Red Ridge?'

'He's not him,' grumbled Dexter.

'Okay,' I shrugged at Dexter, and turned to Liberty. 'Why do you think they called the *racehorse* Profits Red Ridge?'

'Profit means money, doesn't it?' asked Will, leaning forward eagerly. 'They probably hoped he'd make them a ton of money.'

'The racehorse in the paper was a champion wasn't it?' I said. 'So yeah, you're right, tons of money. Maybe he was used as a stud horse, too. That would make them loads of cash. Imagine baby Mintys around, they'd be gorgeous.'

'He is a gelding, idiot,' said Liberty.

'A what?'

'No balls,' sniggered Will.

'Oh,' I replied, blushing.

'The name does fit. He's kind of a reddy brown colour isn't he?' said Will.

'Bright bay,' corrected Liberty.

'What's the ridge bit about then?' asked Will. 'Profits Red *Ridge*.' We all looked around at each other and shook our heads.

'I think he prefers it here.' Dexter looked sad. I didn't realise he cared so much. Then again, he was always first here in the morning and last at night. He spent the most time with Minty than any of us, even Liberty. Perhaps he had nothing better to do.

'How do you know?' asked Will. 'He might miss his home. His stables.'

'Look at him,' said Dexter. We all turned to stare at Minty up in the field. 'He's completely settled. If he were unhappy he'd be tearing about like he did the first couple of days. Whining and all that. But he's not. It's as if he's always been here.'

'Don't you think they'll miss him?' asked Will.

'Who?' I asked.

'The horse trainers and jockeys.'

'No,' said Liberty. 'They've probably billions of horses. He'd just be a number to them. I doubt they'd care.'

'I'm not sure about that,' said Dexter. 'If I were his jockey, I'd certainly care about him. I'd love him. Wouldn't matter to me if he was one of many I rode. I'd still miss him if he went.'

'He's a business to them,' grumbled Liberty. 'They just wanted him to run well and win lots of money.'

'Maybe,' said Dexter. 'But they wouldn't be in the business if they didn't love horses and care about their welfare. And the horses wouldn't perform if they weren't healthy and happy.'

'I disagree,' she argued.

'Fine by me,' he retorted.

'Then what do we do?' I asked, trying to bring the conversation back to the original problem.

'Do we come forward and find out one way or other if he's Profits Red Ridge?' asked Will.

'They'll take the horse off us,' Liberty shook her head.

'Yeah they will. It isn't our horse.'

'Yes he is,' said Dexter defensively. 'He's our Minty.'

'Our Minty,' muttered Will.

'He's ours then,' said Liberty, firmly. 'You're right Dexter. He is ours.'

'What do you mean?' I asked.

'He's ours. Like you said, Raff, this is only a problem if we make it a problem. So it's not. The horse is ours. And as Dexter said, the horse has no injury marks, no features whatsoever to say he's that horse.'

'What about the exact colouring?' asked Will.

'Fluke.' I said. 'There must be billions of big brown horses in the world.'

'What? Horses going missing on the exact same day we found Minty?'

'Exactly,' I said. 'Fluke. Minty is our horse and that should be the end of it.'

'I agree,' nodded Liberty.

'A pact,' said Dexter and held his hand out. 'A pact of complete secrecy.'

'Complete secrecy?' I asked. Dexter's hand dropped momentarily.

'Yes,' agreed Liberty. 'No one can mention this at all. No one can connect us together. We've got to remain strangers in company and discrete at school, too,' she looked pointedly at me.

'Hey!' I protested.

'Basketball? Really?'

I glared down at Will, whose eyes remained fixated on the floor, legs still swinging.

'No excuses to talk at school, none, do you hear? No one can mention a horse, at all, in any form. Mobiles are strictly off limits, nothing searchable. No photographs, no status updates, nothing. Do you all hear?'

'Loud and clear,' grinned Dexter, finally in collaboration with Liberty. 'You're preaching to the converted. It's the weak link here I'm worried about.

'Hey! It was an emergency,' I cried. But there was no point protesting again. They all knew what I was like. I resolved to try harder.

'So a pact,' said Dexter, holding out his hand. 'Are we all in?'

Will hesitated for only a second then put his hand on top.

'I'm in.'

'In.' Liberty put her hand upon Will's and then I did, my hand feeling the warmth of Liberty's beneath it. Soft and warm, her hands felt recently moisturised against my rough ones.

'In.'

'Minty is ours,' stated Dexter, solemnly.

'Minty is ours,' we all repeated. We shook together and then released our hands up high in the air at the rising sun. I tried to linger my hand on top of Liberty's as we all separated, but ended up clunking my fingers into her. She pulled her hand away rubbing hard, and glared at me.

Not what I'd had in mind.

We all left on a high, and for the next few weeks our lives settled into a rhythmic routine.

But peace never lasts.

If I had known how the summer was going to pan out, I would have stopped right there. But I didn't, so onwards I continued, oblivious.

Chapter Eight

'Are you ready?' Liberty asked.

'As I'll ever be,' I replied, and nodded at her before swinging my leg over the stile.

I followed her up the twisty path, negotiating my bare legs past the overgrown thistles and stinging nettles. We reached a clearer patch and continued up the hill towards where Minty stood grazing. He lifted his head as we approached, snorted, and then continued grazing. His long black tail swished around over his back, swatting away the cloud of biting flies.

'Hey boy,' smiled Liberty. She ran her hand down his neck and patted his shoulder enthusiastically. When around Minty her usual black mood seemed to temporarily vanish. 'Here,' she flung the head collar and lead rope over towards me, 'your turn to catch him.'

'How?' I asked. I looked at the bewildering array of buckles and straps. I fiddled with it for a few seconds before holding it up defeated. Liberty rolled her eyes and stepped forward to snatch it back. Rearranging it, she made a loop in the material and held two straps up.

'Here,' she said. 'Put this over his nose and then take the straps around his head and buckle them behind his ears.'

'Okay,' I said. I didn't understand, but I did as instructed. Minty stood still, apart from his munching jaw as I looped the band over his nose and then fastened the buckles. 'Done,' I said, proudly.

'Great,' smiled Liberty, flashing a mouthful of straight white teeth. 'But take it off, turn it around and try again.'

'Why?' I asked, frowning.

'It's upside down.'

'Oh,' I replied. 'It looks okay though.'

'See the fabric running down his nose? That shouldn't be there, it should be under his chin.'

After a few more minutes faffing around with the straps, I had finally managed to catch a horse for the first time. All by myself; well, sort of.

'Now lead him down the side of the hill towards the gate,' she instructed.

'Okay.' I did as I was told. I enjoyed listening to her instructions. Anything if it meant spending some more time with her. It took long enough to persuade her I really did want to learn about horses. She wasn't convinced, but had reluctantly agreed to teach me the basics. On her terms.

'Not that side,' she barked.

'What now?' I asked.

'Don't stand that side of him. Always stand on the left and hold the lead rope nearer his head with your right hand.'

'Like this?' I asked, scooting under his nose and adjusting my position.

'Humm,' she replied. 'That'll do.'

Listening to the constant nag of her instructions, we made it through the field gate, along through a few empty meadows, knee-deep with grass, and finally down to the towpath back towards the boat.

'Now what?' I asked.

'Now I'm going to teach you how to groom him. Do you know anything about brushing a horse?'

'Um,' I racked my brains back to the horse books I'd read. 'A little.'

'What then?'

'Horses need brushing,' I grinned at her, hoping my smile would win over my lack of knowledge.

She frowned back.

'They do, yes, but that's not what I meant. Do you know the difference between a dandy brush and a body brush?'

'They're both brushes?'

'Let's start at the beginning,' she suggested.

For the next hour Liberty talked me through all the grooming equipment, telling me about things I'd never heard of. I listened like a good student, occasionally struggling with boredom but the lull of her perfect voice just about kept me going.

Even Minty dozed off, bored, whilst waiting for the actual grooming to commence.

'How's the teaching going?' asked Dexter, when he arrived on his bike at the boat. He flung his bike down and came over to join us. 'Is Raff being a good student?'

'Good yes…' began Liberty. She reached up and dragged a brush through Minty's thick, black mane, making it lie flat and glossy down his neck. 'But he's certainly not the brightest spark in the class.'

'Oi,' I glared at her.

'Okay,' she grinned, and squatted down to rummage around in the plastic box. She held up two brushes. 'Which one's the dandy brush?' She put her finger to her lips to stop Dexter from answering. He looked at me amused, but kept quiet.

I looked from brush to brush, one wooden with thick red bristles and the other black plastic with smaller smooth bristles, then back up at Liberty.

'Red one,' I pointed to the wooden brush. She frowned.

'Lucky guess. What's a curry comb?'

'Okay, you've got me,' I laughed. 'No idea. At least I'm keen though, even if I don't have the superior knowledge you have. Yet.'

'You'll learn,' Dexter said, solemnly. 'What's his next lesson?'

'Riding,' Liberty said. Dexter snorted.

'No way,' I replied.

'Scared?' she asked. So far only Dexter and Liberty had been up on Minty's back. Minty seemed unconcerned with their attempts so Dexter had begun riding him more often. Liberty seemed more nervous and would only get on when Dexter was there to help. Minty always jiggled around on the spot and found it hard to stand still when they tried to mount him. But once on board, he settled down.

'Too right I'm scared,' I replied. 'Minty's huge. I'm not sure he likes me much either.' Minty looked at me with his big eyes and batted his long eyelashes. He tried to rub an itchy patch on his head onto my leg, so I scratched at his itch with my fingers. He leant his head down and closed his eyes.

'Wuss,' she said.

'Sensible,' I replied.

Liberty cleared up the equipment back into her box and then lugged it up onto the deck. She jumped up and disappeared into the cabin with it.

Dexter's stomach growled and he looked over hopefully at my backpack for an endless supply of chocolate bars and crisps I'd begun to share with him. He was always constantly ravenous like me. But I shook my head. Dad caught me filling my bag in the kitchen and banned me from taking anything unless I asked in advance and gave the reasons why I needed snacks in between set meals. I wouldn't put it past him to make up an inventory, to check I wasn't taking anything.

Bastard.

'Don't be scared of Minty,' Dexter said, rubbing his greasy fingers down Minty's shiny neck. 'He's a big softy really.'

'I've an idea,' I told him.

'Oh yeah?' he replied. 'Sounds dangerous.'

'You don't know what it is yet.'

'Any idea by you is a dangerous one. What is it?'

'Wait and see,' I told him. 'You'll all be impressed.'

'You mean Liberty will.'

'That's what I said.'

'Good luck,' Dexter grinned. 'Let me know if I can help you.'

'Oh you can.' I smiled, more to myself. My idea was bound to work.

Chapter Nine

The last time I entered a library must have been as long ago as during my primary school days. Ages then, considering I'm in the last year of high school. I'm not a big reader, although occasionally a book-related phase will rip around school and curiosity will get the better of me.

The librarian, a girl not much older than me, looked up and smiled as I entered. I smiled back, willing the red flush to keep at bay. I had grown taller in the last few weeks, overtaking my dad by several inches and could easily pass as a college student. Though, biologically that's not surprising, given he's not actually my real father.

'Hey,' I mouthed to her, as I passed.

'Can I help you?' She rose from her chair, in a pleated skirt and white crisp blouse, and spread her hands onto the counter. Her fingers were long and elegant, like a pianist's, but not as heavily manicured as Liberty's.

'I've come to do some research,' I grinned.

'What are you studying?' she asked tilting her head. Her hair was red, long and in plaits, I'm not sure how natural.

'It's not for school,' I said quickly, and then regretted mentioning school at all. 'It's for a project at home.'

'Interesting,' she replied. 'How can I help?'

She reached over for her giant reference book and waited expectantly. She bit her lip and looked up at me. A tiny, silver nose stud glinted in the light, catching my attention.

'Yes, it's for a project.' I repeated.

'About what?' she queried, nodding her head to edge me on. Her eyes were chestnut coloured, like hazelnuts and very round and she looked straight into mine. I leant on the counter and grinned again; stalling for time.

'Do you work here?' I asked.

She looked confused and furrowed her brow. 'On Saturdays. I'm at college. First year.'

'I haven't seen you before.'

'Do you come here a lot then?' she looked surprised. 'Sorry, I haven't got to know all the regulars yet. I only started the beginning of May, a few weekends ago.'

'Well no. Sometimes.'

The nervous red rash was definitely creeping up my neck. I don't know why I hadn't simply smiled as I'd walked past the counter and then walked on by straight upstairs. But something about her manner, open and honest, drew me in.

'I'll just serve this lady,' she said, pointing at an impatient woman, tutting loudly behind me. I hadn't even realised she was there. 'Whilst you think about how I can help you. Take your time.'

I scooted sidewards and let the woman hobble past me to the counter. She lifted her books one by one from the trolley, in a slow, painfully exaggerated manner. She certainly read a lot, she had loads in there.

'Can I help you?' I asked her sweetly, watching her struggle. The woman glared around at me, narrowing her eyes. She looked back at the girl, and continued moving her books at a snail's pace. She'd either ignored me, or not heard what I'd said. Either way, she wasn't going anywhere fast.

I glanced around the library.

The building was three or four stories high. It served the whole county. Although the smaller villages had a travelling library van, which probably came from this as the central hub. I had forgotten how big the place was, but I didn't need help. I knew what I was looking for; it was part of my grand plan to turn Liberty's affections around.

Horses.

The horse section wasn't too difficult to find. Up on the third floor. I came across the pet section first, with the billions of books on rabbits and odd looking dog breeds and then the farm animals. Cows, sheep and pigs, but not the livestock I was interested in. The horses and riding books had their own set of shelves at the far end of the corridor. High windows lined the walls, with a steep drop outside to the carpark. I don't like heights, so I kept to the left, against the bookshelves.

I knew I couldn't take the books home. Couldn't risk the questions from my parents or my sister Abby stumbling across the books and her suspicions arousing. For a nine-year-old she was surprisingly precocious. And horse-mad. There was no way I could get away without telling her if she saw anything related horse-related.

I selected a few suitable books. Piling them up in my arms, I walked around a few aisles until I found an empty table.

Setting the books down with a bang, and making several quiet library dwellers jump, I settled into the seat and began to flick through them one by one. I had a rolled up piece of paper and pencil to jot down the most important notes, or words and equipment I didn't understand, but most I memorised.

After a couple of hours, I had what I needed, returned the books and headed down the stairs.

'I thought you'd gone,' the girl smiled, as I ambled past her desk. 'Did you find what you were looking for?'

'Did the old lady finally get all her books on the desk?' I grinned.

'She changed her mind about half of them,' she laughed. 'I had to take them all back. All over the library.'

'Perks of the job.'

'I don't mind,' she said. 'It's nice being up high in the quiet areas, putting the books away. I sometimes stall for time up there, just hiding away.'

'Hiding away,' I laughed. 'Do you ever come across people, er, you know? Down in the quiet, dark aisles?' I don't know why I asked. She didn't seem the type to find that amusing.

'Sometimes,' she grinned, showing a little gap between her front teeth. Not straight and perfect like Liberty's. 'Is that why you come here a lot?'

'No,' I said quickly. I laughed, blushing. Maybe I was wrong about her, 'I don't come here at all.'

'That's good then.'

'Good? Don't you want me here?'

'Maybe you'd like to come back next Saturday?' she asked shyly, then added, 'I can help you more with your project.'

'Of course. The project. Yes, well, maybe I will see you again.'

'That's good.'

'I'm Rafferty.' I held out my hand to her across the counter. 'Raff.'

'Sorry Raff, I'm not allowed to touch customers,' she replied.

I dropped my hand embarrassed. 'Oh sorry.'

'Only kidding,' she grinned, holding hers up to me, 'I'm Tallie.'

Chapter Ten

'This is a ridiculous idea,' mumbled Dexter. Although grumbling, he'd done as I had asked. Spearmint was standing in front of us with his head collar and lead rope on. He shook his head then rubbed it up and down Dexter's shoulder, sending him almost flying into the canal. Fine red hairs stuck to the arm of Dexter's jumper. Dexter pushed the horse's nose back. 'Oi, stop that, Minty.'

'How do I do it?' I asked.

'Thought you were the expert?'

'The books only taught me so much,' I grinned. 'The rest is meant to be obvious. Hopefully it'll come naturally.'

'I'll move him over so you can stand on the deck.'

'Is it high enough?' I frowned at the side of the canal boat. The side wasn't far from the towpath ground. Minty looked very big up close.

Dexter swung Minty around and backed him against the side of the boat, so his body ran along the side of the wooden edging of the deck. His round belly pushed up against the side and he pawed at the ground. Dust clouded up from his hooves, the ground dry after weeks without rain. For May it was unusually dry. I put my hand up onto the horse's shoulder, like the photograph in the book.

'He's the wrong way around,' I said.

'Who is?'

'Who do you think? Turn him.'

Dexter rolled his eyes, but led Minty forward and spun him around.

'Better,' I said. I thought the boat shifted under my weight. I leant forward against Minty's warm body to steady myself and moved my feet along the edge to regain balance. Minty's hair was smooth and gleamed chestnut in the sun; like Tallie's eyes. Dexter must have been brushing him.

'You going to get on then?' Dexter asked.

'Yeah, give me a second.'

'A second for what?'

'Just a second, be patient, will you?'

'Come on, Minty's getting bored.' The horse was thrashing his head around, Dexter struggling not to be pushed over.

'Okay, ready.' I leant against the horse again but couldn't get the momentum to jump up. I stretched up again but it was no use, the deck was too low. 'I need something higher.'

'Over there?' suggested Dexter pointing to the stile, now cleared of the overhanging nettles. 'You want me to go first?'

'No, I can do this.'

'Liberty won't like you any better even if you do get on the horse.'

I ignored him. 'Come on, this is perfect. Bring Minty here.'

Minty's back felt wide and odd, and when I finally lowered myself down, he shifted his feet under my weight so I grabbed the top of the stile in panic.

'Let go,' commanded Dexter.

I released my hand from the wooden stile and Dexter pulled the lead rope. Minty began walking down the towpath. I wrapped my hand around the hair down his neck and leant forward, my elbows on his shoulder.

'Sit up properly,' Dexter told me. 'Tuck your knees into his shoulders and let your legs relax down a little.'

'Why?'

'It'll feel comfier for you and for Minty.'

'Oh.' I tried to push myself back up off his neck. My legs felt like they were slipping around the horse's belly. I clung on uselessly. 'Don't go too fast.'

'We're barely walking,' laughed Dexter. 'Couldn't go any slower if we tried.' He looked so small down there, walking alongside Minty, with one grubby hand resting reassuringly on the horse's neck. 'Feel better?'

'Yeah, a bit.' I was beginning to get used to the gentle rocking movements of the horse. Like the swaying of a boat. Everything looked so different from up there. I wasn't high off the ground, but the trees seemed more vivid somehow and the grass greener. The perspective of the world heightened everything.

Stupid, really.

'You're a natural,' said Dexter. He didn't smirk or say it with any kind of intent, just a frank uninhibited remark. I looked down at him, walking relaxed alongside Minty. I don't think I had ever seen him look so comfortable and at home.

'You know about horses, don't you?' I asked him.

'A little.'

'More than a little.'

'Maybe,' he shrugged.

'How?' I pressed, trying to understand.

'How what?'

'How do you know more than a little about horses?'

Dexter sighed and patted Minty reassuringly. Minty let out a loud blow from his nose like a sneeze. Dexter laughed and wiped his arm. Minty's head was up high and his ears faced straight forward. They were pricked up towards the way we were walking along the narrow towpath. He seemed happy.

'From my granddad,' Dexter finally offered.

'Does he have horses?'

'Yeah, a few. Big Heavy Horses. Much bigger than Minty. Less poncy, too. Sorry, Minty.' He patted the horse's neck again in apology. 'With massive hooves with lots of feathers.'

'Feathers?'

'You know, the long fur around their hooves.'

'Oh yeah,' I nodded, not really knowing.

'Grew up with Granddad, so spent a lot of time helping him with them.'

'So you *do* know a lot about horses?'

'Yeah a little,' he grinned, those crooked teeth flashing again. 'He taught me everything I know.'

'Do you think he'd help us?' I asked.

'No,' replied Dexter.

The towpath had narrowed, so he was struggling to walk alongside Minty without either ending up pushed down the bank into the canal or against the stinging nettles on the other side. He tried walking ahead, but Minty quickened his pace to a jog and I clung on leaning down on his neck again.

'Lean back,' warned Dexter. 'Or he'll think you want him to speed up.'

I tried but my legs slipped again and I leant across his neck, gripping on tightly to the hair. His body jogged beneath me. Dexter took the lead rope tighter and asked Minty to stop. 'Think it's getting too narrow this bit, we probably need to turn back to the boat now.'

'Good plan.'

I had had enough by then. My knees were aching and my ankles were sore. The purpose of this exercise wasn't to learn how to ride, anyway, though I had enjoyed it more than I thought I would.

'Hold on,' Dexter backed Minty up into the nettles and swung him around, ducking under his neck to avoid being thrown into the canal. Minty took a quick snatch of grass in his mouth before settling back into walking home.

'Why not?' I asked.

'Why not what?'

'Why won't he help us? We could do with his help and experience.'

'Because he's dead.'

I didn't know what to say, so I mumbled 'oh,' and we carried on walking in silence until the boat came into view ahead. Dexter welcomed the silence and didn't offer any conversation either.

As we approached the side of the boat, ready for positioning Minty for my dismount, I spotted Liberty and Will in the distance coming down the towpath on their bikes towards us. I waved furiously.

'Hold on a second,' I told Dexter.

'Ready for the big moment?'

'Don't know what you mean,' I laughed.

I remembered Dexter's advice and sat up tall on Minty, trying to uncurl my hands from the hair and look like I knew what I was doing. When Liberty spotted me on board Minty, her face broke into a huge smile. Just the effect I'd hoped for. But then, as Will squeaked closer on his bike, Minty snorted and backed up a few steps.

'Hold on,' shouted Dexter. But neither Will or Liberty could hear. The path had a slight decline down towards us and their bikes picked up speed. Will make a whooping sound as he free glided towards us, legs out and the wind whipping the hair back away from his glasses.

As the bikes approached, Minty jogged on the spot, snorting and spraying up the dried ground. I felt myself slipping.

'I can't hold him.'

'Try,' I cried.

'I can't. Sorry.'

Dexter struggled on the end of the lead rope as Minty thrashed around. He winced and yelped, as the rope must have torn through the skin on his hand. Minty then spun on the spot, dragging Dexter across the stony ground, before he gave up and let go. I leant forward in panic, re-clutching handfuls of hair.

The wrong move.

Minty took my leaning as the cue to start running, faster than I ever could imagine. His legs pounded the ground under us. Tears streamed down my eyes as I tried to cling on but my bare legs and shorts had no grip. My hair whipped back against my face and for a second I felt light and free.

I began to slip backwards.

Minty, sensing the shift in my weight towards his butt, skidded to a stop, threw up his rear legs like a bronco, and flung me straight up in the air over his head.

The air whistled.

I could just make out the thud of his legs passing me by and disappearing down the towpath before I missed the path and hit the water.

This had to be the perfect movie moment. I couldn't ask for any better.

Liberty arrived, her face a picture of concern. Her pretty, blue eyes wide with worry — for me. Her mouth was open slightly, then biting at those luscious lips.

Head to foot in green slime and mud, I waded out of the waist-high water and crawled up the steep, grassy bank before I collapsed. Through a peeking eye, I watched her fling her bike down and race down towards me. I lay still and reached my algae covered hand up towards her.

I could imagine her reaching towards me hungrily, and us rolling back down the bank together before she would kiss me gently on the lips.

Our first perfect kiss.

I smiled up at her, seconds away from the moment.

'No way, don't touch me,' she burst out laughing and pointed her long finger at the stinking slime covering everything but my eyes. 'You're totally gross.'

Movie moment ruined.

Again.

Chapter Eleven

Dexter laughed as he rummaged in his backpack, then threw me a small hand towel. The towel smelled musty but I accepted it gratefully. I wiped the green from my face and gave a half smile back to him.

'Told you she was a waste of time.'

'She's not, Dexter,' I said, clutching at my heart and exhaling deeply. 'She's not.'

'She really is.'

'Believe me, she's not. She's perfect.'

'I'm not sure she thinks the same about you,' replied Dexter, perching on the edge of the boat. He splashed his skinny bare legs about, frothing up the water.

'She needs more romancing.'

'How you going to do that?' asked Dexter. 'I'm not much help with women advice I'm afraid.'

'I dunno,' I shrugged, defeated. 'Come on, I need some suggestions.'

'Roses,' smiled Dexter. He held out an imaginary rose and then gave a fake swoon back onto the deck. 'Wins over any girl.'

'Too cliché, don't you think?'

'Maybe,' shrugged Dexter, sitting back up. 'But I'm sure all women love roses.'

'I'll save the roses for our anniversary, then.'

'You're living in dream world, mate. Liberty Ashburn will never fall for you.'

'Oh but she will,' I smiled. 'She will.'

'How?'

'That's where I need some help. What else you got?'

'So not roses, erm,' Dexter clenched his eyes before his eyes opened, shining brightly. 'A song!'

'A song,' I frowned. 'What do you mean?'

'Sing her a song.'

'What song?'

'Not any old song. Your song.'

'What's our song?' I asked, confused. '*Your song* means a song summing up the relationship, doesn't it? Or one you've had a kiss to or something? We haven't kissed. Or anything.'

'No, I mean to write her a song. Your own song.'

'Write her a song?' I echoed. 'How?'

'With a pen and paper,' grinned Dexter. 'And your innermost thoughts.'

'Sounds horrific,' I laughed. My innermost thoughts are probably unrepeatable most of the time. 'I'd probably scare her.'

'Then dial it down a notch or two and write from the heart. Bound to win her over.'

'Are you sure?' I asked, unconvinced.

'Yeah, she'll love it. It's dead romantic.'

'You're maybe on to something.'

'My pleasure,' said Dexter.

'Do I have to sing it?'

'Can you sing?'

'Nope,' I said.

'I'm sure just the words will do, then.'

'Great,' I said. I'd totally warmed to this idea.

Just write a song. A song. How hard can a song be? Harder than it sounds, apparently. I sat with an empty page for hours, writing the odd word or two and then scrunching the paper into a ball.

The waste paper bin filled up with the balls as I shot them into it after each failed attempt. One by one.

Mum smiled at me hunched over my notepad when she waved goodnight. *No*, I'm not studying, I wanted to scream at her. But I just smiled and blew her a goodnight kiss before she closed the door quietly behind her. At last, around midnight, I'd hashed up a reasonable-sounding song. I hunted around, quietly, in Mum's cupboard downstairs, until I found an envelope, sealed the letter and finally crawled into bed.

Job done.

I cornered Liberty as she approached the school's library steps. I'd followed her most of the morning, but she always had a gaggle of friends in tow. It was my one chance to catch her alone. My confidence from yesterday had massively diminished, but it was now or never.

'Liberty.' I reached out to tap her shoulder. She swung around, her smile fading as she saw me. This wasn't a good start.

'What?' she frowned. 'We don't talk at school.'

'I wrote you something,' I smiled.

'You wrote me something?' she said. Her face was a picture of puzzlement and annoyance.

'Yeah.' I handed over the envelope.

'Can't this wait?' she asked, then hissed lowering her voice, 'We're not meant to be seen together.'

'Can you read it?'

'What? Now?'

'Yeah.'

'Fine,' she snarled, dropped her backpack to the floor and thrust open the envelope. She unfolded the lined notepad paper and her eyes scrolled down through the words. A smile twitched on the corners of her mouth. She looked up when she got to the bottom. 'What's this rubbish?'

'I wrote it for you.'

'You wrote it?'

'For you.'

'I don't understand. Is this some kind of love note?' She bit at her perfect lips as she tried to contain a smile.

'A song.'

'A song?' she turned the notepaper sideways, and then flipped it over as if she was somehow reading it wrong.

'I wrote it for you,' I repeated. I wasn't sure what else to say. Her smile turned into a burst of laughter. She handed the note back to me.

'Go on, sing it then.'

'What? Now?' I said. My eyes flashed around to the other pupils rushing in and out of the library doors, glancing at us as they passed.

'Yeah now,' she pouted.

Words failed to form on my lips as I glanced down at the childish scrawls across the paper. She stood waiting, hand on her hips.

'I can't,' I said, finally.

'Loser,' she laughed, tossed her hair and bounced up the stairs away from me. I stood, note in hand, and watched her go.

'Lusting after the unattainable, are you?' Nigel appeared behind me. One of my only mates away from the courts. Years of unlikely school friendship between the athletic and the couch potato had endured the test of time. 'What you got there?' He tore the note from my grasp and read aloud, word by horrendous word.

'Don't,' I cried, my arms flailing at him. He blocked me with a stocky arm as he finished the song. He was surprisingly strong.

'Who's this for?' he asked.

'No one,' I replied.

'Good,' he said, laughing. 'It's awful.'

'Really?' I whined, snatching the note from him. 'Great, I suck at everything.'

'Not totally.'

'I do.'

'Nah, it's not bad. I could help you finish it if you like?'

'I thought it was finished.'

'Oh,' he said and patted my back. 'Sorry mate but no, it's not. Not in the slightest. Come on,' he nodded towards the library. 'Let's go inside and I'll take a look at it.'

'How about the benches?' I said, trying to draw him away from the library. And Liberty.

'Okay,' he nodded. 'Lead the way, Maestro.'

'Who?' I asked.

'Never mind,' he grinned, shaking his head. 'Just lead the way.'

Half an hour later, just as the bell went, we had finished. I gazed down my transformed words with almost pride. I grinned at Nigel.

'It's great. Thanks.'

'So who are you giving it to?'

'A good question,' I said, tucking the newly-written song into my pocket.

'Is there an answer you can give me?'

'Not yet,' I grinned. 'Not just yet.'

Chapter Twelve

A few Saturdays later, I woke up early. No alarm clock needed this time. As my eyes flickered awake, I felt a little fluttery inside and the sleepiness vanished instantly. The flutters became more intense as I headed out on my bike towards the library.

But as I passed the reception, the flutters vanished, and disappointment took their place. A grey-haired lady manned the desk. She was serving a customer but glanced up as I entered. I smiled politely, resisting the urge to wave liked I'd planned. Then I headed up the stairs towards the horse section.

I had a job to do.

As the ride had turned out a little disastrously, and after Dexter had brought Minty home, I was forbidden to set foot, or bottom as it were, anywhere near the horse again. Minty wasn't too scathed by the incident. But I'd liked the feeling up there, and as I still didn't know much about horses, I guessed it wouldn't hurt to learn more.

So off to the library I went.

I had been reading books and taking notes for almost a couple of hours, beginning to give up hope, when I heard shuffles of footsteps coming down the aisle towards where I sat. I held my breath and waited for the inevitable. But nothing happened.

Silence.

I turned and grinned. An old man, toothless and reaching shakily up for a book, grinned back and nodded.

'Lovely day isn't it?'

'Oh just marvellous,' I replied. The man tipped his cap in agreement and turned back towards the shelves. I heard shuffling as he slowly moved away down the aisle. I breathed noisily and rolled my eyes to the ceiling.

'Just marvellous isn't it?' her voice mocked from behind me.

I spun in my chair. There she was. Her hair, previously plaited, now hung in curly red rings around her face. I couldn't understand why I looked forward to seeing her. But I clearly did.

'Back so soon?' she asked.

'Yep,' I nodded smiling.

'For the project?'

'Yep, the project.'

'Which is?' She glanced down at my open book before I could conceal the page. The book was a little basic, probably aimed at children under ten. But the photographs helped to explain the gibberish words. She frowned, looking puzzled. 'Horses?'

'It's just research.'

'Research for what? What's the project?'

'What are you doing tonight?' I spun my best smile, the one to make the girls beam, bite their lips, and giggle wildly. At least that's what I imagine them doing. Except for Liberty. Nothing works with Liberty.

'Looking after my sister tonight. She's eight. My parents are going out.'

'Oh.'

Maybe my smile didn't work after all.

'The project?' she pressed again. 'My sister likes horses. Do you have one?'

'No!' I answered. I ruffled the pages in the book to disguise my lie.

'You're full of mystery aren't you?'

'Everyone likes a little mystery.'

'I don't,' she replied. 'I prefer an easy life with no complications. No false pretence or atmosphere. No tension or walking on eggshells, day in and day out.' She sighed, looking out of the window, before turning back and searching my face with those big chestnut eyes. 'I guess I had too much tension, before, at high school. Easy life, that's all I want. No mystery or secrecy needed here.'

'Sorry,' I mumbled. I blushed at her honesty. 'It's just, this project is…well, it is a secret, sorry. I wish I could talk about it. But I can't. Sorry.'

I felt like a five-year-old talking about secrets. The conditions set by Liberty seemed ridiculous when faced with reality. But, some sense of loyalty towards our little friendship — just the four of us — stopped me from telling Tallie.

'I've just promised someone…' I shrugged apologetically.

'Fine by me,' she nodded, her eyes round and serious. 'Then I won't ask about it again. Off limits, okay?'

'Okay,' I smiled, relieved. 'Thanks.'

There was a pause. I thought she might leave me then and carry on filing books back from her trolley, but she didn't. She stood looking out the window as I kept my hand across the pile of books, hiding the racehorse manual. I felt a cross between relief that she stayed and apprehension as the silence remained between us.

'I've a sister, too,' I volunteered, finally. 'She's nine.'

'Does she like horses?'

'She does indeed.'

'Would she like to come and meet mine?'

'I'm sure she'd love to.'

'Then we can leave them to the horse talk and think of something else, less forbidden, to talk about.'

'I'll let you decide the subject.'

'I hoped you would think of something.'

'I'll try,' I promised. 'I'll bring a DVD just in case I can't.'

'Good plan,' she laughed. 'And pizza?'

'Meat feast? And garlic bread?'

'You're on.'

Chapter Thirteen

The tension had been building slowly at home. Nothing too obvious; nothing confrontational, but it hung in the air all the same. The hushed voices whispering in the lounge, and the sudden silence as I entered.

They were onto us.

My sister, luckily, remained oblivious and would break the atmosphere with her shrill voice and carefree affections.

I tried hard to keep to a routine. To not arouse suspicion. I left early for my paper round as usual, but I had dropped a couple of routes, and only took the far houses past Petersfield lane. I had more time, by at least an hour. Bill hadn't minded. There are always eager boys to take up the rounds.

My wallet noticed the most.

After school was the hardest to find time without my absence being noted and questions asked. The study group sessions 'excuse' hadn't washed with Mum. Although detentions were more believable, too many and Mum might get anxious enough about my upcoming exams to take a trip to the school. I just had to find the perfect balance of deceit and pretence, mixed with a tiny bit of truth, to get by.

Of course, the others were doing the same, so it wasn't all left down to me. We all had jobs to do; mine just checking, cleaning and refilling the metal water bucket. Hardly rocket science or time-consuming. Usually Dexter had done all the chores anyway, so we just sat talking or brushing Minty.

No matter how early I arrived, or late I'd leave, Dexter was always there before and after me. I guess he had nothing better to do.

I fussed around in the kitchen, pouring myself a large glass of cold milk and brushing burnt toast crumbs onto the floor. Mum stirred something on the hob. She is not the greatest of cooks, more the homely warming type of cook, perfectly edible but completely bland. She tutted as she reached past for the sieve.

'Rafferty, love, move over will you.'

'Mum?' I asked.

'If this is about the new bike, Dad says he will think about it. But you can't blame him for not giving in to you with your behaviour recently.'

I bit my lip at the remark. Dad was still clinging onto the detention excuse, but really he had no intention of buying me the bike anyway.

'No Mum, it's not about the bike.'

'What then? Excuse me.' She leant past again and reached for the plates. Her hands slightly shook as she steadied herself whilst down on her knees at the cupboard. I took the plates from her and began to lay the table. Our large farmhouse-style table dominated the middle of our kitchen.

'Is it okay if I go out this evening for a couple of hours? I won't be late.'

Mum looked up at me, already shaking her head softly. 'I don't know what Dad will say.'

'He's not here,' I said. 'What would you say?'

'You know, love, I'm worried about you and your detentions recently.'

'There's only been a couple.'

'Even so, it's a slippery slope. Dad is right to be worried and we think you need to focus on your studies.'

'Are you worried?' I asked.

'I know you always do your best, Rafferty, I just wish you tried harder to show Dad your best.'

'I don't study just to please him you know.'

'I know. I know.'

'Obviously you don't.'

'Don't be silly. Just all the school trouble has him worried.'

'And not you?'

'It has got us both worried, Son.'

'It's a Saturday night. I'm nearly seventeen, Mum please.' I could see her resolve weaken. After all, I am nearly seventeen and unlikely to look at any type of school textbook on a Saturday night. I had completed my weeks of punishment for the bunking-off day, without complaint.

'Where would you be going?'

'There's good news,' I smiled up at her. My smiles are always a winner with my mum. Who can resist your own offspring's gorgeous smile? 'Abby can come, too.'

'Where are you going?' she asked, suspiciously.

'I met a friend in the library and she's minding her kid sister tonight. The sister is Abby's age, too. We are all going to watch a DVD and eat pizza,' I paused trying to think up more good reasons. 'Abby needs some more friends. She hardly goes out at all.'

'Your Dad won't like it.'

'Why not?'

'Abby's too young to go out.'

'She's nine, Mum.'

'Exactly.'

'When I was even younger than nine, you were out dating, drinking, meeting Dad and you left me with anybody that would take me. Or alone if they wouldn't.'

'That's not true, Rafferty.' Mum's neck turned a reddish colour as she bit. She ran her fingers through her greying, unkempt hair, and sighed. I can't remember the last time she'd gone to the hairdressers for a cut and colour. She had always loved going with her friends. A pamper 'treat' day she'd call it.

'But you were out more often than you were in.'

'I was a single mum, Rafferty. Your father had been gone years. I needed to start dating again. Getting back out there, reclaiming a life. As much as I loved you, Rafferty, you couldn't expect me just to stay at home and look after you all the time.'

'I didn't,' I softened, 'I didn't mind Mum, really I didn't. I liked the time by myself and I liked the babysitter. We had fun. But Abby is treated like a little princess. She's just a kid and needs to get out there and socialise a little more.'

'I wanted to do better the second time around.'

I laughed. 'You didn't do such a bad job the first time around. I hope.'

'Of course not, love,' she smiled and planted a kiss on my cheek. She smelt of peach and creams, and the familiar smell from childhood always comforted me. 'I didn't do such a bad job at all.'

'So is that a yes?' I grinned again, risking a quick hug to cement the deal.

'Home by nine.'

'Ten?' I pushed. 'It's a one off, Abby can sleep in late.'

'Nine thirty,' Mum insisted. 'Dad will be home from his shift by ten so it's best she's home.'

I shook my head with frustration but agreed.

'We are being picked up by her parents at six.'

'Okay,' Mum looked resigned. 'Please be careful.'

'Am I anything but?'

'Hmmm,' she smiled. 'Careful is not your middle name, Son.'

Chapter Fourteen

'Have you seen Dexter recently?' Liberty asked the minute she arrived at the canal. She dropped her bike down onto mine with a crash, then walked over to the boat.

'Not today, why?'

'No reason.'

'There's always a reason,' I grinned and patted the boat edge next to where I sat. I swung my legs into the water, making ripples across the still water. 'Come sit down.'

'No reason you need to know anyway.'

'Oh,' I replied, slightly crestfallen. She heaved herself on the boat and rejected my seating plan, sitting opposite me. I pretended to ignore her deliberate snub.

'When did you last see him?' she asked.

'Dunno,' I shrugged my shoulders, before adding, 'depends on the reason?'

'Grrr,' she growled at me in frustration. Her black ponytailed mane flicked around her shoulders like a whip. 'Wilbur just mentioned something, that's why.'

'What did he say?'

'What's it worth?' she asked. Probably nothing, I thought. I couldn't care less where Dexter was or had been. I didn't even care what Will had mentioned or seen. But Liberty caring, well, that made me interested. I scooted over, across the boat, and sat next to her.

'A kiss?' I tried, puckering my lips. I knew some girls at school found me good looking, I just needed Liberty to realise what she was missing.

'Er no thanks,' she laughed. 'I think you've misunderstood. I need to benefit from this somehow. I don't benefit from your kiss.'

'My kiss will be totally worth it.'

'Is that so?' she asked. 'But no. What else is it worth?'

'Err,' I thought quickly. There wasn't much else I could sell to Liberty. Certainly not my riding skills. 'You're crap at maths aren't you?'

'Yeah great, thanks, Raff,' she groaned, slapping her forehead. 'Way to make me feel good. How will your observations on my mathematics skills benefit me?'

'I can give you some revision sessions to prepare for the exams?'

'Really?' she asked surprised. 'I'm not awful, it's just the algebra.'

'That's not too bad then. I can help you with the algebra.'

'And… statistics and probability,' she said, sheepishly, 'and maybe percentages.'

'Okay, so a lot of maths help needed.'

'Yep,' she agreed. 'A lot. So in exchange for the gossip from Will, you'll really give me the revision sessions? Starting from now as the exams are only a few weeks away?'

'Yep,' I smiled. 'Starting from now.' I was onto a win-win here. I really didn't care about the information from Will, but in exchange, I would get hours and hours of time with Liberty. I could barely contain my excitement. I cleared my throat before beginning, 'I will give you the maths sessions you so obviously need. If it helps you, Liberty.'

'Thanks, Raff,' she smiled warmly. 'I really appreciate it. So…Will was at school today in the canteen and he heard lots of shouting and cheering from the kids over the other side of the room.'

'Dexter?' I asked.

'Shhh, listen,' she said. 'Yeah, Dexter. He went over to have a look and Dexter was being pinned up against the wall by Josh Taylor, from Year Nine.'

'Josh is such a moron,' I groaned. 'Why?'

'No reason, as usual. Dexter probably caught his eye by accident. It doesn't take much to rile Josh. Anyway, Dexter managed to scramble under the table and head towards the door. Straight into Will. Will caught Dexter's arm, but he was in no fit state to listen to anyone, so he shook Will off and scarpered. But before he did, he looked straight into Will's eyes. Will said he'd never seen fear in someone's eyes before. And that Dexter's face, beneath his blonde mop, was bruised to shit.'

'From Josh?'

'No, old bruises,' Liberty said. 'They were all yellow and green. All around his eye sockets and forehead. Cut lip, too.'

'Who did it?'

'Dunno,' she paused with an elaborate roll of her eyes, probably for effect.

It worked.

I leant over the deck towards her, straining to listen. She smelt of summer flowers and linen, probably just her washing powder fragrance. Heavenly.

'So, I wanted to know when you last saw him? Because a few days ago he was beaten up. Badly it seems. And not by anyone at school.'

'Why do you think that?'

'We'd have heard, wouldn't we? Someone would have spread rumours. Taken photos of it. People like to laugh at his misfortunes. The bruises have to be from someone out of school. Someone he's had an argument with.'

'Guess so.'

'So when did you last see him?'

'I haven't seen him,' I told her. 'Promise. Actually, I can't remember the last time I saw him.'

'Like this week?'

I scrunched up my eyes thinking, 'Maybe not even this week.'

'Where is he then?'

'Do you really care?' I asked her. 'Since when have you and Dexter actually liked each other?'

'I don't,' she said. 'But I care about Will and he was worried. I've never seen him frightened before. Will is always, always so serious and cynical. Frightened, no. Dexter must be in big trouble.'

'How will we find him then?'

'Minty, of course,' she said. 'He's been here. He never misses seeing Minty.'

'Okay,' I agreed. 'So we'll wait.'

'We may be in for a long night.'

'I'm sure I'll cope,' I said, smiling inside, but trying to keep the grin off my lips. 'Just.'

Chapter Fifteen

Dexter's grip loosened only slightly when I placed my arm on his shoulders. Will's eyes bulged and his glasses fell to the floor. His feet flailed, trying to touch the ground as Dexter had lifted him off the floor by his neck. He was surprisingly tough despite his short stature and skinny arms. He pressed Will up against the side of the boat, his eyes blazing

'Drop him,' commanded Liberty. Fear tipped into her voice, betraying her usual authoritarian tone.

'Dexter,' I cried, shaking at his shoulder. 'Look at him, he's terrified. Please.'

'Please,' Liberty pleaded, looking around us uselessly. There was no one to help us out here. Dexter groaned, then lowered Will to the ground before he released his grip. Will sunk to the floor choking, his fingers pulling at his neck, willing the air to go in faster.

'I didn't…' he stuttered. 'I didn't mean to upset you Dex. I was just worried.'

'Right,' said Dexter, and he kicked at the dirt around Will. Will scrambled backwards away from his kicks, and propped himself up against the side of the boat, heaving.

'I didn't Dexter. Promise. I was worried.'

'Worried about what?' Dexter spat.

'You,' I said. 'We were all worried about you.' Dexter glanced over at me, his eyes showing a flicker of sense.

'Ganging up on me are you?'

'What do you mean?' asked Liberty.

'All of you. Waiting here for me. It's none of your business what's happened.'

'Are you okay though?' I braved. 'We heard what happened at school.' I tried my best to put on a concerned voice and soft expression. I'm not very good in conversations like these. Even when I'm being genuine it doesn't come across that way. Like people who laugh when someone dies. I think it's a nervous reaction, not them being mean. That's like me.

Anyway, I must have been better at my concerned face than I thought. Dexter's eyes stared into mine and softened slightly. His face was worse than I had imagined. The cut on his lip had nearly healed, but the bruises staining his eye sockets were a horrible shade of yellow and green. It made him look sick.

'I'm fine,' he said. He lowered his hand down to Will and pulled him up. 'Sorry, mate.'

'It's okay,' replied Will, sniffing slightly and trying to hide it behind his hand. He readjusted the wonky glasses on his nose.

'Shouldn't have grabbed you.'

'Sorry, I had just wanted to help. I will keep my mouth shut in the future.'

'Probably best,' he grinned, flashing his teeth and his blackened gums. 'I've a wicked temper.'

'Oh really,' sneered Liberty. 'I would never have noticed.' Dexter smiled over at her sweetly, but she scowled back with no forgiveness. He rolled his shoulders, looked to the heavens, and slumped back against the boat.

'You going to tell us what happened then?' I asked. 'Why the bruises?'

'No,' Dexter replied, pressing the bruises with his fingers. His nails were short and dirty. 'Not now, not ever.' I knew better than to pursue it. I tried to change the conversation.

'How's Minty doing?' I asked. We all turned to gaze up the hill where the horse stood grazing.

'He's content,' replied Dexter.

'How do you know?' Liberty asked.

'He told me,' said Dexter. I saw the twinkle behind his eyes but it completely went over Liberty's head and she turned to frown at him.

'He told you?' she asked.

'Yeah, I'm getting good at horse language business. Learnt it all from a book. Horse whispering it's called. Like in the film.'

'Really?' she asked. I couldn't tell if she was humouring him or actually believed him.

'Come on,' Will said to me. 'Let's leave these two discussing horse talk and go for a walk.'

'Good plan,' I agreed and followed Will down the path. The heated discussion behind faded out as we climbed over the stile and made our way through the undergrowth and up the hill.

'You okay?' I asked Will. I held back a tall patch of brambles to let him pass before it whipped back behind us.

'Just about,' he replied, fiddling with the edge of his glasses. 'Wasn't expecting him to go mad.'

'Neither was I,' I agreed. 'He just launched at you. I've never seen him lose the plot.'

'Why doesn't he do that at school?'

'What? Fight back?'

'Yeah,' Will said, frowning. 'He's certainly got more strength than I thought.'

'He just cowers and takes it. Never hear a sound from him.'

'I don't get him,' said Will, shaking his head, the curls flapping around his head. He needed a hair cut. I liked mine as short as possible in the summer, to keep the heat away from my neck.

'Makes two of us. He didn't hurt you?'

'Neck's a bit sore,' he said rubbing at his throat, 'but no, I'll live.'

We reached the end of the path and headed up through the grass towards the far end. Minty ambled over as we approached the corner of the field. He started running when he recognised us, giving a small whine before skidding to a stop in front of us. He snuffled in our pockets and pawed at the ground impatiently.

'Dexter's been feeding him too much,' I noted. His head shoved at my leg, and I stumbled away from him. 'Oi.'

'Yeah, he always expects something to eat from us.'

'Lucky I came prepared,' I said, pulling out some mints from the bottom of my pocket. I held Minty's nose away whilst I unpeeled one then held it flat on my palm. Minty's bristly nose brushed across my fingers. He slobbered on my hand trying to reach the mint. I offered the packet to Will to give to Minty, but he declined.

'You don't like horses much?' I asked him.

'Don't mind them,' he shrugged. 'Just a bit scared of them.'

'So why come here?'

'Cos Liberty loves it here.'

'So? You don't need to come.'

'Would be left out otherwise,' he said. 'I've my mates at school and stuff but don't do much out of school. I used to spend lots of time with Lib, but now she's always busy. She doesn't talk to me like she used to.'

'So coming here gets you time with her?'

'Yeah, something like that. And I like spending time with you and Dexter too. You more than Dex,' he grinned. 'It's nice having a hobby. My mum always says I need a hobby to get out of the house and away from the books and computer.'

'Does she know you come here?' I asked.

'No,' he replied, laughing, his breath misting up his glasses. He took them off to wipe. 'Don't worry. She thinks I've taken up cycling. She's so happy me and Lib are always out in the countryside together. Not sure she'd be too pleased if she knew what we were up to.'

'Think we'd all be in trouble,' I agreed, grinning. Minty nudged at my arm, and bared his teeth, annoyed the mints had run out. 'Come on, let's head back down.'

'He's totally mad,' Liberty said to us when we finally returned down the hill.

'Knowledgeable,' replied Dexter. 'You just don't want to admit you know less about horses than I do.'

'I *do* know more about horses,' she began, her cheeks blazing.

'You two!' exclaimed Will, shaking his head in despair, glasses jingling. 'We've been gone ages and you're still arguing. Enough.'

'I bet you haven't even had riding lessons,' Liberty mumbled. 'I have.'

'Yeah, you did Libby. Years ago, though,' said Will. 'Come on, I've had enough. Can we go home?'

'Agreed,' I said. 'It's getting dark and Will was sent to find Liberty anyway. Your parents must be getting worried he's not returned. My Dad will probably be livid too.'

Earlier, Will had interrupted the magical moment blossoming between Liberty and me whilst we waited for Dexter. Well, sort of blossoming, more like a de-thawing of ice. When Will arrived, the thawing had halted.

And begun to re-freeze.

'Fine,' said Liberty. She turned to Dexter and held out her hand. 'Agree to disagree?'

'Fine by me,' said Dexter, ignoring the hand and winking over at us. 'Sorry again, Will. I'll control my temper around you guys. Promise.'

We lifted our bikes up one by one from the pile, my hand stinging as I brushed fingers against nettles.

'You not coming, too?' I asked, noting Dexter's bike remained the last one, sunken into the long grass. He was hovering around the boat, tidying up the already spotless deck.

'Going to go up and say 'goodnight' to Minty before I go,' he said.

'Make sure he says 'night' back,' I grinned. I looked over at Liberty, who frowned and then tried to swat me with the back of her hand.

'Horses don't talk.'

'Not to you they don't,' I agreed, grinning.

I jumped onto the bike, pedalled fast, and sped away down the lane.

'Night, Dexter,' I yelled over my shoulder. 'Bye, guys.' I could hear the whirring of wheels close behind, so tucking my head down and my chin into my chest, I pedalled as hard as I could. By the time I'd reached the bridge, I'd lost them.

I propped my bike up against the bridge, pulled myself up on the side and waited as casually as I could.

Surely she'd be impressed.

Chapter Sixteen

'I just don't understand.' Liberty sunk her head down into her book.

'What don't you get?' I asked. I scratched at my hair. To me this stuff was simple, basic mathematics; I hadn't even approached the complex formulas. I just didn't understand how she didn't get it.

'The equation part?'

'That's the whole point.'

'So I have to find out the value of the letters?'

'Yes.'

'And do the same action on both sides?'

'Yes.'

'Okay,' she said. 'Let's try again.'

I wrote down a simple equation on the paper and leant back to allow her to solve it. I glanced around her room and smiled. I couldn't believe I was there again.

'Done,' she smiled. I glanced down at her answer and cringed inside.

'Okay,' I started. 'Look again. You've subtracted the six but what about the other side?'

'Oh yeah,' she reached for her pencil, chewing on the end. 'Give me a minute.'

'Take your time,' I mumbled and pushed back my chair to wander around the room. I mooched over to the window and looked out. Liberty's house sat in a small, private estate on the outskirts of the village. It had a mishmash of dormer bungalows and small, detached houses, with Liberty's house tucked in the corner of a cul-de-sac. Her bedroom overlooked the shingle driveway, with a side window looking out onto a veggie patch. I couldn't picture Liberty gardening, her manicured nails cloaked in gardening gloves. I smiled.

'Finished,' she said and rose up to join me.

'Will's a good kid,' I said, toying with a small, wooden framed photo of the two of them, as kids, arms around each other and squinting in the sunshine. Liberty with silly star shaped sunglasses on her head. I placed it back down and looked back out the window.

'Yeah he is,' she replied, pulling her hair from its clip and letting it fan over her shoulder. She followed my gaze out the window to the climbing bean cane. 'Annoying as brothers go, but basically good.'

'I'd like a brother,' I said.

'Maybe your mum will have one someday.'

'No chance,' I laughed. 'She's enough to deal with having Abby and me. And Dad has enough trouble liking kids as it is. He wouldn't want any more.'

'Troublesome, are you?' Liberty grinned, twisting hair around a nail. 'I'd have liked a little sister. I guess you always want what you can't have.'

'Guess so.'

'You can borrow Wilbur though if you like.'

'I may do,' I smiled. 'And likewise, Abby is always there for the taking.'

'Little brothers and sisters don't do much for your image though do they?'

'I don't know about that,' I replied. I ran my fingers through my recently cropped hair, enjoying the spiky sensation. 'But, well, I suppose Abby is much younger than Will. She has never bothered me in that way. She's always been in a different school to me anyway. Didn't think Will bothered you much either?'

'He doesn't. Just having a geeky little brother doesn't help me much. Especially when he's a bit odd sometimes and those friends he hangs around with…'

'I don't think anyone cares whether you've a geeky little brother. I certainly don't.'

'Well, you don't count.'

'Thanks,' I said, and frowned at her. 'Who counts then?'

'Just everyone at school.'

'Why do you care so much about what others think?'

'You don't get it, do you?'

'Get what?' I asked.

'It's okay for you, running around without a care in the world. Throwing basketballs about on the courts and with girls hanging around you like flies. You don't even need to try.'

'Nor do you. You're Liberty Ashburn. Every girl wants to be you.'

'It wasn't always that way,' she sighed and rolled her eyes. 'But now it is, and I don't want Will ruining things for me.'

'Just be lucky you've got Will, even if he ruins your image. Like you said, he's a good kid, though a little odd at times. I like odd. I'm odd too. Remember? It's unique, don't you think?'

'Whatever,' she replied and turned away from the window. She always took two steps back whenever I thought I was getting a little closer.

'Come on. Let's have a look at your answer.' We went back over to the desk and looked down at her blue pen scrawls and crossings out across the paper.

'How did I do?'

For a split second, I felt slightly satisfied with life when I saw the incorrect answer on the page. Even if it did reflect poorly on my teaching skills.

'I think we need to have another go at this one.'
'Really?' she groaned, slapping her forehead.
'Yes really,' I smiled, smugly. 'You suck.'

Chapter Seventeen

I slid each beer inside a sock before slipping them into my backpack gently. One by one. A trick I had learnt to stop the bottles from clinking together and giving the game away. Too many and it would be too obvious and too few would be pointless so I stopped after eight, two each. Dad hasn't drunk beer in a while, so I doubt he would notice. I weighed up the options of taking something stronger, but memories of a previous evening debacle stopped me so I stuck with the beer. Taking anything else of Dad's might arouse suspicion anyway. His taste being the stronger stuff.

I crouched down as the voices in the lounge grew louder, tenser. My knees ached as I waited for the right moment to cross back through the dining room door, across the hallway, to the kitchen.

I caught a glimpse of Will through the window and motioned to him to duck down. I had told them to wait for me in the lane. Waiting for mum and dad to settle in the lounge after dinner had taken longer than I'd wanted. Mum fussed about, washing up in the kitchen for ages, and Dad seemed reluctant to come in from the garage.

But at last, they'd taken up their evening positions, a sofa each in front of the television.

Footstep by painfully slow footstep, I inched through the kitchen towards the back door.

'Where are you going?'

I spun around. Abby stood sleepily in her nightie, in the archway of the kitchen door, rubbing her eyes.

'I wanted some milk," she continued. "Why are you dressed?'

'Go to bed, Abby,' I smiled at her, unwilling to say anymore. I reached for a glass from the cupboard and poured her some milk.

'Do Mum and Dad know you're going out?'

'I'm just going to play in the garden.'

'Liar. I don't believe you, Raff. Why do you have your backpack? Where are you going?'

'Please, Abby, do you want me to take you to see Holly and Tallie again?'

Abby considered this for a moment or two. She tilted her head to one side and put her hands on her hips, weighing up the options. 'Yes,' she finally said. 'But I want to know where you're going.'

'Nowhere important,' I ruffled her hair. 'Just to meet some friends. Can you keep it a secret? Please.'

'It's late.'

'Not for me, Abby, it's only half seven.' In the height of summer, the evenings stayed light until nearly ten. Plenty of daylight, although we hadn't planned to return until morning anyway. 'Go back to bed. I won't tell dad if you want to read in bed tonight.'

'When will you take me to see Holly again?'

'How about we go to the library tomorrow and we can see when Tallie is free next? We can get some books out, too?'

'Pony ones?'

'Yep.'

Abby beamed up at me, and then put her finger to her lips warningly. I froze and strained my ears.

'Go,' she whispered. She nodded towards movement from the lounge. Abby spun around quickly, skipping across the corridor and blocking the entrance to the lounge before mum could leave. 'I've a tummy ache,' I heard her say before the kitchen door softly clicked behind me and I disappeared down the garden path.

'You took your time,' Liberty tutted when I took my bike from her. Dexter had slipped into our garage and had brought the bike around the back, ready for our getaway.

'Patience,' I winked.

'Did you get it?' she asked.

'Yep, did you?'

'Yep,' Will grinned. 'We did. Come on, race you there.'

Chapter Eighteen

I lay back in the grass and let the warmth flood through me. It wasn't the first time I'd had a beer, but the effects of the first few bubbly sips still coursed their way through my blood quickly, dulling my senses and fogging my brain. Liberty took a big swig from the bottle and sat watching Dexter and Minty up in the meadow.

Dexter sat astride the horse, the two of them looping together gently in circles. Almost like dancing. The horse had his neck arched and his tail held up high. Dexter was a natural bareback rider.

Despite my disastrous first ride, Dexter finally relented and allowed me back up on Minty.

Only for a second.

I didn't have Dexter's natural grip and balance, or any kind of control on the horse like he did. He barely needed a touch on the rope or squeeze with his legs and Spearmint would bend easily this way or that. I sat awkwardly, with Minty rolling his eyes and dancing about below my slumped posture. Dexter shook his head and asked me back down. Minty clearly remembered how badly our first ride had gone.

I wasn't forgiven.

'Can I have a beer?' Will asked.

'You're too young,' Liberty told him, taking the bottle from him as he held it expectantly.

'Oh come on, Lib, I'm only a couple of years younger than you.'

'A couple of years is a huge amount in high school.'

'Please.'

'No.'

'But that's not fair.'

'Life isn't fair, Will,' Liberty took a huge swig of her bottle and gave a wry smile.

'How's the fire going?' I asked.

'Not great,' mumbled Will, tossing the beer back into the backpack. He crouched down over the pile of gathered twigs and branches with his lit match. The flame flickered around the wood, almost licking at the edges, and then died.

'Let me have a go.' I rolled over to my side and propped myself up on my elbows. 'Watch the master.'

I winked at Liberty. She rolled her eyes and turned away. I scratched the wooden tip against the strip on the cardboard box and the match roared to life. Then it had the same effect for me as it did for Will, and it too soon withered away and died.

'Only a couple left,' noted Will, shaking the packet, the last unlit matches rattling inside. 'Couldn't find any more at home. Except for the fire lighter. If we don't get it lit, there will be nothing to eat tonight. I'm starving.'

'Won't your mum notice anything missing?' I asked, looking at all the food spread out on the rug.

'No, there were tons of it. They'll never notice.'

My stomach groaned at the thought of sausage sandwiches. Liberty and Will had brought other things from their fridge, marinated chicken thighs and spicy burgers, sauces and relishes. But it might just be dried bread for dinner at this rate.

'Good ride?' I asked Dexter, as he plonked himself down next to me. He was all red and sweaty with a huge grin on his face. Blonde hair plastered across his damp forehead, flattened down from the riding hat. His dirty fingers, caked with grease from Minty, left a smear across his forehead as he pushed back the hair.

'Epic,' he smiled. 'That horse is amazing. Complete class, not like Grandad's cart horses.' He looked guilty for a second. 'As magnificent as they were. They were like riding a sofa bed and driving a tractor. No grace.'

'Don't you want to ride with a saddle?'

'Nah, don't need one. Prefer *au naturel*.'

He stretched out on the grass with his hands behind his head. 'Pass me a beer, will you?'

I tossed one over, which he popped open with his teeth.

'Thanks,' he grinned and took a gulp.

'That's really bad for your teeth,' Liberty shook her head at him disapprovingly. 'You'll end up with chips and everything. Maybe even missing teeth one day.'

'Don't care.'

'Your dentist will.'

'Haven't got one,' Dexter grinned again, his crooked teeth giving his grin a mischievous edge. 'Why? Is your daddy offering?'

'My dads a private dentist, you couldn't afford him.'

'Not even for mates' rates?'

'You're not a mate.'

'Oh, so you wouldn't mind me mentioning Minty around school then, would you? If we're not mates and all.'

'You wouldn't dare…' began Liberty, pink spots appearing on her cheeks.

'I might.'

'You wouldn't.'

'Would so.'

'You two, pack it in,' I said laughing, rolling onto my tummy and flicking grass at Liberty, trying to be playful. 'You both know Dexter wouldn't do that.'

'I wouldn't put it past him,' grumbled Liberty.

'He wouldn't because he cares just as much about the horse as you do.'

'Probably more.' It was Dexter's turn to grumble.

'How come Dexter gets a beer but I don't?' Will said, noticing Dexter sipping at his. 'He's only a year older.'

'But way more mature,' grinned Dexter.

'Doubt that,' Liberty said. 'Fine. Just one.' She used her keys to flick open another beer and passed it over to Will. 'Just take it easy, please.'

'Don't you think we need to put the tent up?' I asked. 'It's getting dark.'

'I prefer it under the stars anyway.' Dexter lay back, looking up at the sky.

'You would.'

'I don't mind the stars, too,' Will nodded in agreement. 'And it's warm tonight. No harm in sleeping outdoors.'

'Well I'm not,' replied Liberty.

'You best get started on the tent then,' grinned Dexter.

'Fine by me.' Liberty stood up and went over to the bikes to grab the tent bag where it rested up against the tree. She glanced back at us lying on the ground, beer in hands before disappearing down the path towards the canal.

'Go on, Romeo,' Dexter nudged me. 'The perfect opportunity to get the ice-queen into bed.'

'Sometimes, I understand why you get thumped daily at school,' I laughed at Dexter. I noted a quick drop in his face before the smile bounced back.

He shrugged and winked, 'I'm right though.'

'Maybe you are,' I agreed. I wanted to jump to my feet quickly and dash after her but waited for a second or two before sauntering slowly upwards. 'Just maybe.'

I walked over, past the bikes and down the little path, to where Liberty was struggling with the tent poles on a flat bit of grass by the canal towpath.

'Need any help?' I asked. I blocked out the sniggering I thought I could hear from where Dexter and Will lay, glugging beer in the increasing darkness.

She turned to glare at me and I grinned back.

The winning smile.

Chapter Nineteen

By the time I had figured out which tent pole went in what hole, and faffed around in the undergrowth trying to fit the tangled guy lines, the fire at the camp had been lit.

Liberty was no help.

She watched in sombre silence as the sunlight disappeared, occasionally passing over a pole or two when asked.

The conversation, revolving over and over in my head, hadn't happened. She hadn't, as yet, invited me to share the tent or indeed warmed to me in any way whatsoever. The night was still young though.

I remained hopeful.

'Who lit the fire?' I asked. 'Looks good.' The two boys lay stretched out on the ground, their faces lit with the dancing flames. The heat radiated out making the air on my back feel chillier than it actually was. They had gathered more twigs and branches into a big pile to keep feeding the fire for the evening, too. I was impressed. I'm not sure I could have made such a roaring fire so quickly. I was glad to see the two getting on so well after the neck incident.

'Wilbur Ashburn is a genius,' Dexter said lazily sipping at his beer. His voice was beginning to slur with the effects of the alcohol.

'Er, I don't think I did anything,' blushed Will, poking Dexter. 'It was your bright idea for the dry leaves. And you had the lighter in your pocket. We'd used the last of Dad's matches,' he told us. 'The firelighters were useless too. It was all you, Dex. I just gathered all the twigs and stuff.'

'Oh yeah, maybe I am the genius.'

'You are,' nodded Will, eagerly. 'Couldn't have done it without you. Have you lit a fire before? You just seem…an expert at all this outdoorsy stuff.'

'Maybe.'

'Well I could tell, you seemed to know exactly what you were doing.'

'Thanks,' grinned Dexter, finally accepting the compliment. He glowed from it.

'Now then boys, bromance over, who is going to cook the meat?' Liberty interjected.

'You?' I suggested, giving her a wink. Wrong move. What I meant as a light-hearted comment came out with unfortunate undertones. Not the effect I had envisioned or even meant in the slightest.

'Oh, is *that* all I'm good for?' came her dry reply. 'All you think women are good for? Nice one, Rafferty Lincoln. Good to know how you really feel.'

'No,' I said quickly. 'I meant, I would help you.'

'Mmmm,' she replied, not convinced. She allowed me to help anyway and soon the smell from the fire wafted around the small camp area.

My stomach growled in anticipation.

'You still awake?' Will poked me in the ribs.

'Mmmm,' I replied. 'Just…can't…move. I'm sooo full.'

'Me too,' mumbled Dexter. He passed around the last of the beers and bit the cap off his. I winced. Liberty's blue eyes furrowed but she held her tongue this time. 'I can probably fit in one more sausage though.'

'You eat like a horse,' I laughed. 'More than Minty. Don't you ever get fed at home?'

'Nope,' he grinned, tomato sauce trickling down his chin. 'This is too good.'

'Fancy a swim?' Will asked. He folded his glasses beside him and beamed wide-eyed at us.

'You've got to be kidding?' laughed Dexter, finishing off the sausage with one large bite, then reaching for another. 'That isn't water. It's green slime and filth.'

'Might be refreshing?' shrugged Liberty. I hadn't taken her to be that kind of girl. All lipstick and nails usually, not the throwing-herself-into-filthy-water-in-the-dark kind of girl. 'It's so muggy tonight. Good idea, Will. We could do with a dip.'

'Really?' asked Dexter.

'Yep,' nodded Liberty. 'And then we could try something a little stronger than the beer you brought.' She frowned at me.

'I liked the beer,' protested Will.

'You're a child,' she said. 'Wait till you try what I brought. Make you a man.'

'Oh really?' I smiled.

'Well, maybe not you,' she frowned and pursed her lips. 'Who's up for a dip then?'

'I'm up for it, if you are,' I nodded in agreement. 'Someone pull me up though, I can't move.'

It was another twenty minutes, whilst we finished our beers, before we finally staggered to our feet. The sunlight had completely disappeared and the haze replaced with bright stars and a half moon, lighting up the dark. It illuminated our path down through the field, past Liberty's lone tent, and overgrown stile to the towpath. The canal water had a reflective, shimmery quality. The sky looking like it had almost fallen down into the water.

Dexter jumped neatly up onto the boat, his lean frame athletic despite his shorter stature. He could easily do well in sports at school, but somehow I doubted he would be interested. I'm not sure the sports teams would welcome him either.

His popularity at zero.

I made a mental note to probe Liberty more about him. There was something she was holding back.

Dexter lowered his arm to help pull us all up. Liberty shrugged off his arm and pulled herself up. She was the first to shake off her trainers and lowered a foot over the side into the water.

'It's freezing,' she cried and flicked water off her foot at me. 'No way I'm jumping in.'

I laughed and pulled off my trainers, too. 'Mum always said the bottoms of canals are filled with rusty bikes and sharp metal. Never ever enter a canal. Drilled the warning into us.'

'Do you always listen to your mum?' she asked.

'Do you?' I grinned at her.

'Never,' she replied with a smile. 'Will's the goody two shoes.'

'Oi,' protested Will.

'What about you, Dexter?' she asked.

Dexter just looked at her but didn't respond.

'Who's going in first?' I asked. 'Will? It was your idea?'

'Why not,' grinned Will, flinging his socks onto the deck and reaching up to pull his T-shirt off over his curly hair. 'Always like a chance to shake off the goody two shoes image.'

Chapter Twenty

When I walked into school the next morning, the world had changed. I smiled at people, strangers, in the corridor — they frowned back. My step was lighter, I glided down the hallways, nodding and grinning at everyone, music bouncing around in my brain. I swung my shoulders and shook my knees.

I could imagine the high fives. The pats on the back, and handshakes, and although none came, I still felt giddy.

It radiated from me.

'You look pleased with yourself,' Jake Martin said to me as I entered the changing rooms. I was early for basketball practice so I was surprised to see anyone there. He paused to lean down and tie his trainers tighter. 'Good weekend, mate?'

'The best,' I smiled up at him as he stood up. '*The* best.' I am tall, but Jake towered above everyone, students and teachers alike. He was the master on the courts, mainly due to this. Jake would understand if I told him, he would be envious but he'd understand. I think he may have once had a thing with Liberty, but I'm sure he wouldn't care. He moved on to the next one pretty quickly.

'Going to share?' he asked. '*The* Rafferty Lincoln finally get laid?'

I blushed, 'Not quite.'

'Oh,' he frowned. 'So not that good a weekend then? Don't worry mate, there's always another chance. You should have been around Rudy's instead. Intense party. Amazing. The bollocks. Everyone who was anyone was there.'

'Sounds great,' I said. I felt deflated. I always heard about parties after they happened. Never invited, but never uninvited. Just completely forgotten. Time and time again, unless I managed to catch wind of something early. 'Maybe next time.'

'Yeah cool,' Jake said, flexing his arms, muscles bulging. Disinterested already. 'So what did you do then?'

'You know, this and that. Out on my bike. A bit of camping. Was good fun.'

'Sounds fun,' Jake smirked and patted my back. Finally the pat on the back, but not for the reasons I wanted. 'Not as much fun as Rudy's. Come to the party next time yeah? Find you a special someone.' He winked as he left the changing room and me, dejected, behind him.

The only ray of hope in my otherwise dampened spirits were Jake's words. Anyone who was anyone was there. Well, Liberty is definitely someone at Rhynside High, and she wasn't there. She was with me.

And something did happen.

Chapter Twenty-one

I struggled to remain calm. History whizzed by in a whirr of names, faces, and horrific deaths. Our teacher loved the horrific deaths in particular. I think he laboured on those points just to grab some semblance of attention from us bored students.

The numbers swam in front of my eyes during math. The whizzing slowed to a grinding trickle. I needed the day to speed up, the laborious hours to tick by faster than they were. I had hoped a ripple of excitement would be spreading around our year group by now. Smiles, whispers and nudges as I passed.

Nothing.

No one lifted up their head and nodded as I entered the canteen. No back slaps or high fives, I would pretend weren't appropriate but would secretly enjoy. This wasn't how it had panned out in my mind or in my dreams. I cursed myself for not spreading the seed of rumour into Jake's head this morning in the locker room.

And there formed the plan in my head. The plan that would lead me into all kinds of shit, but seemed the most obvious and successful thing to do at the time.

I started my own rumour.

'Hey, Nigel,' I settled down next to who I would call my closest friend during the end of lunch break. My legs sat astride the bench. 'Good weekend?'

'Raff,' he smiled at first, which turned to a frown. 'Why weren't you at Jake's party? He asked where you were?'

'Heads up next time please,' I shook my head at him. 'A heads up would have been good.'

'Doh,' Nigel slapped a big palm across his equally big forehead. 'My bad, I was going to give you a buzz on the way over. Completely forgot.'

'It's okay,' I said.

'So, a bad weekend then mate, sorry.'

'Not necessarily,' I smiled.

'Oh yeah?' he leant closer. 'Tell.'

'Can you think of a certain lady that wasn't at the party either?'

'Errrr.'

'Someone you know I like.'

'Suzy?'

'Urgh no,' I groaned. Suzy would give Frankenstein a run for his money. 'Why would you think that?'

'Just kidding, mate,' he laughed. 'She's out of your league.'

'Cheers.'

'You're welcome.'

'Think again.'

'Give up, mate, sorry. Anybody who is anybody was at the party. I can't think of anyone who wasn't.'

'I wasn't!' I protested.

'Yeah but you're not anybody.'

'I will be after this news gets out.'

'What news? Come on, spill. What did you get up to?'

'Miss Ashburn,' I said.

'Liberty?' he said. 'She was at the party.'

'No, she wasn't,' my voice raised up an octave.

'Yeah, she was,' he frowned again. 'No wait, you're right, she wasn't. Tilly was having a moan about it. Then tried her best to fill Liberty's place in the pecking order. Didn't go down too well. She's not even half of Liberty. Wait, she was with you then?'

I nodded. 'Exactly.'

'You dirty dog!' exclaimed Nigel. 'So whilst I was getting wasted on knock-off beer weakened down with lemonade you were with Liberty Ashburn. You lucky bastard. So the song worked? I take all the credit for this.'

And that's how easy it was.

By the time I left the first period after lunch, I had my first back slap, then another and another. As I entered the gym hall, a roar of approval sounded from across the courts. Yes, this is what I had waited for all day. I hadn't even needed to go into details. Details were insignificant here. Just the fact I had been with Liberty excelled my social status beyond anything comprehensible. I had finally made it in high school. This is what it was all about.

I just hadn't factored one thing into my plan.

Liberty.

Chapter Twenty-two

I cycled down the towpath, after school, towards the canal boat. I'd just had time to dump my bag into my bedroom and grab my bike from the garage when Mum swung up the drive in her car.

'Where are you heading?' she shouted at the retreating bicycle.

'Won't be long,' I called back over my shoulder.

'Dinner at six…' I heard before I was out of earshot. I pedalled hard and fast towards the country lanes.

The day had passed without a glimpse of Liberty. My one final hope to see her would be at the boat. The sun had dropped in the sky, directly in front of my bike, colouring the canal's usual murky brown a reflective yellow and white sheen. If it wasn't so tricky riding whilst half-blinded, I would have stopped to admire the beauty of the calm, still, waters and sounds of the insects and birds in the pretty wildflowers. You may think teenagers don't stop to admire such things, we do, we just don't bore each other with talking about it.

'Dex,' I called, as I approached the boat. Usually, his head and crooked smile appeared over the low sides before he'd wave and jump down. This time, nothing but the sound of shrill birds filled the air. 'Dexter, are you in there?'

I skidded my bike over to the side of the verge and threw it on the bank, where it disappeared into the thick nettles and purple thistles.

'Oi, Dex?'

I pulled myself up onto the boat and peered down into the dark cabin. The hay had been stacked to the back and down the sides, blocking the small boarded windows from the footpath. On the boat floor, in the small square gap of floor-space, was a scattering of blankets and Dexter's bag. I kicked at his bag with my foot but resisted looking inside. A faded grey washing up tub perched on a bale, and had a few plates and plastic cutlery inside.

Returning outside, I looked up the hill towards Minty. The horse wasn't grazing in the stretch leading down to the towpath. He must have been higher up around the corner.

'Minty,' I shouted, cupping my hands to make my voice travel as fast as it could. Usually, there would be a piercing whinny and thunder of hooves as the horse plunged down the hill towards the stile, hoping for an apple or mint we all stuffed our pockets with. 'MINTY!'

'Can we help?' Dexter's call startled me. I swung around. His voice came from just around the corner, but there was no one in sight.

'Dexter?'

'Who else?' He appeared into view, with Minty, walking slowly on the grass verge of the path towards us. Dexter astride, a knot of horse mane casually twisted around in his grip. His thin legs hung down either side as he motioned the horse to walk towards me, then stopped.

'Still riding bareback?' I noted. Minty reached over to try to nip my leg. I dodged out of the way.

'Have you bought us a saddle then?' Dexter asked. 'It's fine without one. We make do.' He slid down Minty's side and held the lead-rope as the horse bent his head down to stretch for a mouthful of grass.

'Where have you been?'

'Just walking along the towpath as far as I could go until we reached the dual carriageway bridge. It's too low to ride Minty underneath and I couldn't be bothered to get off and walk under so we just swung back home.'

'Lovely evening for it,' I kicked at the dust around my feet. Yeah, there is a good reason teenagers don't talk about nice things like the beautiful scenery, it just seems stupid and awkward.

'You want a go?' offered Dexter.

'Nah,' I replied. 'Minty's probably done enough for today. Next time.'

'Okay.'

'Didn't see you at school today?'

'Weren't in, that's why.'

'Why not?' I braved. Dexter glanced up at me then frowned. He spat onto the dried ground and kicked it around with his foot until it disappeared. Minty rubbed his head against his leg then carried on grazing from the tall grass on the verge.

'Hiding.'

'Huh?' I said. 'Hiding from what? Or who?'

'Doesn't matter. Just hiding.'

'Won't you get into trouble?'

'From who?'

'Your parents? For bunking off?'

Dexter just shook his head in response. 'Might go to school tomorrow. Maybe.'

'What about the school? Don't they mind you missing all the lessons you do? I barely see you at school.'

'Stalking me, are you?'

'No, just don't see you about much.'

'Keep myself to myself,' he shrugged. 'School don't mind too much. They know I come in when I can.'

'Why do the other kids give you so much trouble?' I probed.

'Do they?' Dexter stared into my eyes, his face grim and determined. I could detect a glimmer of something in his large brown eyes. Sorrow? I wasn't sure. Maybe fear.

'Yeah, they do.'

'Can't say I've noticed.' Dexter turned back towards Minty and stroked his neck. 'I'd better get him back in the field. It's such a trek going around the farmer's fields. We need to sort out making the stile into a gate, to get him in and out straight onto the towpath.'

'Want me to come?' I asked.

'Nah. Will try not to be long.' He disappeared up the towpath, Minty ambling alongside.

I sat back down on the boat edge, my legs swinging over the water's edge and leant back, propping my elbows up to keep an eye on the towpath over my shoulder. The soft thuds of Minty's hooves faded out as they had turned off the path and headed through the fields, up and back along towards the gate into Minty's meadow.

I closed my eyes and let the sun pour down onto my face.

A few minutes later, I heard footsteps coming down the path towards the boat.

'You weren't long at all,' I grinned, eyes still closed. 'Don't know what you were moaning about with the long trek. Why didn't you just hop over the stile on the way back, though?'

Before I had an answer to my question, or could even open my eyes, two hard shoves pushed on my shoulders from behind. I barely even had time to yelp before I hurtled off the boat edge and into the water.

Whenever you jump or dive into water, your body is fully prepared for the sensations it's about to receive. But if you've ever been caught by a rough wave at the beach or pushed into cold water by surprise, you'll understand what I felt.

Complete, utter shock.

Water went up into my nose, eyes, and down into my throat. I struggled to surface from the water, completely disoriented. My feet flailing at the soft squidgy mud beneath me. Gasping, I reached a hand up and grasped the rope tied around the boat. Tugging on that, I pulled myself out of the water. I lay heaving as I looked up at the person who pushed me.

Liberty Ashburn.

'That,' she said, pointing a finger down at me, 'is only the start of what you deserve.'

Chapter Twenty-three

Liberty was correct. That was only the start. For the next day at school, I wished I'd died. Humiliation doesn't quite cover it. If starting your own rumour for people to twist and turn into their own story was bad enough, what Liberty did was worse. She not only started her own rumour but left it so open to interpretation that the whole school joined in with mocking me.

It's not like I even lied. I just let the truth hang in the air, so others filled it in with their own version. She certainly chose to punish me for that.

And punish me she did.

Thousands upon thousands of lies were now spread around the school about me. Okay slight exaggeration, but tons were.

When Dexter finally appeared back on the boat that evening, Liberty had gone.

'Why are you wet?' he asked, as he pulled himself onto the boat.

'Liberty,' I said, my breath still rapid as I lay on the deck panting.

'Ah,' he nodded, as though I'd explained everything. 'Doesn't take fools gladly that one.'

'Am I a fool?' I asked.

'Exactly,' he said. 'Where is she?'

'Gone,' I replied. Dexter pulled me up to my feet.

'You okay?'

'Just about,' I replied. I grabbed my bike in silence and rode back home, wet clothes and all.

The next evening, when I returned to the boat, Dexter already sat waiting for me.

'I heard what happened.'

'Even you heard?' I slapped my forehead and rolled my eyes. 'It's bad if even you know.'

'Thanks,' he grinned. 'I don't even need to be at school to get all the gossip. I kind of expected it after what happened to you last night. Liberty certainly did you over, didn't she?'

'It was childish.'

'Well, we are children,' he shrugged and then laughed, flashing a mouthful of jumbled teeth.

'It's juvenile,' I grumbled, hoping the change of word might get Dexter's approval. He just laughed harder, clutching at his stomach, his long blonde hair flying.

'Funny, though.'

'No, it's not.'

'Come on, you have to agree. It's so childish, it's laughable. And it was ridiculously easy for her to do.'

'Pathetic.'

'Who knew it would take off like that?'

'People love some sort of craze. Idiots.'

'And now you're the craze,' his eyes twinkled. 'Come on, Raff, you have to agree. It's kind of funny your name is now spread everywhere around the school.'

'Rafferty Lincoln loves…' I said and cringed. 'You should see what some people have filled up the ending with. It's so embarrassing.'

'She didn't write them all though, did she?'

'No. Nigel said she started one off in the girl's loos, scratched into the toilet door with a compass she'd stolen from math. Then another couple scraped on desks and walls. It just took off from there. People started doing it everywhere…or else just completing the sentences started by others.'

'So who do you love?' asked Dexter.

I ignored him.

'I even caught Nigel trying to scratch the sentence on my locker,' I said, shaking my head. 'He looked completely guilty for a second then just laughed at me and said he was following the crowd. Peer pressure. He made a 'baa' noise and ran off. Even my own friends are joining in, how can I compete against that?'

'Genius.'

'It's not,' I fumed.

'She is pure genius.'

'Evil.'

'Maybe.'

'Someone's even scratched the sentence into the tree outside our house. With a fucking love heart. Dad will go mad. I need to cut off the bark, tear it off or something when I get home.'

'Don't do that,' Dexter frowned.

'Why not?' I asked. 'I don't want Mum and Dad knowing I'm the laughing-stock around the school. Dad's already pissed at me as it is.'

'It'll damage the tree.'

'What? A bit of bark missing?'

'Bacteria and insects will get in. The bark protects the phloem layer. It's like the circulatory system. So if it's damaged then the tree can die. That person shouldn't have done that to a tree. You need to treat the tree with soap and water to stop the pathogens.'

I frowned at him, 'How do you know all of that?'

'Science class.'

'But you don't come to school.'

'Yeah, but when I do, I pay extra attention.'

'Hmmm,' I replied. I'd never heard anything about trees and bark during Science. I wasn't sure if he was having me on or not. 'What do I do then?'

Dexter thought for a second or two, 'You need to squash the rumour.'

'What does that mean?'

'Complete the sentence yourself. Then it'll become old news and people will move on.'

'Don't know if I agree with you. I might fuel the flame.'

'Have you any better ideas?'

'Well, no,' I said. There weren't any better ideas. 'Do you know what Abby asked me when she came home from school?'

'What?'

'Who is Charlie?'

'Haha,' laughed Dexter. 'Charlie as in cocaine?'

'Yeah. Either that or someone wants to set me up with a nice guy called Charlie. I hadn't the heart to tell Abby about drugs and corrupt her perfect little world, so now she thinks I'm in love with a boy. Great.'

'Nothing wrong with being gay.'

'I know. Just don't want Liberty thinking I'm not interested in her.'

'I'm sure she knows you're interested,' he laughed, ruffling up his blonde hair. Scratching like he had fleas. 'More than interested. Don't worry, Raff. Could be worse.'

'How? Even my sister, at a different school, had read the sentence. My life is over.' I flung myself down onto the deck, peeling off my socks ready for the swim. 'Completely over.'

'Look on the bright side,' said Dexter, fumbling with his own socks. Peeling one off over a grazed ankle.

'Is there one?'

'You've only got a few weeks left and you've finished anyway. Everyone knows your name. I'd say high school was a success for you.'

'Everyone knows your name, too,' I noted.

'Yeah well,' mumbled Dexter. 'I'm not sure that makes it a success for me. Your life can't be as bad as mine, can it?'

'You're right! There is a bright side then,' I grinned. 'Thanks, Dex.'

I pushed Dexter off the boat into the water, tucked up my legs and bombed into the water beside him.

Chapter Twenty-four

It wasn't long before I came to the attention of a teacher. I had spent next day in a foul mood, rage surmounting inside at the rejection. I'd successfully avoided all company from friends and kept to myself during breaks and lunch. Just sat silently fuming outside on the benches until the break was over and then returned straight to the next class. To my dismay, no one in my year had noticed or cared. It was if my outer self always displayed a sullen moody teenager.

The final class had been the last straw.

Liberty was already seated, surrounded by her friends and chatting relentlessly before the teacher banged her hand on the desk sharply, to signal class had begun. The class began to settle. Books opened and pens ready.

I had slipped in late and took a seat at the back. Science was one of the only classes we shared together. Usually it would be my favourite class of the day, and not due to the science at all. I longed for Thursday afternoons to arrive. But today, I just wasn't in the mood to be within ten miles of her, let alone ten feet. I struggled to stop from blurting out the torrent of hurt from within me. I practically had to hold my lips together with my fingers to stop from saying anything.

But I didn't try hard enough.

I glanced over from time to time as the lesson progressed, trying to catch her eye. The humiliation of the previous day was still etched on my face. She either deliberately or unknowingly ignored me. I tried something more obvious and pathetic. I knocked my textbooks noisily to the floor. Made a big fuss of scraping back my chair, knocking it over as I went. The chair clattered down, metal onto wood. Some of the class turned to stare as I fumbled around picking everything up and glowering.

'Mr Lincoln,' the teacher scolded, glaring up at me from behind her desk. 'Please be more careful.'

Liberty hadn't batted an eyelid and continued talking animatedly to her science partner. I returned to my seat, dumping the textbook down with a bang, and mumbling under my breath.

'Mr Lincoln,' she continued. 'As you have disrupted the class, please can you read and explain the last answer from your book?'

'Erm,' I looked blankly up at her.

'The answer from the question I just asked. We have just talked and answered questions about messenger RNA and now we have moved onto transfer RNA. Please, could you elaborate?'

'Sorry, could you repeat the question?'

I heard giggling from the tables in front of me. Others turned to stare at me. I struggled to keep the red from flushing my cheeks. My fingers tingled.

Liberty finally glanced around, caught my eye, and then looked away quickly. I could see her shake her head, then giggle and push the girl next to her. She put her arm around the girl's shoulder and pulled her in close. She pointed at something on the desk. The beats of my heart pounded within my chest. I gritted my teeth.

'The question I have just asked you,' the teacher said, her patience beginning to waiver. 'The question that should already be written in your book.'

'What?'

'Pardon,' she corrected. 'The cell biology question that should already be written in your book.'

'The question,' I fumed. Liberty whispered into the girl's ear and laughed. She glanced back at me. 'And what question might that be? I have a good question; perhaps you'd like the answer.'

'Just answer my question, Rafferty,' she said.

'Wouldn't you like to know my question?'

'Not particularly, Rafferty. Just answer the science question, please.'

'It is in a *way* a science question. And of a biological nature. Though not about cell biology, more of a personal, intimate, biology reproductive question.'

The giggling hushed around the room and eyes turned wide as they stared. Heads shook.

'Rafferty,' said the teacher, exasperated. She spread her fingers out on the desk and stood up. 'Just answer *my* science question please. The structure of RNA. Would you like me to repeat it, in case by some sheer mishap it's not written in your book?'

My words finally held Liberty's attention. She turned to flash a warning at me, with her brows furrowed and venom in her eyes. Her lips pursed. Those lips that I once wished to kiss and touch, and longed to know what they felt like.

No longer.

'I don't give a fuck about your question,' I raised my voice, still glaring at Liberty, her eyes wide and boring into mine. She shook her head, trying to stop me or shake me away. As if I would vanish if she closed her eyes tightly enough. 'I want to ask my question and you to answer it.'

'Rafferty Lincoln, are you not feeling well, should I get someone?'

'I'm feeling fine and fucking dandy, thanks for asking.'

'Do I need to report you?' she said, reaching to her desk for her internal phone to the office.

'No, if you let me ask my bloody question, you won't need to.'

'Rafferty, I'm shocked at your behaviour today.' Her face went pink as she picked up the phone and began hastily punching in the extension number to the main office. 'There is no need for that awful language in this school. You should be ashamed of yourself.'

'Why?' I continued, not breaking my line of sight. 'Is my language upsetting you because I usually just lie down and take it like a fucking doormat? Let you shit all over me when I laid out my heart for you?'

'What?' she said. The teacher paused in her tracks, phone in hand.

'Pardon,' I corrected her, standing to my feet.

'That's enough, Raff,' Jake stepped up from his desk and laid his hand warningly on my shoulder. 'What's got into you?' he murmured.

'Her,' I pointed, not at the teacher, but straight into Liberty's mortified eyes, before swinging my bag onto my shoulder and walking straight back out the door. My shoulders and arms shook and legs trembled as I slammed the door behind me.

Oh shit.

What have I just gone and done? I took three deep breaths before turning down the corridor and taking myself to the school welfare office to turn myself in.

So that's why I stood in front of the board, chalk in hand, about to complete a task that would fling me right back to Victorian times. There is nothing like a schoolteacher who thinks that time has stood still for the last century. Tweed jacket and cap on head, he smiled as he passed over the thin piece of white chalk, before tapping the clock and sauntering out of the room.

'Switch the lights off as you go,' he called over his shoulder. 'I will inspect your work tomorrow.'

Fifty lines in fifteen minutes, if I was to get out on time to catch the last bus.

The first forty-five minutes of the hour detention had been the lecture. The long, long and mind numbing lecture. Needless words that washed over me. A phone-call home ensured my punishment would continue on late into the night and a full day's suspension, where I was to be locked into my bedroom revising.

I knew, and Mr James now knew, that the foul language from my otherwise usually clean mouth had never been aimed at the poor Science teacher. As I had mentioned before, I don't swear, unless deliberate or used in anger, both of which were the case this time.

I agreed on a face-to-face (and supervised) apology to the teacher in question with a hand-written and slightly childish sorry card. Then, later, some community service, cleaning up the mess around the school, my name etched into every surface.

A punishment for the crime I didn't commit.

He left me to the rest of the detention; meaningless lines, written not on paper but on a board. And not any old board, but a chalk board. A relic of times forgotten that Mr James must get some sort of thrill from. He was the only teacher not to swap the old boards for whiteboards, and then again in recent years for an interactive whiteboard linked to the computer system. Something to do with English being the language of medieval England and they didn't have laptops around then so why should he.

Whatever gives him kicks.

Just the feel of the dusty chalk between my fingers sent shivers down my spine. Without even placing the end anywhere near the blackboard I could hear fingernails grinding down.

Fifty lines with the words, 'The subtle art of using the English language effectively and politely,' squeezed onto the board before I left the room. It was Mr James' idea of a play on words from the infamous self-help book, fitting my bad language outburst perfectly. He laughed heartily at the irony.

I had completed only one line when I stood back and stared at the board. An idea, no matter how ridiculous it seemed, had already entered my head. Mr James' tutor group would be in the room first thing in the morning, so whatever I wrote on the board would remain until the morning for the group to see.

Including Liberty.

A one-chance opportunity to win her over and make amends for the outburst of today. For her to know that despite her reaction and humiliating retaliation, my love still burnt blindly for her. Of course, Mr James could arrive early and see the board, thus increasing my nightmare, but I was willing to take the risk.

I found a cloth and wiped away the first line from the board, and then redid the sentence, changing the ending. A subtle nod towards Liberty's own sentence from the toilet door, but with a finished ending. Half an hour later, my bus for home missed and right arm aching, I had finished.

I stood back to view my masterpiece and smiled before tossing the stump of chalk into the bin and sauntering out.

I reached up to flick off the light as I went.

Job done.

Chapter Twenty-five

Nigel filled me in on what had happened earlier. His description made me feel like I was there, witnessing the horror of it all, in the front seat of the car crash, and in slow motion. I cringed and blushed despite not having set foot in the tutor group this morning.

Mr James had arrived early to class. Usually, he waltzed in just before nine when the entire tutor group had already assembled. He would clear his throat and flick open his brown notebook before giving the group his 'thought for the day.' Handwritten probably on his commute in. Something wordy, confusing, and meaningless. Then he would rush the register and dismiss everyone as the bell rang, usually before he had reached the last name.

No time for questions or concerns by anxious pupils — just the way he liked it. After all, as he told the group, the school had counselling services for all of that. He was just there to note whether everyone had actually turned up for school.

But, for once, he'd arrived on time, as only a few people were wandering in, chatting, to take their seats.

Nigel included.

Mr James glanced at the board before taking his swivel seat behind his desk, then spun in his chair away from the class. He threw out his legs and read the board slowly. He obviously had clocked the incorrect words on his way in.

He sat in silence, waiting. As the room filled one by one, the chatter ceased. Most were surprised to see him already in his chair. Students took their seats and stared at what Mr James studied with a tilt of his head.

Liberty arrived.

The silence became a bubble of murmuring voices. Students touched heads as they frowned, then laughed and whispered to each other. Liberty looked confused before taking her seat.

'What's going on?' she asked Tilly. Tilly nodded towards the board. Liberty's face paled a shade or two before recovering and flushing intensely.

'That little …' she rose to her feet.

'Sit down, Miss Ashburn,' boomed Mr James. It was the first time Nigel had heard him use a commanding voice. Liberty sat.

'Well,' said Mr James. 'As we have plenty of time this morning for discussion, all of ten long horrendous minutes with each other, I'd like us all to discuss this.' He pointed to the board.

'I don't think that's very fair,' started Liberty.

'Don't you?' inquired Mr James.

'No.'

'And why not?'

'Because it's about me.'

'And if it were some other name smeared across the board, would you be joining in with the babble of whispers around the room? Would you be laughing, too?'

Liberty flushed further, if that was possible. 'Well no of course not. I wouldn't.'

'You would,' laughed Tilly, leaning forward onto her elbows. 'You'd be first to laugh and then jump in with a point of view.'

'I wouldn't.'

'You so would,' grumbled Tilly, slightly defeated. She sunk into her chair and muttered, 'You laughed at the sentence in the loos.'

'Well said, Miss Farrow,' interrupted Mr James. 'So, Miss Ashburn, imagine that it doesn't say your name, but that of another, what would be your point of view? Give me your opinion.'

Liberty took a moment or two to think. Mr James glanced at his watch and sighed.

'Go on,' he urged.

'I think that the author of the message has some serious issues.'

'And why's that?'

'Firstly, it's the same thing is written over and over again. So, either they are insane or they were involved in some kind of line-writing punishment — namely, detention. And for whatever reason they had detention means they are stupid.'

'Stupid?'

'For getting caught.'

The class laughed.

'Is that so?'

'And,' she continued. 'There is no way EVER to win over Liberty Ashburn or get her to fall in love with you, so writing that was a delusional waste of time.'

'Well. Said. Liberty,' Tilly laughed and clapped her hands. Liberty shot her a dirty look. Clearly, she wasn't forgiven.

'No way at all? Ever?' cried a boy from the back, rising to his feet and mock fainting back into his chair. 'My life is over.'

Other boys joined in whooping, gasping, and swooning in mock horror.

'Enough of that thanks, Mr Corbett.'

'Devastated,' the boy whispered and rose back up in his chair sheepishly.

'So if I were you, Mr James,' continued Liberty, unbothered by the commotion. 'I'd bring back that idiot to redo their detention with you. Clearly, they have completely missed the point and blatantly not completed the task you set either.'

'I might well do,' he agreed. 'Or maybe not.'

'And think hard about what you say to someone in detention next time, as your words obviously didn't cut it with him either.'

'Him?' he raised his eyebrow, nonplussed by her overt criticism. 'How do you know it was a *him*?'

'Her, him, whatever,' she flustered.

'Well thank you, Miss Ashburn, your insight has been very helpful,' he glanced back at his watch. 'And as we still have five blasted minutes left in this hell hole, would anyone else like to add something?'

This is when I warmed to Nigel even more than I did before. I wanted to lean over, as he told the story, and give him a bear hug. But that would seem weird and an overstep of our friendship. We were on purely handshake and back pat terms. But Nigel's my mate and has been since we were once neighbours. Despite us going in slightly different ways since starting high school, him the spelling bee club and me the furthest from this possible, true mates always stand up for you.

Nigel rose up his arm.

'Nigel Harris. This is an interesting time for me to hear your voice for the very first time this year. Go on. I can't *wait* to hear your thoughts.'

'I think the author had different intentions. I agree with Liberty,' he nodded over to her for approval, 'about the detention. Maybe a public display of words, clearly from the heart, wasn't the greatest idea ever. But I think she's missed the point of the words. They are, yes, slightly over-eager, even confident, cocky, but don't you think they are endearing?'

'Elaborate.'

'I think we are in a time where romance is well and truly dead and big gestures, like this one, are seen as odd and creepy. Didn't Romeo go to Juliet under her balcony? Nowadays Juliet would have called the police for some guy she's only just met hanging around outside her window. Then, maybe she would have missed out on the love of her life … err and a horrible death, but we won't go there. Yes, stalking and odd behaviour needs caution, but something as harmless as words on a board? I just think it's romantic, that's all. Doesn't anyone else?'

The boys whooped, jeered, and laughed, but some of the girls went oddly silent and gave little cute smiles at each other.

'Thank you, Mr Harris, for those tremendously wise words. I think we all feel better about life now. Well there you have it, folks, class dismissed.'

'What? Wait?' Liberty said. The class scrambled to their feet, most already disappearing out of the door. 'Is that it? Aren't you going to talk about our answers? Give your opinion? And tell us the consequences of his disregard of authority?'

'No. Off you go.'

'Not even tomorrow morning?'

'No.'

'Really?'

'No, I'm not, now shoo. I have a class arriving in a minute and I've wasted enough of my life as it is. Now excuse yourself and leave.'

'So,' I asked, my hopes only slightly raised by the end of his story. 'Was Liberty one of the girls giving the little cute smiles at each other?'

'No.'

'What was she doing?'

'She was frowning. Angrily. Then she glared at me as if I had killed her mum, and told me to 'drop dead you fucking creep' as she left the class.'

'So my words didn't work?'

'Nope, sorry mate. Not one bit. The ice queen hasn't thawed in the slightest. She now thinks you're a liar, a total loser and probably a nut job as well.'

'Great.'

'You'll probably receive the restraining order in the post, along with her dad at your door.'

'Fabulous.'

'Good call, though, with the sentence on the board. Completely got revenge for the rumour about you. Ingenious.'

'Really?'

'Nope,' laughed Nigel. 'It couldn't have gone worse.'

I take back the bear hug sentiment.

Chapter Twenty-six

After all the shenanigans (as Mum would say) of the last week, I should have hidden my head in shame and been totally and utterly defeated in my quest to win over Miss Ashburn. But I am Rafferty Lincoln, and I am never defeated. Well maybe a little with the winning aspect, but I resolved to bounce back quickly to hide my humiliation.

Easier said than done.

I figured if I acted fine, everyone would think I was fine, and then the gossiping would stop. Life would continue as usual. Liberty continued to ignore me at school. I dared not approach her for fear of her backlash, so I ensured we were never in the same room together. Obviously, my way of apology was completely off the mark and had angered her further so keeping my distance, for the time being, might be wise. I'm not sure I'd completely forgiven her for what she'd done to me either.

Science proved the only tricky subject to avoid her, but, as the teacher wasn't my greatest fan either, no one mentioned my absences.

Only another couple of weeks and our year group will be off on study leave until the exams.

A few people would laugh when I entered a room, most would look confused as if they themselves weren't entirely sure of the truth or what was going on. It gave me enough distance to plaster on a smile and continue as usual.

The school had come down hard on all the graffiti and it slowly disappeared without being replaced. Walls were being painted for the new year, desks scrubbed clean and wooden surfaces re-sanded.

I had been hauled up again by Mr James to explain why my name was plastered all around the school. I shrugged and blamed it on kids having a laugh. He dropped the community service punishment. I don't think he wanted to see me again.

'You're brave,' Will caught up with me in the corridor.

'Brave?' I asked.

'To show your face around here,' he laughed.

'It's old news now, isn't it?' I said as nonchalantly as I could. He'd noticed the whispers, comments, and graffiti, despite being a few years younger and not within any real social circles. Then again, if my sister had heard, then obviously he would have.

'Not quite,' he frowned. 'It's only just happened.'

'Well, it will be soon,' I replied.

'People are being sneakier,' he said.

'What do you mean?'

'The Rafferty Lincoln sentence. It's now a game to see where it can be written around the school without being removed. Without being caught by a teacher. There are bets going, too.'

'How have I not heard this?' I frowned.

'Think people are afraid you'll get rid of it. There's a lot of money going on it.'

'Great,' I replied, shaking my head at the idiocy of it all. 'Whatever. School ends soon, thank fuck for that.'

'Have you seen Libby around?'

'No, why?' I asked. I looked around in panic. Was she meant to be here with him? Will was leaning casually against the door frame by the entrance. 'You're waiting for her, aren't you?'

'She said she'd cycle home with me.'

'I'd best get going then.'

'Why?'

'Why do you think?'

'Don't be silly, you can't avoid each other forever anyway. You'll see us down at the canal later.'

'Not sure Liberty will like me coming, too.'

'Why don't we ask her,' he nodded his head down the corridor. 'Here she comes.'

I debated scooting across the hallway and into the toilets but that would be too obvious. There was no way to avoid her. Liberty had flung on her backpack and pulled her hair up into a band ready for the cycle home. She smiled when she saw Will, but the smile faded as she noticed me next to him.

'What are you doing here?' she asked.

'Just leaving,' I said and turned to Will. 'See you at the canal over the weekend.'

'Okay, Raff, see you soon.'

'Don't leave on my account,' she said, glaring at me.

'I wasn't,' I told her. 'I've the bus to catch.'

'Oh,' she replied. 'I guess our revision sessions are off then?'

'Guess so,' I said. 'Wouldn't want to take up the precious time of the great Liberty Ashburn.'

'Don't be like that,' said Will. 'Come on Libby, you really needed those sessions and said they were helping. I know you looked forward to them.'

'Really?' I asked, surprised. I couldn't remember Liberty making progress with anything I'd been trying to teach her. Not one single thing.

'A little,' she admitted, frowning. 'It's good to go through things with someone else. But I'll ask Tilly to help.'

'The offer's there if ever you need it,' I said, kindly. 'I don't mind helping you out.' I was surprised I actually meant it.

But I was prepared to let bygones by bygones if she was, too.

'I doubt I'll need it,' she said stiffly. 'I only let you tutor me because I felt sorry for you.'

'Sorry for me?'

'You're always so desperate for people to like you.'

'Okay,' I said quickly. 'Bye, Will.' I gave him a quick salute before turning and walking back through the corridor towards the side exit and bus stop. Throw a carrot and get a slap back. From that moment, my heart left Liberty Ashburn.

Maybe it was never hers to have.

Chapter Twenty-seven

Saturday night I went around to Tallie's, this time without Abby. It had been a couple of weeks since the pizza night and I'd missed her.

Mum raised her eyebrows as I mentioned my plans, but for once didn't interfere. I knew nearer exam time this wouldn't be the case, so I planned to take advantage of things whilst I could. The exams were creeping nearer and nearer and I had done little in way of preparation. Dad was working late again anyway, so less chance of a refusal. He was known for giving blanket refusals to anything asked at the moment. Mainly due to my recent behavioural issues, or so he said. He was basically being a dick as usual.

Tallie opened the door with a quirky smile and tilt of her head, then ushered me inside. Her usual plaits were gone, replaced by funny sticky up tassels, tied with coloured bands. Her parents were home, in the kitchen cooking. I smiled and waved at them. Her mum came across to the doorway to give me a hug, beaded jewels jangling around her neck. I was taken aback, as I didn't realise I had made such a good impression the first time around. Holly waved happily from her position in front of the TV then turned back to her programme.

'Hi,' said Tallie.

'Hi back,' I said.

'Do you want something to eat?' her mum asked, going back into the kitchen and stirring something nondescript in

137

the pan. Maybe sauce and some kind of meat, I wasn't sure. I am used to the meat and veg kind of dinners, so whatever was cooking, although it smelt heavenly, I had no idea what it was.

'Er, thanks, only if there is some left.'

'Plenty,' her mum reassured me, smiling. She wore a red apron tied around the middle and feathers for earrings. 'You two go off and I'll call you when it's ready. You can eat upstairs if you'd like. I will make up a tray.'

'Don't be silly,' said Tallie. 'We'll eat together.'

'Of course,' I echoed, not so sure about the family dinner situation. I'd done well so far to not slip up and say something stupid, but over a dinner, I wasn't sure I'd last. 'That would be lovely.'

'Come on.' Tallie grabbed my hand and led me past the kitchen to the stairs. Her hand warm and soft in mine. I wasn't sure what I was expecting a female's hand to feel like. Like mine, but nicer. I think Liberty's would be just as soft, but her long nails would probably stab me if she gripped too tightly. Tallie let go of my hand as she took the stairs two at a time up to her room.

'So,' she said. 'Which one?' She held up two DVDs in front of me. I squinted my eyes, looking at each of them then widened. Oh dear. Girly rubbish I presumed.

'Er…' I said.

'Which one?'

I glanced at the DVD cases. Both had loopy but slightly different pink writing with unidentifiable but good-looking (in my honest opinion) men on the covers and a smiling girl. Practically had glitter and sparkles flung over the cases. I could smell the sing-a-long music and joy within the cases. I shuddered involuntarily.

'Can I say neither?' I replied, grimacing.

'You pass,' she smiled.

'Pass?'

'The test.'

'And the test was?'

'Whether you have taste or not.'

'And I do? I'm not so sure about that.'

'True. But you passed the first test. These are my sister's DVD's.' She flung the DVDs back into the shallow, wicker box by the bed.

'Phew,' I grinned. 'I can tolerate a rom-com on occasions but those were sickly to look at. So, what are we going to watch?'

She shrugged. 'Dunno.'

'You choose,' I insisted.

She turned back to the box and started rummaging around. Her room was different than Liberty's. Completely different. Although she had the same vanity table cluttered with bottles and bits and bobs, there was a different, more subtle edge to her room. She didn't have the usual pop stars lining the walls and pink, sparkly girlishness I had expected. It was as if the year between the end of school and starting college wiped all the high school-ness from you.

Instead, she had a large painting of an African elephant over her bed, painted in silver and gold swirls on board rather than canvas. The other walls were bare, apart from the odd pinned up sketch, presumably her own artwork. There were sketches of trees, houses, and people I didn't recognise. Thick black pen lines outlined an old man smiling down at a child handing him a flower.

'You drew these?' I asked.

'Yes,' she mumbled. 'Back in my dark and moody stage.'

'Oh yeah?' I grinned. 'Tell me more.'

She glanced up quickly, 'My early high school days when the dramas of the world were too much to handle.'

'Oh,' I replied. 'Sorry.'

'Don't be,' she smiled. 'It was mainly when Mum and Dad divorced. I was embarrassed to tell anyone when Owen moved in. Turned to scrawling dark oppressive drawings instead.'

'Who's Owen?'

'The man downstairs.'

'Oh,' I said. 'He's not your real Dad?'

'No,' she replied. 'Though he's been as good as a Dad to me, so I don't think he's not anymore.'

'Really?' I asked.

'Of course. I'm lucky, I have two great Dads. Why do you ask?'

'No reason,' I said. I guess it's not normal to have such issues with your step-dad. Maybe I'm the issue. Tallie obviously recovered from her childhood dark days. I haven't.

'I'm over with all the drama now,' she continued, head back down in the box. 'I know it's here somewhere.'

'They're good,' I said. But she didn't hear. Maybe I should have drawn out my moods in vivid charcoal. I regretted choosing woodcraft over art, as useless as I am at that, too. You should have seen my mum's expression when I presented her with the wooden photo frame I'd made in class.

Priceless.

I let Tallie keep looking. I glanced around the room towards the large windows. She lived up the valley, on the other side of the town, as the hill sloped back away towards our school. The houses were bigger, more spaced out with more unusual interiors than the more common semi. Some houses began on the middle floor, with the kitchen below. Tallie's house had three levels, with her room on the top of the last twisty staircase.

Tallie's room was light and airy, no clutter lining the sides or piles heaped within the wardrobes. Her window had the view across endless fields. I leant on the windowsill straining down to see her garden below.

'Careful,' she warned.

'Huh?' I asked, and then noticed the only clutter in her room, lining the windowsill, which I had either squashed or sent fluttering to the floor. 'Sorry.'

She shook her head at me, tutted, and turned back to the box. I bent down to pick up the paper from the floor. I twirled one in my hand before returning it to the windowsill but another was seriously squashed.

'Sorry,' I said again. 'What was this?'

'A horse,' she replied, finally turning towards me.

'A horse?' I asked.

'Yeah, they're origami animals.'

'Ori…what?

'Origami, you know, craft made from paper. It comes from the Japanese words for paper, and to fold. So basically it's folding paper into shapes.'

'Oh,' was all I could respond. Her shoulders dropped slightly so I added, 'How did you get into that?'

She smiled, showing the cute little gap in her teeth. 'I'm not some kind of paper freak. I like making them. I looked it up once after I was roped into watching an episode of Prison Break.'

'Prison break?' I asked, confused.

'The guy in it makes paper cranes,' she said, before adding (after noting my even more confused face), 'you know, the crane bird.'

'Oh yeah.'

But I didn't know. Cranes to me were a type of machinery.

'Most people thought it was a swan,' she said, shrugging. 'But it wasn't, it was a crane. It has a meaning in Japanese; the crane represents a long and happy life. They can also be a sign of happiness and good luck,' she said, then smiled. 'Also there's a legend, too. A wish granted.'

'A wish?'

'If you fold a thousand cranes, a wish will be granted.'

'Interesting,' I smiled. 'You'd better get folding.'

'I think I'd need some help.'

'So you're quite a little paper freak after all,' I said. She laughed and pushed lightly at my shoulder.

'I don't use the special thin paper sheets or anything; just whatever I can find lying around. Keeps my hands busy. Here,' she picked up the one I had squashed and fiddled around until it bounced back to shape, just. 'This horse was just made from one of my old envelopes. And this one,' she laughed. 'This one is from Mr Burton's maths lesson last year.'

I recognised the school's squared paper, now twisted into the shape of a duck. I laughed, too. 'I'm sure Mr Burton will be thrilled to know what happened to your algebra homework.' I picked up another and studied it. 'I like them.'

'Would you like to try?'

'No way, I'm all thumbs when it comes to anything crafty. That's why I suck at art, and at woodcraft. There weren't many other options.'

'Food tech?'

'Wait till you see my mum's cooking. I have her skills.'

'Is that an invite around to dinner?' She bit her lip and sucked in air through the gap in her teeth. It whistled, reminding me of the strange sounds I make.

'Would you like it to be?'

Tallie laughed. 'Enough of us flirting, I've found the perfect DVD.' She waved the case in my face. I grabbed at it from her and studied the title.

'Alien!' I grimaced. I am not great at horror kind of films, especially in company. Scream like a girl, I think was Nigel's comment about me when we watched it the first time around. I'd probably rival any girl's scream. 'Do you want to scare me into cuddling into you?'

'Maybe,' she winked softly and then blushed at her brashness.

I liked it.

'Was that my second test?'

'Huh?'

'You said the first test was about my taste in DVDs, so what was my second?'

'This,' she said, leaning over and kissing me on the lips.

I was taken aback. It took less than a second to block Liberty from my mind before I responded and kissed her back.

'Do I pass?' I asked.

'Humm,' she murmured, leaning forward again. 'I think you need another try.'

Chapter Twenty-eight

'I'm not sure he's ever going to like me,' I moaned to Dexter.

'That's because you're frightened of him. He can sense it.'

'I'm not frightened,' I replied.

'You so are.'

'Just cautious,' I said, grinning. 'After the fall, Minty hates me. It's easy for you and Liberty. You both know what you're doing around horses, and Wilbur, well, he's not bothered one way or the other.'

'And you are?'

'Yeah, I guess I'm bothered. If we're going to spend all this time here and doing all the jobs, I want to get some benefit out of it.'

'Now the Liberty benefit has gone?'

'Something like that,' I laughed. 'I guess she wasn't much of a benefit after all.'

'So you want to learn about horses?'

'Yeah, properly this time. Not just to impress Liberty but to actually learn something.'

'Come on then,' he said, hopping down from the side of the boat. 'Let's do lesson one.'

'What's lesson one?' I asked.

'The basics,' he replied.

'How basic?' I asked, frowning. This didn't sound fun.

'Let's start from the very beginning.'

'Oh,' I said. 'I was afraid of that.' I followed him over the stile and up the windy, overgrown path towards the field.

Dexter, with grubby hands, handed me the lead rope and head collar and pushed me towards Minty. The horse paused from grazing and snorted. His nostrils flared.

'First job. Catch him,' he told me.

'How?' I asked.

'Have you not learnt anything?' he said and frowned. 'I'm sure we covered this before? Didn't Liberty go through this with you? God knows why I ever let you ride him in the first place.' He positioned the head collar in my hands so all I needed to do was slip Minty's nose into the loop and buckle behind his head. Then he pushed me towards Minty. 'Go on.'

I approached the horse, hands out wide with the rope. Minty pawed at the ground and then backed up a few paces, tossing his black mane about.

'Come on boy,' I whispered and then clucked with my tongue against my cheek. Minty pricked his ears at the sounds and stretched his neck towards me. I reached forward to loop the band over his nose.

'Gently,' called Dexter. With the band looped over his nose, I went to pull the strap around his head to buckle up. Minty swung away, dragging me around with him. Then he pulled back, tossing the head collar and me to the ground. He turned, kicked up his back legs and then galloped up the hill towards the farthest corner. Clods of mud flew up, spraying down all around me.

'What went wrong?' I asked Dexter, sitting up and hugging my grazed, grassed-stained knees. I must stop wearing shorts to the canal.

'You,' laughed Dexter. 'He just really doesn't like you.'

'But you said that was just because I was frightened.'

'Were you frightened today?' he asked.

'Yeah,' I said. 'But Minty didn't know I was.'

'Of course he did,' he smiled. 'Horses can tell a mile off.'

'Then I've no hope.'

'Don't give up yet,' said Dexter, and he pulled me to my feet. He brushed down the mud from the back of my T-shirt and then patted my back. 'He'll respect you for trying again.'

'What? Now?' I asked, shuddering.

'Yep,' he said and nudged me up the hill. 'Now or never.'

'Do I have to?'

'Yep,' he called after me. 'You do. And don't be timid this time. Just stroll up to him, maybe offer him a mint if you've got one, and put the head collar over his head. No bullshit, be in charge.'

'Easier said than done,' I grumbled, turning up the hill towards the grazing, oblivious animal. I rummaged in my pocket for a sticky mint. 'Bloody horse.'

'I heard you,' called Dexter. 'He probably did, too. Try being a little more friendly and he might like you.'

'Bloody Dexter,' I mumbled loudly, turning to flash a sweet smile back at him. 'You wait, I'll be a horse whisperer before you know it.'

'Yeah likely,' said Dexter, waving me away. 'Now off you go.' He turned and walked down the path towards Will and Liberty, who were winding their way up to us from the stile.

Great, an audience.

I breathed in and swung back up towards the horse. Come on, Minty, don't let me down. Minty munched on grass and watched me approach, occasionally swishing his long, black tail from side to side to squash the odd fly or two. His red coat gleamed in the evening sun. He stood statue still. I marched up and buckled the head collar over his nose before he could even protest. He didn't even flinch. His eyes had a bored, solemn expression. Jaw grinding the grass.

'Well done,' I grinned, and patted his silky nose. 'That wasn't too hard. Now come on boy, walk on.'

I pulled on the lead rope. Minty just stood motionless and munching, hooves rooted to the ground.

'Come on, boy.'

I pulled again, the rope straining on the metal hoop under the head collar. Minty lowered his head for another mouthful of grass and stood staring at me. His black lashes blinked over his huge brown eyes. His hooves didn't budge an inch. I turned to see Liberty, Dexter, and Will laughing up at me. Liberty looked particularly gloating. Anger began to boil inside.

'Bloody horse indeed. Little shit more like,' I whispered into his ear. 'Move.'

Minty pricked up his ears and took off down the hill towards them, dragging me along the ground behind. My hands burned as I gripped the rope, refusing to let go. He skidded to an abrupt stop in front of Dexter and lowered his head back to the grass. Groaning, I rolled away from the horse, over onto my back and peered up at the cloudless sky.

'Lesson one complete,' grinned Dexter, the blonde mop of hair appearing above me in the skyline. 'You okay?'

'Yeah bloody marvellous,' I replied, looking at my torn, bleeding palms. 'And what is lesson two?'

'Wait and see,' he laughed.

'Oh. I can't wait,' I said. 'I really can't. Count me in for more torture any day.'

'Torture?'

'Sorry. Learning. Count me in for all this fabulous horsey learning any day.'

Chapter Twenty-nine

Tallie hadn't mentioned the word 'horse' again since she spotted me with the book in the library.

I wasn't sure if the word still hung in the air between us or she'd completely forgotten. Forgotten about how we met that day in the library and why I was in there in the first place. There had been no more library visits, mainly to stop any questions. Further research was done through a library book I'd borrowed and hidden under my mattress in case Abby came snooping.

Brushing up on my horse knowledge for Liberty was pointless but I had started to enjoy learning about Minty and using this to chat to Dexter. There wasn't much else Dexter and I had in common. It gave us some middle ground to break the awkward silences.

There were many of those.

So when Tallie asked her question, it took me by surprise. I struggled to come up with any kind of answer without giving the game away.

'When are you going to tell me about the horse?' she asked, as we lay on her bed side by side, as the credits rolled on our evening movie marathon.

'Huh?' I said. Lies and excuses swirled around my brain, and I was unable to form a coherent sentence. I looked over at her. Her eyes remained focused on the ceiling.

'The horse?' she repeated. 'When are you going to tell me about the horse? I think I've been very patient,' she chuckled, and looked over at me, biting her lip. 'I haven't asked, but I still know something's up. So when are you going to tell me?'

'What horse?' I asked.

'Come on. I think you know me well enough by now to not keep secrets.'

'This secret I can't share,' I said carefully.

'Are you buying Abby a horse?'

'No,' I laughed. 'What? With the money from my paper round? Bill's shop doesn't pay that well.'

'Suppose not,' she grinned. She rolled over and propped her head up on her hand. Her freckles splattered her nose. 'So what is it then? Why are you learning about horses? It's an odd thing for a teenage boy to care about.'

'I told you the conversation was off limits,' I warned.

'Yeah, when we were strangers.'

'It's still off limits.'

'That's not fair,' she said crossly. 'I shared stuff with you. Private things, too.'

'I didn't ask you to.'

'So you wish I hadn't?'

'That's not what I'm saying,' I told her, getting frustrated. 'I do share things with you. Just not this. And I like you sharing things with me.'

'Is this to do with Liberty Ashburn?'

'What?'

'Liberty Ashburn.'

'What have you heard?' I looked over at her sharply. She shrugged her shoulders.

'Rumours.'

'What rumours?'

'Nothing in particular. Just rumours about you and her together.'

'Liberty and I are just friends. *Were* just friends. I'm not sure we're close anymore. Probably not even friends.'

'Because of me?'

'No, Tallie,' I said, shaking my head. 'Nothing to do with you. It was a stupid rumour. Well, lots of rumours. There has never been anything more than friendship between me and Liberty. Friendship is probably too strong a term to describe it anyway.'

'Okay,' she said. She seemed satisfied. I didn't have to go further into exactly what happened with Liberty or the disastrous after-effects of my pathetic behaviour. I'm beginning to think it's a distant dream anyway.

'Okay now?' I asked her. 'Shall we watch another movie? My choice this time?'

'How do you know Dexter?'

'Dexter Forrest?' I asked. I knew full well he is the only Dexter I'd ever heard of.

'That's the one.'

'I don't really know him.' A lie and she knew it. I'm not great at lying, my face colours quickly and my voice gives me away. I swear my balls curl up inside me, too. Probably too much information. 'He's a year below us at school.'

'Just wondered,' she said. 'I heard you knew him.'

'Who told you that?'

'Rumours again,' she smiled and shook her head. 'No one in particular.'

'Nope, don't know him apart from at school. How do you know of him?'

'I don't,' she said. 'He'd only just started at the school when I left for college. Transferred from another school. He's just one of those kids you hear about, isn't he? And wonder his story.'

'His story?'

'Yeah, you know, how he's got into the situation he's in. I hear all sorts about how he's treated at school. Poor kid getting bullied every day.'

'He's alright,' I told her. I think of the different Dexter I know from the boat. 'He can stand up for himself.'

'Hardly,' she said. 'Poor kid's getting picked on all the time. He's already bruised to shit before he gets to school anyway. Must knock him right back down when the same happens at school, too.'

'What do you mean?'

'Oh nothing,' she said. 'Just what I heard.'

'Go on. What did you hear?'

'It's nothing. Just I hear his home life wasn't very happy. He wasn't treated nicely, wasn't fed and washed properly, that kind of thing. Lives with his Granddad now apparently.'

'No, he doesn't.'

'Yeah, he does.'

'No,' I shook my head confused.

'He does,' she insisted. 'That's what the papers said. His Mum and Dad were physically abusing him so Social Services took him away from them a few months ago. Don't think they do that often and only in the worst cases. His Granddad said he'd take him in and look after him until he's old enough to live on his own. He'd been practically raised by him anyway.'

'Raised by his Granddad?'

'Yeah, between the Granddad and his parents. He's better off living with the Granddad now anyway. Poor kid.'

'Yeah,' I agreed, nodding. My mind had wandered off to the conversation Dexter and I had during our ride out with Minty. 'How do you know all of this anyway?'

'My mum works for them.'

'Who?'

'Social Services.'

'And she's allowed to tell you about the cases? I'm surprised she can just tell you about it.'

'No she can't, she's not exactly allowed to.' Tallie's face flushed. 'The files are all confidential. Mum never talks about any of them to me. Not even if I ask.'

'Then how do you know all of this?'

'Mum brings home the case files sometimes to read in the evenings. Paperwork like letters that aren't on the computer. She catches up on the reading before meetings the next day and types up the notes. She leaves the papers on the kitchen table…'

'And you snoop in them?' I exclaimed, my eyes wide in surprise. I couldn't see Tallie doing that.

'Only the once. I just recognised his name when the files were stacked on the table ready for Mum to take back. I wouldn't normally but he's one of those kids everyone talks about. His name was on top on a sticky label. I couldn't help myself.'

'I'm disappointed in you,' I grinned. 'Very disappointed, Miss Phillips. You should be ashamed of yourself.'

'I am,' she nodded, solemnly, twiddling with her hair. 'Really, really ashamed. Mum would kill me.'

I believed her.

'Naughty girl,' I said, tutting. I'm not sure if I would have had any self-control either if I had seen the files just sitting there, with Dexter's name blazed across it. But I liked teasing her. She swatted me with the DVD cover.

'Ouch!' I protested at her battering, holding her off by her arms.

'Please don't say anything.'

'I won't,' I promised. 'Your secret is safe with me.'

'What about your sordid secret?' she smiled and ruffled my hair.

'That's still off limits.'

'No way,' she protested. 'After all the sharing, I would have thought I'd earned your secret. Go on, tell.'

'Sorry,' I leant over and kissed her on her lips. 'The secret dies with me.'

'We'll see about that,' she said, before kissing back. 'I am good at finding out about secrets.'

I seriously hoped she was wrong.

Chapter Thirty

'So what's lesson two?' I asked, not wanting to know. I stood behind Dexter reluctantly. Minty hooked up to the boat, munching hay Dexter had tied up in some kind of wide-holed net. The horse's big eyes were upon me.

'Lesson two is basic horse care,' he replied, dragging out a plastic box. He opened it to reveal tons of different brushes.

'This looks familiar,' I said, recognising the equipment. 'I think Liberty went through all of this with me.'

'So we can skip to lesson three?' asked Dexter. He held up a brush and raised his eyebrows. 'What's this?'

'A brush,' I replied.

'Yeah, but which one?'

'A fucking horse brush, Dexter, okay?'

'Shall we stick with lesson two then?'

'Fine,' I mumbled. I tried to concentrate as Dexter ran through the names of all the brushes again and their purposes. He showed me how to use a funny bent metal hook to clean the mud from his hooves and how to get him to lift up each foot in turn. Minty kept his hoof welded to the ground for my turn. Dexter just had to click and he'd lift it for him.

I think this time the lesson sunk in.

Maybe.

But I certainly didn't want to have to start the lessons all over again. Finally, he passed me a brush and we began to clean the mud from Minty's smooth red coat. His body shone the same colour as Tallie's hair. Beautiful flaming red; just like the missing racehorse. Profits *Red* Ridge wasn't it? I quickly dismissed the thought.

We worked in silence for a good half an hour, whilst Minty just munched and finished up his hay. It was hot work and I sweated through my T-shirt. Dexter took a wide-toothed comb and dragged it through Minty's black mane until it lay flat and silky.

'Lesson two complete,' he said, standing back to admire the shiny, clean horse.

'Really?' I asked, glancing at Dexter. 'I was just beginning to enjoy myself.'

'A great way to spend a birthday,' he smiled, and patted the horse, before flinging his small, thin arms around the horse's huge neck. His T-shirt rose slightly, showing a huge purple bruise spreading across the top of his hip. I didn't know he'd fallen off Minty, too. He buried his nose into the horse, who lowered his head and waited with half-closed eyes.

'Birthday?' I asked. 'How do you know it's his? Thought you said all racehorses have the same birthday?'

'They do,' he said. 'January 1st. But no, it's mine.'

'Your birthday. What, today? Why didn't you say?' I asked.

'I just did,' he shrugged, letting his arms drop from around Minty.

'No. I mean earlier on. So we could have planned something.'

'What like a party?'

'No. Well, yeah, something like that. Not a childish party, but maybe another camping trip down here or something.'

'Didn't see the point,' he said, simply. 'Minty's had enough. He's finished the hay. I'll take him back around to the field.'

'Okay,' I replied, watching him untie the rope and spin the horse back around onto the towpath. Minty ambled along beside him. 'I'll clear up.' I watched him go and shook my head slowly.

I didn't understand Dexter. Who wouldn't want to celebrate a birthday? I vowed to make it up to him another day, to throw a celebration for him. But somehow as the summer progressed, my vow got forgotten.

I'd just finished putting the brushes back into the box when Will arrived.

'Hey,' he said, screeching his bike to a stop, gravel spraying. 'What you up to?'

'Finishing up,' I said. 'Dexter had me brushing Minty. Apparently, I needed to start my horsemanship lessons right from the very beginning.'

'That good are you?' he laughed.

'Apparently.'

'You look boiling,' he noted.

'Sweaty,' I replied.

'Yeah. I didn't want to mention it but you're really red and sweaty,' he laughed and sniffed the air near me. 'And smelly. Yuck.' He flung his bike down and pulled himself up onto the boat deck. I lifted up the box to him and he heaved it on board, then pulled me up after it. 'Coming in for a swim?' he asked, pulling off his T-shirt.

'Maybe,' I nodded. 'I'll just sit on the edge and have a breather for a minute though. I'm knackered.'

He pulled down his jeans and folded them, placing his mobile phone and glasses on top. Then he ran and bombed into the canal, spotting me with droplets of algae green water. Smiling, he rose back up to the surface.

'It's amazing,' he grinned. 'Like a bath. So warm. Come on.'

'Not yet,' I replied. I leant back and let the evening sun wash over me.

'Help me back up,' called Will. He held out a wet hand and I reached down to him. I gripped with both of mine to tug his slippery body on board.

'Why?' I asked.

'I've an idea. Can you help me?'

We pulled over a couple of bales to the edge and Will stacked them up, one on top of the other, against the edge. He climbed to the top and looked down into the water. He looked around at me, grinning, his floppy, curly hair partly covering his eyes.

'Careful,' I warned. 'Is it deep enough?'

'Think so,' Will replied. 'I've swum down to the bottom and it's at least a couple of metres or so. Should be enough.'

'Still,' I warned. 'Just be careful. No higher okay?'

'Okay,' he cried and launched himself off the bales into the water. The sprays faded back to calm water before his body pierced up through the surface again, hair now swept back off his face. He swam, treading water and grinned happily. 'Amazing,' he called. 'Plenty deep enough.'

He swam back over and pulled himself on board, using the rope around the edge of the boat. 'One more bale,' he said. 'Please?'

'Really?' I asked. 'You sure it's safe?'

'Yeah. Just one more? Promise.'

He dragged over another bale and stack it up on the top. The bales wobbled together as he climbed up, holding onto my shoulder.

'Ready?' I asked.

'Yeah!' he cried, leaping high and blasting the water with his body. His beam arrived up through the water a few seconds later. 'Fucking amazing, Raff.'

'Looks it,' I agreed.

'Come on in. The water's gorgeous.'

'Think I'm too tired,' I told him, looking sceptically at the swirling brown-green liquid. I felt drained from all the brushing, and just wanted to lie back on the boat and watch. 'You keep going though, and I'll watch.'

'Can you take a photo?'

'A photo?' I asked. It had never even occurred to us to take photos down by the canal. I didn't even have one of Minty. 'What? On your phone? You shouldn't have your phone here. You know Liberty's rules.'

'Bet you have your phone?' Will retorted.

'Maybe,' I grinned, feeling my phone case in my shorts pocket. I didn't always take the phone when I was on my paper round, but I had today. I had been bringing the phone more often recently. 'But I never use it here.'

'The rules were not to bring it here.'

'Then why do you have yours?' I asked, raising my eyebrows.

'Good point,' laughed Will, swimming over to the boat side and holding onto the rope. He kicked his back legs out and lay floating. 'Just don't like leaving it behind. We're always down here alone, what if something happened?'

'That's why I've started to bring it,' I agreed. 'Just one photo then.' I leant back and reached the phone off his pile of clothes.

'Hold on,' he asked. He swung back out of the water and positioned himself on top of the bales. 'Wait till I'm mid-air.'

'I'm not a photographer,' I laughed. 'I'll do my best.'

'Three, two, one,' he called, before leaping off the top. As I pressed the button in the middle of the phone, he'd already disappeared under the water.

'How'd it look?' he asked, pulling himself up out of the canal.

'Sorry,' I said. 'Missed you. Try again.'

'Press the button on the count of one this time.'

'I'll try,' I shook my head, grinning. I waited until the exact moment he jumped before I pressed the button.

'Better?' he asked, treading water beneath me.

'Keep trying,' I said. Clearly, I'm not meant to study photography at college. Lucky, I wasn't. It took another five times, and an exhausted Will, to get the perfect shot. Will, mid-air between bale and water, with a gleeful expression on his face. He flopped down next to me and took the phone.

'Perfect,' he said, admiring the shot. 'Bound to get tons of likes when I post this one.'

I smiled at his enthusiasm. Maybe photography could be a choice after all. Dad had a good couple of cameras. An old, vintage Polaroid and a newer digital make with tons of different zoom lenses for the perfect shot. I'd not ever been allowed near them. I wondered if he'd miss one of them if I brought it here one day, just to capture the perfect shot.

'Think it's a good idea to put on Facebook? It might cause some awkward questions.'

'Photo is bound to be a winner,' he smiled, ignoring me. 'Can you take some more?'

'You BETTER not put the photo anywhere near Facebook. You hear?'

The voice behind made us jump.

Liberty.

'And why do you have your phone here, Will?' she asked, pulling herself up onto the deck. 'You know the rules. No phones. No social media. Nothing to ever indicate we've ever been here.'

'He's got his, too,' Will said, pointing at me. I raised my eyes to the sky. Thanks, Will.

'There's no law about bringing phones down here,' I said, jumping down from the boat. I'd better things to do than be around her, especially when she was in one of her moods.

'We agreed,' she said. 'We all agreed. Remember?'

'Whatever,' I said, picking my bike up and mounting. 'Bye, Will, have to be heading back.'

'Bye, Raff,' he replied, still looking shameful. 'Sorry for getting you in trouble.'

'You didn't,' I replied, averting my eyes from Liberty's stare. 'No one's in charge down here. Just remember that.'

I cycled away feeling the boring eyes into my back.

Chapter Thirty-one

The tension still hung heavy in the air whenever the whole group was together by the canal boat. Liberty and I usually just blanked each other as we went about our chores in the field or on the boat. She occasionally muttered about the phone under her breath, but we ignored her. To make our lives peaceful, Will and I agreed to leave the phones behind. We tried to always come down, or at least swim when someone else was around.

'School any better?' asked Will. He paused in his task of clearing the brambles from the stile and looked at me with concern.

'Bearable,' I told him.

'She still giving you a hard time?' he nodded over his shoulder towards his sister who was half the way up the hill, wearing yellow marigolds, with a wheelbarrow and spade. She saw us talking and scowled back down at us.

'No, of course not, she's completely won over by my charm,' I laughed.

'That's a yes then?' he asked.

'Yeah, still a hard time.'

'I'm on your side, by the way,' he lowered his voice, despite Liberty being far enough away she wouldn't be able to hear even if he shouted.

'Really?' I asked, surprised.

'She doesn't mean to be cruel,' he said. 'She's just scared about losing her social status at school. Up high on her pedestal. Means everything to her.'

'What do you mean?' I asked.

'She does like you. More than like you, I think. She's been so happy now Minty is here; nice even, and much more fun. Like she used to be when we were younger; jumping in the river and stuff, and camping. She would never have done that a few months ago. But at school, she changes back to being the same old Liberty. I prefer her being nice.'

'She's like a different person?'

'It's the group she's with.'

'Her friends?'

'Yeah but it's not their fault, it's how they are together,' Will put his hand on his forehead and scrunched his eyes together. 'It's hard to explain.'

'I think I understand,' I told him. 'She has to change herself a little bit to fit in?'

'She changes a lot. Totally changes into a different person and I think she mostly likes who she becomes. She's not like that at home though. Still has a foul temper and stuff but she's more human.'

'So there's hope?' I asked.

'No,' he grinned. 'I'm not saying this so you think you're in with a shot, so don't start all hopeless romantic crap again.'

'Harsh,' I said and chuckled. I helped Will to pull back a thick patch of brambles, whilst he chopped at it with a stick. I winced as a thorn tore through my finger, drawing blood. I sucked at it as Will finally defeated the undergrowth.

'Just the truth. I'm just saying, don't take it personally about how she reacted to the rumour and how she treats you sometimes. She was just protecting her reputation. Even if the rumour was true.'

'Why does she care so much about her reputation?'

'Don't we all?'

'Yeah, suppose so, but it means so much to her, doesn't it?'

'She's worked hard to build it up.'

'But why try so hard?'

Will looked back down the track, as if she'd appear and hear we were talking about her.

He lowered his voice, 'She used to wear braces at the start of high school. Kids were mean to her all the time. Proper mean.'

'Ahh, that's why her teeth are so perfectly straight,' I said, surprised. Liberty's beautiful smile is what drew most people around her. Why didn't I remember her with braces? I don't think I noticed Liberty back then.

'Totally perfect.'

'But lots of kids wear braces. It's nothing unusual.'

'It completely took away her self-confidence. And some of her friends back then found out what she needed to wear with it at night. She was so embarrassed by the headgear.'

'Headgear?'

'Yeah, some kind of torturous-looking orthodontic device thing she had to wear at night. Dad had her wear it. One of her friends around for a sleepover saw. Kids were laughing at her since then. Liberty took it badly and kind of went quiet since. Faded into the background until the treatment was over.'

'I didn't realise.'

'She doesn't talk about it...ever. All the kids can't remember she wore it at all now. They just laughed at the time and forgot. But the embarrassment always stuck with her. She doesn't want to remember the old Liberty Ashburn. Totally changed herself. But I liked her before.'

'Seems silly to change yourself like that. Doesn't excuse how she treats others now.'

'It's not an excuse. A reason. So don't take it too personally how she is with you and what she did. Doesn't mean she didn't like you.'

'So she did like me?'

'Are you even listening?' Will looked frustrated. 'Liberty isn't worth getting yourself the laughing-stock of school for. She can do worse than a silly scratched message in a toilet door. Believe me.'

'Okay,' I admitted, slightly defeated. 'I've moved on anyway.'

'Oh yeah? Tell.'

'Probably best I don't.'

'Very wise,' agreed Will. He battered down the last of the nettles with his stick and stood back to admire his handiwork. The track from the towpath to the stile was clear.

'Maybe all of this has taught me a good lesson.'

'You? Learn a lesson?' laughed Will. 'Never.'

'Thanks.'

'Anytime.'

'Where's Dexter?' I asked.

'Out riding,' Will pointed up the towpath leading west around the corner. 'He wanted to try taking Minty under the low dual carriageway bridge so he can ride out for longer.'

'He'll get seen,' I frowned.

'He'll be careful,' said Will, pushing his glasses further back onto his nose. 'Dexter's probably got his wits about him more than we have.'

'Yeah, I heard he's pretty tough.'

'Tough doesn't cover it. What have you heard?'

'A few things I didn't know.'

'Go on.'

I hesitated for a maybe half a second before I made up my mind and pushed the promise with Tallie from my mind. Liberty had walked down the hill to join us as we turned back towards the boat. She nodded in approval at our cleared area as she hopped over the stile, hot and flustered from all the shovelling.

'About how things are for him.'

'What things? Who are we talking about?' Liberty was quick to ask, catching onto our conversation. She leant her spade up against the boat and swung herself up onto the side.

'Dexter,' said Will. 'Raff's heard something about Dexter.'

'Haven't we all,' said Liberty, dismissively. 'That's nothing new.'

'Really?' I asked, surprised. 'What have you heard then?'

'He's a loser,' said Liberty.

'Yeah that's what everyone thinks, but what do you actually *know* about him?'

Liberty coloured slightly, irritated by my response. 'Well, I *know* he has no friends and always eats alone. He gets into a lot of fights and is rude when you talk to him. Doesn't he live in the housing estate past the chip shop…?'

'You've still not told us anything new.'

'Then there's the rumour.'

'What rumour?'

'About his little brother.'

'I didn't know he had a brother.'

'He doesn't anymore.'

'Why, what happened?'

'Rumour is Dexter killed him or caused his death in some way.'

'Bullshit,' I said.

'It's not.'

'How?'

'No one knows,' Liberty shrugged then shivered and wrapped her arms around herself. 'He's weird and creepy. That's why he gets picked on at school.'

'No he's not,' said Will. 'I like him.' Liberty gave him a sharp look.

'Is there any truth behind these rumours?' I asked.

'Kids have been saying it for ages, years even.'

'But is there any truth?'

She shrugged, 'Does there need to be?'

'I've not heard these rumours before. Dexter has been beaten at school for as long as I've known of him. Probably for longer. Of course, there needs to be some truth,' I said, my voice slightly raised. 'There isn't any truth is there?'

'Probably not,' she said. 'But who cares? You turn a blind eye when he's getting punched. Don't go acting all shocked now.'

'Well, I shouldn't turn a blind eye then.'

'But you do. And if you said anything or tried to stop it, you'll be in for the same treatment, too.'

'Well, maybe I should. See if it's true.'

'Don't expect us to stick up for you,' snapped Liberty. 'Nobody associates with Dexter.'

'You wouldn't stick up for me anyway would you?' I fumed. 'We all know what happens when I try and stand up to the truth. Liberty Ashburn lets you drown without even throwing a life raft. Been there, done that. Think I will survive doing it again.'

'On your head,' said Liberty, shrugging nonchalantly at me. She smoothed back wisps of hair in her ponytail. 'Don't say I didn't warn you. And it won't just be me and my friends laughing at you for being pathetic. It'll be the whole bloody school.'

'Guys, guys.' Will said. He got to his feet and tried to stand on the path in between us. 'What are we arguing about?'

'Dexter,' we both shouted.

'Ah,' said Will, pushing his glasses firmly down his nose. 'Dexter. And I thought we'd gone off track. I'm not sure he will care you're both fighting over him.'

'It's not fair,' I protested, looking at Will for support. 'The poor kid has done nothing wrong and all he gets is shit at school and then shit at home. I'm angry, that's all. Angry at the situation. Not at you,' I glared up at Liberty, swinging her legs to and fro on the boat. Surely she'd understand, considering the treatment she received at school in the past. 'I'm angry at everyone at school who just joins in regardless. Because of some stupid rumour.'

'Shit at home?' said Will, his eyes large with concern. 'What do you mean? Is this what you heard? You haven't told us about it yet.'

'Shit, as in beaten up.'

'He's not been beaten up at home,' said Liberty, sneering. 'Complete rubbish.'

'Haven't either of you noticed the bruises?'

'So?'

'He's always bruised. You saw them yourself, Will,' I turned to him.

'Aren't they bruises from school?' said Liberty. 'He's always got bruises from all the fights.'

'Have you two not noticed he hardly ever goes to school?'

'I saw him there last week,' frowned Will. 'Or maybe it was the week before.'

'And what about all those other bruises?' I asked. 'The ones he already has before he even goes to school.'

'We were just guessing,' said Will. 'He never told us how he got those ones. Could have been from another fight, days earlier.'

'Go on, tell us then,' said Liberty. 'You're obviously leading onto something with all this. What did you hear?'

I was pleased to see the smug smile disappear off Liberty's face as I told them about the file.

'Thought you said his Grandad was dead?' said Will, finally.

'Yeah exactly,' I replied. 'Think Dexter has some secrets of his own.'

Chapter Thirty-two

It didn't take even two full days before I paid for my betrayal. I couldn't possibly see how it could get back to Tallie.

I was wrong.

Like in the old-school Friends episode 'The trail'. Yes, yes, I know. I like Friends, the repeats on Comedy Central are addictive; my guilty secret pleasure. Not quite the Big Bang Theory, but good enough. Anyway, the episode where you need to track through the trail to find out how a mistake ends up back at the source. I didn't think through my trail properly.

Tallie rang my mobile just after I had jumped out of the shower. I raced back into my bedroom and slammed the door before lurching for the phone. I answered, breathless.

'Rafferty?' she asked.

'Hi, Tallie.' I slumped down onto my bed and kicked out my legs, which stuck over the end of the bed. 'Missed you,' I smiled.

'How could you?'

'Huh?' I sat back up in bed and frowned. I hadn't noticed the edge to her voice.

'You promised you wouldn't say anything.' Her voice sounded strained and tearful.

'I didn't…' I began.

'Don't you dare lie to me, Rafferty.'

'I'm not,' I tried to say, but I knew it was hopeless. I tried a different angle. 'I didn't say you told me.'

'You didn't have to.'

'How did you find out?'

'Once something gets out, you can't stop who people tell. You didn't think, Raff.'

'I don't understand,' I said. 'I didn't tell anyone who would spread rumours.'

'You didn't tell anyone who would *purposely* spread rumours. But they did anyway.'

'Like I did,' I realised.

'Yes, like you.'

'How did it get back to you?'

'The usual,' she sighs. 'One friend tells another. Someone else overhears. An adult finds out. A responsible adult. One that has to pass on such information. Mum gets a phone call. I get into deep shit. All thanks to you, Raff. Mum could have lost her job or at least been reprimanded. I had to confess everything. You're such an idiot.'

'I know,' I said. 'I'm sorry, Tallie, I didn't think Wilbur or Liberty would talk to anyone. I trusted them.'

'You're still seeing Liberty?' Tallie's voice changed again, becoming more monotone and shut down.

'No, Tallie. Not like that.'

'Like what then?' she asked. 'What possible reason could you have for talking to Liberty? I thought you said you weren't friends anymore, and the rumours I'd heard were just rumours.'

'It's complicated.'

'Try me.'

I paused, thinking as quickly as I could. 'I can't Tallie,' I said finally.

'What's the point then?'

'The point of what?'

'The point of us?'

'What do you mean?' I asked. I knew what she meant and I knew where this was leading, but I couldn't stop this happening without betraying the pact.

'If you can't trust me to talk to me, there is no point in us, is there, Rafferty?'

'I guess not,' I told her.

'So this is goodbye then?'

'If that's what you want.'

'Bye, Rafferty,' she said softly. She went silent, apart from light breaths.

'Wait. Tallie?' I called.

A sharp click sounded as the phone went dead.

Chapter Thirty-three

Dexter sensed my seething, bad mood as I slumped on the boat. He skirted around me, fiddling with hay bales and sweeping the stray wisps of hay from the deck. I had done nothing but moan and sit about restlessly since I arrived.

Liberty and Will had yet to join us, their evening visits becoming less frequent as Liberty's exams approached. Revision. As I should be doing, too.

'What's up?' he finally asked, kicking my foot with a frown on his face.

'Nothing,' I said, and groaned, rolling onto my side. 'Nothing that can be fixed.'

'Try me?' he asked.

'I need women advice.'

'Ah, well then maybe I can't help,' he laughed. 'As you've probably noticed, I'm not much of a hit with the ladies at the moment … or the men for that matter.'

'Great. No use then.'

'Well you can try anyway, it might be good to voice your problem, even if we can't find a solution to it.'

'Maybe,' I agreed. I sucked in the air through my teeth in a long drag.

'Go on then,' he said before adding, 'This better not be another moan about Liberty.'

'Not this time,' I grinned. 'But I'm sure that time will come again.'

'So about your new lady friend?'

'Yeah. I've messed up.'

'How? It's barely got off the ground. How have you messed up already?'

'Messed up badly. I need to think of a way to make it up to her.'

'Have you ever heard of saying sorry?'

'I think this will take more than that.'

'How badly did you mess up?'

'Completely and utterly fucked up.'

'Wow,' he replied. 'Not sure I can help you.'

'You're no help.'

'Sorry, mate. You're not explaining yourself very well, are you? Man up, say sorry, show you've listened to her and then wait for her to come to you. That's my only advice.'

'Show I've listened to her…?' I repeated, my thoughts trailing off.

'Yeah, that's what I said. Show you have listened to all the mundane, boring, little details she has ever talked about. Women love that kind of shit.'

'I think you're on to something,' I smiled. 'I've an idea. Thanks, Dexter.'

'See,' grinned Dexter. 'I'm more than good looks and charm.'

'Oh much more,' I laughed.

'Now get off your arse, stop moping around, and help will you?'

'Yes, Sir,' I said, jumping to my feet. Dexter winked at me before jumping down off the deck and heading purposefully towards Minty's field, head collar in hand.

Chapter Thirty-four

I knew exactly what I had to do. When I got home I rummaged into the back of my wardrobe searching for the shiny, white box I knew would be there somewhere. Once located, I dragged it out and tipped the contents of the box out over the bed. A jumble of assorted old footwear bounced out onto the bed and I put the box flat again, using my hand to swipe the shoes onto the floor.

I just needed the box.

Shallow and rectangular, it once contained new wellies for a Christmas long forgotten. Now, as I had the container needed for Tallie, I set about filling the contents. This needed more preparation. I looked around my room for something suitable. I pulled open drawers and flicked through the books stuffed into my school bag.

Nothing.

Shaking my head back and forth, I hit upon an idea. I pounded down the stairs and into the lounge.

'Mum, where are the old, used newspapers?'

'The what?' she looked up at me from the sofa and smiled. 'Sorry love, pardon?'

'You're in the way,' Dad grumbled. He peered around me towards the television. His head darted left and right trying to see the screen. Then his hand flicked at me back and forth, gesturing at me to move sideward, out of his way. I stood still to annoy him further. 'Why do you want my papers?'

'Just a school project.'

'They're my papers.'

'I need the old ones, Dad. The ones you've finished with.'

He looked up, dragging his eyes away from the screen for a second, to catch my eye.

I held his stare.

'What project?' he asked suspiciously.

'An English journalism essay,' I lied. 'I want to browse the news for inspiration. We need to write an article.'

'Sounds interesting,' nodded Mum, encouragingly. She loves sharing. I think she hates I rarely tell her anything anymore. A part of her role is slipping away and she's desperate to remain in my life. 'Is this for your coursework? I thought you had finished all of your paperwork now. The exams are soon. Do you have to be a reporter? Publish an article? Sounds great, Rafferty.'

'Something like that, Mum,' I nodded, itching to get away and find the papers. I inched back towards the door slowly, a foot at a time. 'Do you know where they are?'

'What article are you going to write?' she continued.

'I don't know yet, Mum. The papers?' I asked, again.

'You could write about that horse,' Dad said, eyes finally returning to the screen. The horse. Oh god, they know. My heart stopped beating I swear, and my palms felt suddenly tingling.

'What horse?' I asked. I tried to keep the squeaky shakiness from my voice.

'You know, that missing racehorse,' Mum joined in, excitedly. 'Yes, you should write about the horse. Some say the horse must have come this way, towards the village. From the position the horsebox was in, the horse must have come this way. Hoof prints into the woods from the dual carriageway. Would make a good mystery story wouldn't it love?'

'Pah,' spat Dad. 'You don't know what you're talking about, Maureen. I heard down the pub that the horse has been stolen. People have been hearing a horse neighing down by those old barns. Behind the playing fields. And if you'd been listening, he's writing an article, not a bloody mystery novel.'

'I was just…' began Mum.

'Just what, Maureen?' Dad crushed her further.

'Why would anyone steal the horse?' I asked, interrupting the usual verbal bashing, which had become more and more a regular daily occurrence. I don't know how Mum refrained herself from hitting him. Or why I hadn't yet for that matter.

Dad shook his head, disbelievingly, 'Why do you think, Son?'

I shrugged. 'Dunno. To race?'

'Have you never heard of Shergar?'

'Who?' I asked.

'Don't worry yourself,' he turned back towards the television and flicked the volume up a notch.

'Was Shergar stolen?'

'Don't worry yourself about bloody Shergar. And don't slouch,' he corrected, frowning at my posture. 'Sounds like you need those papers as you don't seem to know anything.'

'Language, Michael, please,' soothed Mum. 'Wasn't a ransom asked for Shergar?' He frowned and continued staring at the screen.

'What was in the papers?' I asked. As far as I was aware, the missing racehorse story had flat-lined several weeks ago. Had become old news. People moved on, new stories had taken over.

'The reward, of course.'

'The reward?' I echoed.

'That's what I said, Son, are you deaf or something tonight? Go and see for yourself, the old papers are stacked down behind the kitchen bin. Return them when you're finished.'

I turned and raced towards the door, barely hearing Mum's call as I left, 'Let me read your article when you finish. I'm sure it'll be fantastic.'

I grabbed the stack from behind the door and took the stairs two at a time back to my room. I shoved the box over onto the floor.

The plan for Tallie could wait.

I smoothed out a paper onto the bed. It wasn't until I reached the fourth newspaper that I found the article. I read it slowly before reaching over to my mobile to text the same message three ways. Liberty had warned us not to link each other in any way by phone and to make sure any internet searches didn't contain horse-related words (which I have stuck to), but an emergency called. She replied first, within seconds.

'Why r u texting me?'

'We need 2 meet.'

'This is not in the agreement.'

'Sod the fucking agreement. We all need 2 meet.'

'Usual place in 20?'

'Ok, bring Will.'

'U get Dexter.'

'He'll already b there.'

'C U THERE.'

Dexter was already there, as predicted. As my bike squeaked along the narrow tow path, he jumped down from the boat and stood in my way. I screeched to a halt in front of him and smiled.

'Good evening, Dex.'

'Evening, Raff. What brings you this way so late?' he looked at me anxiously. 'Anything up?'

'Didn't you get my message?'

'I've lost my phone,' Dexter replied.

'Liberty said she'll be here by 8.'

'And Will?'

'She's bringing him.'

'What's up then?' Dexter looked anxious. 'Why is everyone coming here?' He was still in shorts with a small T-shirt showing his painfully thin arms. He noticed me staring and turned back onto the boat, grabbing for his hoodie. I noticed more purple marks behind his armpits before they were enveloped in clothing.

'I have some news,' I told him.

'What?' he asked. 'We have been sprung, haven't we? I knew it.'

'Why?'

'Some old couple cycled past the other day. Stopped and stared up at Minty for a minute or two before carrying on down the track. The lady had pointed up at the field. I had ducked down into the boat so couldn't hear what they were saying. Don't think they saw me.'

'No, don't think they've said anything. It's just another horse in a field. No one will bat an eyelid.'

'Are you sure?' Dexter asked anxiously.

'Yeah don't worry. That's not the reason I'm here.'

'What is it then?'

'What till the others arrive?' I pointed towards the bridge. 'Oh look, there's Liberty.'

'Where's Will?' Dexter called to her, as she neared us, her bike bouncing down the stony path.

She pulled up next to us panting.

'This better be worth it,' she looked accusingly at me. 'And no, Will couldn't come. It's bad enough me trying to sneak out this late in the evening, but Will is younger, there was no way I could get him past the parents this late, without a planned excuse. He got spotted straight away. I managed to duck down and hide so he covered for me with a lie,' she paused for breath. 'So no, he's not here.'

'You can fill him in then,' I told her.

'Go on then,' said Dexter. 'Tell us what's so important. He sat on the edge of the boat, feet hanging over the towpath side. Liberty pulled herself up next to him and I stood on the path, addressing them.

'I was looking for some newspapers and I saw something,' I began.

'Old newspapers or new?' said Dexter.

'Does it matter?' asked Liberty crossly.

'Let me start again,' I said, patiently. 'I was looking for some newspapers and saw something from a paper from last week. Any better?'

'About Minty?' asked Dexter.

'Yes,' I said. 'Well, about that racehorse.'

'Minty then,' said Dexter.

'Minty isn't the racehorse,' mumbled Liberty. 'Why are you still going on about it?'

'What did the paper say?' asked Dexter.

'It went over the original details from other articles. Missing horse, car accident, blah blah, and now, that the racehorse is believed stolen. And then it offered a reward.'

'A reward?' Dexter's eyes widened. 'How much of a reward?'

'A fuck off, huge reward.'

'It doesn't matter what size the reward is, Minty isn't the racehorse,' said Liberty. We ignored her.

'How huge?'

'Like really huge. Monstrous. More money than we will ever have in our lives.'

'Whoa,' whistled Dexter. 'Imagine what someone could do with that.'

'I know,' I nodded.

I could see cars, lots of convertible cars. A vintage red Austin Healey. Shiny new mountain bike or even a moped — whilst I waited to pass my driving test. A fluffy pony for Abby and the most prestigious art college for Tallie, with all the best art equipment. Mum could finally have the thatched cottage with a country rose garden she'd always wanted. Have the money to pay Dad to get out of our lives. I'm not sure what else I could buy, but I'm sure I'd think of something.

'We are not turning him in,' said Liberty, jumping down from the boat and turning to Dexter and me. My bubble burst. 'Not now. Not ever, and not for any amount of money.'

'I agree,' said Dexter. 'But that's not the point.'

'The point?'

'What is the point?' I asked him, the Austin Healey driving away out of reach.

'It's not you, Rafferty, Will and Liberty, or even me, rushing off to claim the money we have to worry about.'

'What do we worry about then?'

'The others.'

'What others?' I asked and Liberty echoed my question with a scowl on her face.

'Anyone seeing the horse. Anyone seeing *any* red brown horse within a hundred-mile radius is going to wonder whether it's the horse that will bring them the jackpot. This horse is like a lottery ticket. One sitting in a field waiting to be spotted. And believe you me, anyone that sees him and thinks he's the missing racehorse will turn him in. Whether it's your own blood and guts family. That amount of money overrides everything.'

'What can we do then?'

'Be more careful,' warned Liberty, looking at me. 'No more texting of *anything* between us. No mentioning the word 'horse' to anyone. No more working on the farm anymore, Dexter. It's too suspicious.'

'But we need hay,' protested Dexter.

'We've so much hay, I'm not sure Minty will ever eat through it all,' I laughed. 'It's filled up his whole boat stable.'

'I like working there,' grumbled Dexter.

'Well you can't,' said Liberty.

'Who says?'

'I do.'

'I'm sure if he's careful, working on the farm can't do any harm. Just don't work for free hay anymore,' I added. 'Liberty's right, it's too suspicious. No rabbit on earth could eat that much. Do it for free or pocket money.'

'What about the field?' Liberty asked. 'It's too close to the towpath.'

'We need to fence off the section of the field running down to the stile. The top bit, around the trees opening up wider to the corner. He can only go up there.' said Liberty.

'Not big enough,' protested Dexter, shaking his head. 'He'll get bored.'

'Then we need to ride him more,' Liberty said firmly. 'He can't be seen.'

'Okay,' I agreed. 'We'll have to find some fencing from somewhere.'

'I can try the tip for wooden posts or stakes. Sometimes they have wire or pallets. Anything would do to block off the bit running down to the path.'

'It's not too wide a gap anyway, probably a load of pallets would do. Wouldn't it, Dex?'

'I'll see what I can find,' Dexter nodded at me. He turned to look at Minty, who had ambled over to the stile and had pushed his head over, nuzzling at Dexter. 'All this for you, aye, boy.'

'You knew, didn't you?' I turned to Liberty. 'You saw the article already and you knew.'

She had the good grace to blush. 'Why do you think that?'

'Because you didn't react to the money, like I did. Or even Dexter. I love Minty, and all, but for a minute or two, when I saw the amount in the article, in black and white, it's all I could think about. You didn't have that moment.'

'I love Minty too much to think like you lot,' she said.

'I don't buy it,' I laughed.

'Okay fine, yes, I'd seen it. And I knew you all might react like I did when I first saw the paper. The money could buy us each a horse, land, our parents big, new, shiny houses. Clothes, bags, shoes, the possibilities are endless. That's why I didn't tell you.'

'We could have stopped people seeing him earlier,' muttered Dexter, shaking his head at her. 'If you'd told us earlier.'

'People?' asked Liberty. I explained about the couple cycling by. 'Oh, I didn't think,' she said.

'You never do,' said Dexter.

Chapter Thirty-five

The moment, filling me with such bubbling excitement in the pit of my stomach, all but vanished once I returned home. My desperate attempt to prove or show Tallie something, I'm not sure what, seemed childish and laughable. I sat on the bed, leant over, and threw the shoes from the floor back into the wardrobe one by one. They hit the wooden panel with a thud.

Crumpled newspapers lay spread over the bed like a blanket. Shaking my head, I scooped them up and rolled them angrily into a ball to hurtle them, too, into the depths of the wardrobe.

I slumped back onto the bed again, my energy gone. I rubbed my forehead with the palm of my hand, trying to think.

'Come on, Rafferty,' I said, aloud. 'Do what needs to be done.'

I puffed out a loud exhale of air into the room. I might as well just continue the plan. This summer couldn't get much worse. Another rejection from a female would just add to the testing times they call 'growing up'. And you never know, it might not be a rejection. Okay, that's probably hoping too much.

But you never know.

My new alarm clock said midnight already. Although we parted ways before the lanes hit complete darkness, I had to walk the final way back across the meadow towards our

RAFFERTY LINCOLN LOVES…

house due to a puncture. Our semi-detached lay nestled in a maze of similar houses towards the end of the village, nearer the village shop and last remaining post office. As I threw my bike back into the garage, I caught the twitch of curtains from my parents' room.

Dad, more than likely.

I went straight up to my bedroom and shut the door. The telling-off could wait until the morning. I knew I'd broken curfew, it being a school night, but I had hoped he wouldn't notice my disappearance.

The plan would take serious time. It was now or never before I lost my nerve.

Retrieving the pile of papers and smoothing out salvageable crumpled ones, I began cutting them into squares, roughly 10 cm by 10 cm. This process itself took well over an hour, cutting more or less a thousand squares of newspaper. The quickest and easiest way was by marking out a template, then cutting through several pages at once.

I made a few extra, for practice.

Looking up the step-by-step instructions on my phone, I spent an agonising half-hour mastering the technique. By the time I'd finished, the paper crane matched the photo on my phone perfectly.

I set to work.

It was three in the morning. My eyes felt heavy. I wondered, briefly, whether I should abandon the whole stupid idea and crawl into bed.

I quickly realised, even when taking just over a minute per crane, making a thousand wasn't possible by the morning. My technique had improved but I could only shave a second or two off the time.

Two hundred cranes in, I fell asleep, surrounded by mounds of paper.

'Rafferty,' Mum shook me awake. 'Rafferty, your alarm has been ringing for twenty minutes. Wake up, love.'

'Oh,' I stumbled my hand out towards the clock. But she'd already switched it off.

'You'll miss your paper round.'

'I'll do it later. Bill won't mind if I do it after school,' I sighed. 'I'll ring him.'

'Are you not feeling well, love?' she pressed her palm to my head and sat down on the edge of the bed. 'You feel very warm.'

'Just tired, Mum.'

'Is this about Tallie?'

'Why?' I asked, confused. What did Mum know about me and Tallie?

'Her mum rang up a little concerned about you.'

'What did she say?'

'Nothing much. It was mainly asking about another play date for Abby to see Holly, but she mentioned Tallie being upset about something. Apparently, they'd had some strong words, too. I wondered if you knew why?'

'They had?'

'Yes, Tallie and her mum. She didn't say why.'

'No,' I shook my head. 'I don't know why she's upset. The usual teenage stuff probably.' I brushed the conversation off. Mum stared at me for a moment or two and then carried on.

'You been up studying all night?' she frowned as she looked at the flutters of newspaper all around the bedroom. 'You look like you've been busy hunting for the perfect article.'

'Something like that.'

'Dad will be pleased,' she smiled, her eyes tired, 'and he thought you were busy out gallivanting, too. He had a right hump this morning about it. I've a good mind to bring him in here to show him how hard you've been working.'

'Don't do that,' I pushed myself up on my bed. 'I'll clear up after school.'

'No, Rafferty, dear, you lie down. You look worn out,' she gently pushed me back down again. I didn't have the energy to complain. 'I will ring the school and tell them not to expect you as you're poorly.'

'But the exams start in a couple of weeks,' I said, thinking solely of Liberty and Will, and nothing of the exams. 'I need to be in school. There are only a few days left before study leave.'

'You're so dedicated, Son,' my mum soothed. 'But you must rest.'

I lay back down and smiled. 'Thanks, Mum, you're the very best.'

She beamed.

Mums are big suckers, aren't they?

Maybe, with a pause or two for a late morning nap, I would have the time to finish. I would be able to drop the box over at Tallie's, to sit it on her doorstep, by the time she returned from college. I could see her response, as she would look around, trying to spot who delivered them. She'd be smiling as she carried the box inside. Of course, she'd know they were from me. I would be waiting, opposite, in the bushes to watch. Not in a stalker-ish way, mind. Just to check she'd got them. Then I would dash off and wait for my mobile to ring.

All forgiven.

Mum puttered around the room for a moment or two, whilst I lay, looking through half-closed eyes. Retrieving a few cups and plates, she paused at the door.

'Sleep well, Rafferty,' she said. She closed the door softly.

The sleepiness now gone, I leapt to action. Doubling my production time, I was done by just after lunch. I counted and recounted the thousand paper cranes before sealing them in the box with brown tape. I used a final crane to scrawl a quick note upon before sticking it on top of the box as a label.

Then I lay back down exhausted. Sleep soon followed.

Chapter Thirty-six

In the cold light of day, everything always feels different, doesn't it? I had serious doubts as I walked, box tucked gingerly under my arm, towards Tallie's house. Why oh why does nothing ever pan out as imagined?

Maybe it's just me.

The time approached quarter to four. By my calculations, and of my watch, the bus returning from college should round the hill into our village in three minutes time. It would take Tallie a couple of minutes to walk from the nearest bus stop to her house, so that didn't leave me long to set up what I had planned. I climbed up the steep hill towards her upside down house and reached the top slightly puffed.

I could see the bus rise above the brow of the hill and then disappear into a dip before it would then rise again towards the first stop.

Tallie's.

I darted quickly down her lane and sprinted towards her doorstep. Her parents' cars were both missing from the driveway, a good sign my plan might go as expected. I set the box down on the mat in her arched porch-way and then backed away across the road. I looked left and right for anyone around, before tucking myself behind a tall enough tree to hide my towering head. Tallie's house and grounds were big enough that the nearest neighbour didn't have much of a view her way. All was well.

I waited.

I heard the drone of the bus engine and then a hiss as it settled down into the stop. A few seconds later, a roar as the bus started up to life. My ears strained, trying to pick out footsteps crunching down the lane towards her drive.

None.

I looked at my watch. The seconds ticked by. Again at the house. Nothing. I peered around my tree at the lane.

Empty.

I leant my head against the tree and closed my eyes. I counted to a thousand slowly. I heard a faint flicker of sound and forced myself to count to ten before looking up. It must be her. Still nothing. I looked at my watch again. Five more minutes then I would give up.

'What are you doing?'

A voice from behind scared the shit out of me. I clutched at my heart as I stumbled backwards, tripping over my big feet and landing on my arse. I heard a giggle. A very familiar giggle.

My sister.

'What are you doing here!' I exclaimed loudly, making her jump. I pulled myself to my feet and grabbed her shoulders. 'Why are you here?'

'Mum said I could go home with Holly tonight, as you were poorly.'

'Where's Holly?' I asked suspiciously.

'Here!' Holly giggled, peering around from the tree. 'What are you doing? We could see you a mile off so we crossed the road to jump out on you.'

'Funny,' I said, rubbing my knee, blood spotting from where I'd grazed it on the tree bark. 'Do you always walk home from school alone?'

'No. Mum picked us up and dropped us at the playing fields. She said we could walk home together as long as we were both sensible. We saw your friends, too.'

'Who?' I asked, not caring. 'Nigel?' I strained around to see behind her. They had come from the opposite direction from where I expected Tallie, from a footpath leading up from the playing fields. Where was Tallie? Surely if she had been on the bus she would have been here by now.

'Liberty and Will,' squealed my sister.

'They're not my friends,' I told her harshly. How did she know about them?

'Yes they are,' she continued putting her hands on her brattish little hips. 'They always hide behind the gate out the front waiting for you. Then you disappear off with them when you're not supposed to.'

'Great,' I said, defeated.

'But I won't tell,' she added. 'I promised, didn't I?'

'Where did you see them, just now?'

'They cycled home from school; we saw them pass the playing fields a few minutes ago. Why don't you cycle to school?'

'Because I'm too lazy, Sis. That's why.' She had a good point though, cycling would shave time off the wait for the bus and I could cut across the country lanes towards the canal. Liberty didn't seem to take the bus anymore, perhaps I didn't need to either.

'What are you doing here?' asked Holly suddenly. 'Outside my house?'

'Going for a jog,' I told her. 'I stopped to lean against the tree, as I was out of breath.'

'Since when do you jog?' asked Abby.

'Since now,' I hissed at her.

'But aren't you poorly?' her precious hands went back to her hips.

'I needed the fresh air.'

'You never like fresh air.'

'Now ladies. I must leave you two and keep jogging. I don't want my muscles stiffening up.' I jogged on the spot and waved. 'So long girls.'

'Bye, Raff,' giggled Abby. 'Enjoy your run.' They turned and crossed the lane towards the front path. I smiled as I watched them. My smile slowly faded to stone.

The box.

I peered around them, straining the see the brown cardboard on the mat. I frowned and stumbled forward.

'Raff?' Abby turned to stare at me running down the driveway towards them. 'What are you doing?'

'Where's the bloody box?' I screamed.

'What box?' asked Holly, confused, with slight panic across her face. She looked ready for tears.

'The white box sat on your doorstep, Holly. What have you done with it?' I accused, pointing a finger at first her and then at my sister. 'I'm not kidding, you two.'

'Promise, Rafferty.' There were tears in Abby's eyes, too. 'Promise. What box? We haven't been to Holly's house yet. We haven't seen your box.'

'Where's Tallie?' I asked. I softened with relief. She must have come home or been home all along. She could have spotted the box ages ago. I'd been outside the house for at least half an hour.

'She's at piano in the town.'

'What?' I spun around at Holly. 'What?'

'She's at her piano lesson in the town. Til five,' Holly stuttered. 'Is your brother okay?' Holly looked pleadingly at Abby.

'Is there anyone else home?' I asked. 'Is there anyone else home?' I shook her shoulders.

'Raff, please,' Abby's eyes were round and wide. She stepped towards us and placed her hand on the arm clutching Holly.

'Is there anyone else home?' I shouted.

'No,' Holly sobbed, her shoulders heaving. Big tears dripped down her face, steaming up her glasses. 'No. Mum's gone to the town to pick up Tallie, and Dad works late. Please let me go.'

I let go and she stumbled towards Abby who took her hand. They look back at me in silence as they walked together towards the front door. They slammed the door behind them.

Fucking shit. I had messed up big time. But there was one thing more important than my sister and her friend's feelings.

Where was that box?

Chapter Thirty-seven

I expected to hear Dad's hard, angry footsteps outside my bedroom door within seconds of getting home. They didn't come. Instead, I was surprised to hear gentle knocking on the door, and the muffled sound of slippers on wooden boards, half an hour later.

'Rafferty?' came Mum's soft voice. She tapped again. 'Are you in there, love?'

'What do you want?' I asked, not caring how I sounded. I knew what was to come. I closed my eyes and waited for the inevitable.

'Can I come in?'

'If you must.' I look up at the door, but it didn't open. I raised my voice, 'I said if you must. Come in, Mum.'

'Sorry, love,' her face appeared around the door. She had her dressing gown on and her hair wrapped in a towel. 'I didn't want to disturb you.'

'Bit late for that, isn't it?'

'Rafferty, I need to talk to you.' Mum perched gingerly on the edge of my bed. My revision books were spread across the covers. Faking the impression I'd been spending an evening studying.

Alas, a ploy.

I did need to fit in some studying, but it could wait until I'd sorted the mess of my life out.

I inched the television remote under my pillow and leant over to clear a space for Mum to sit properly. She tied the knot on her dressing gown tightly and slid down more onto the bed.

'Shoot,' I said.

'Pardon?' she frowned.

'I mean, what do you want to talk about?'

'Dad is concerned…' she began.

Wrong move.

'Just Dad? So you're not then?' I retorted. I lowered my head and ran my fingers through the short stubbly back of my hair. 'Been sent upstairs, have you, so I shoot the messenger instead of him?'

'Rafferty,' she seemed exasperated. 'I've had a call from Holly's mum. Again. This seems to be a recurring theme, you upsetting the Phillips girls. But it's one thing to be upsetting a teenage girl, nearly an adult, but a child, Rafferty? What's got into you?'

'I didn't mean to upset her.'

'Accusing her of stealing something of yours, a box? Then shaking her senseless? Rafferty, love, I'm surprised her parents didn't call the police.'

'I'll apologise,' I said.

'I'm not sure that'll be good enough.'

'What then?'

'That's for you to work out. I can only guide you, not tell you what to do. You need to figure it out for yourself.'

'What happens if I can't?'

'Then you'll need to try harder. But in the meantime, you need to stay away from the Phillips household. You're not welcome there at the minute.'

'What about Abby?'

'Holly and Abby have become close. I'm not stopping her going around there and neither are her parents. It's *you* they have concerns about.'

'What happened with Tallie isn't my fault,' I whined.

'Maybe not, Son,' she said. 'But it's still deeply hurt Tallie and she'll need time to process her thoughts and see if she's ready to forgive and forget.'

'You think that might happen?'

'Depends on how badly you have hurt her.'

'Did her parents not say why?'

'No. Tallie's mum said it was between you and her. I respect that. She said it wasn't her business what went wrong between the two of you, just to protect her daughter from getting hurt again. When she's ready to see you, then her parents will give their blessing.'

'Okay,' I said.

'They're being very lenient, Rafferty, you need to understand. If some teenage boy with raging hormones and a crazy look in his eye had shaken my Abby, I'm not sure the outcome would have been the same.'

'Why are they?'

'They must know, deep down, what I know, love,' she said. 'That you're a good kid. Misguided and silly at times. I'm not too pleased about you skipping school either with those sickness excuses. Then telling the girls you were out jogging. Something doesn't add up.'

'Sorry, Mum,' I blushed. 'I didn't mean to lie to you.'

'Well,' she fiddled with the corner of my duvet. Her eyes were heavy and puffy. 'I was a little surprised you did.'

'Sorry,' I said, again. 'I've got a lot going on.'

'Okay, love. Don't make a habit of it.'

'What does Dad think?' I asked.

'Let's keep this between us.'

'Really?' I asked, surprised. Mum does nothing without Dad's consent.

'Yes. Dad doesn't need to know.'

'Why not?'

'Don't you concern yourself,' she patted me on the leg. 'Now, young man, I will leave you to your studying. Exams start in a couple of weeks, right? School finishes on Friday?'

'Yes, Mum.'

'Then you best get onto it sharpish.'

'Okay,' I grinned at her. 'Thanks, Mum.'

'Night, Rafferty.' She closed the door softly behind her before her voice sounded through the keyhole. 'And please don't reach back under your pillow for your TV remote.'

I stopped, remote in hand and smiled at the closed door. 'Of course not, Mum,' I called back. I heard her chuckle and then disappear back down the stairs.

Chapter Thirty-eight

Seriously, who actually remembers any of their high school lessons? Who remembers erosional landforms, or how to manage tectonic hazards? I certainly won't remember anything beyond the summer; possibly as soon as the day after the exam, let alone long enough to regurgitate the information back again for a future job interview or career years down the line.

No chance.

I flicked absentmindedly at the pages of the textbooks, flitting from subject to subject, unable to settle down to any of the revision. The clock was ticking by, minute by minute. The grains of time dwindling away. My note pad lay empty beside me.

'Think, Rafferty,' I said, but it was no use. Mum's words echoed through my head.

She didn't say I couldn't try to apologise to Tallie, just Mrs Phillips didn't welcome me at the house. In fact, Mrs Phillips had been quite 'lenient'. Those were her exact words. Mum obviously wanted me to try to make amends and so did Mrs Phillips; how I was going to do that was the tricky part.

A plan began to form slowly in my head. I know what you're thinking. Not another plan. But I'm a teenage boy.

Plans are all I have.

Whatever had happened to my box it was too late now to win Tallie over with that idea. Tallie doesn't trust me. I needed to win her trust big time. Dexter's advice had prompted the box idea, so I scrunched my head trying to remember his wise words to see if would spark any more ideas. And it did. The idea hit me.

I fumbled down the side of the bed to the stack of papers discarded on the floor. Dragging them up I spread them all over the bed.

Please don't say I'd already cut it out when I made the cranes.

I flicked through the pages, hastily trying to find it, before remembering what Dad had said. The paper was only last week's. Checking each date, I threw the papers back down onto the floor, one by one, until I found the one. I thumbed through the pages.

There it was.

Reaching for the scissors, I cut the article out into a square. I read it one more time, biting my lip until I drew blood. I pulled at my lip with my thumb, feeling for the cut and then frowned at the article. The word 'reward' jumped out at me. Scrambling into my drawer, I pulled out the original article when the racehorse first went missing. I looked between the two articles then choose the old one. Again, I cut out a square.

Doing this meant betraying the pact, breaking the promise among the group. Was she worth it?

I decided yes.

Guided by a quick tutorial on my phone, I perfected the folds I needed on scrap paper, before bending the newspaper article into the shape. With a final, outside reverse fold, I gingerly held the little origami shape on the palm of my hand.

A perfect little racehorse concealing our momentous secret.

With two more days until the weekend, I had to wait for Tallie to be working at the library. The wait was torturous. I debated approaching the house with the paper horse. I didn't. Any slip-ups and the game would be over for good.

When Friday came, the Year 11s were given the afternoon off lessons to collect autographs from fellow students and generally mess around until the bell went. I decided to avoid the gathering masses in the courtyard and fields and wait it out in the deathly silence of the canteen. A few others loitered in there, too, and looked surprised to see me enter. I ignored the stares and ate in the corner away from prying eyes.

As the final bell went, an hour earlier for us leavers, the sound of cheering spread around pockets of the school. I slunk out the back way and headed home.

No more school.

A week of exams lay between me and a summer of freedom, before college in the local town would begin. A college Tallie also attended. I couldn't wait.

'Wait up,' her voice called. Footsteps clipping behind me.

'Liberty,' I said, surprised. She ran up the path to join me.

'You heading for the bus?'

I nodded, 'Yeah.'

'You made a sharp exit,' she noted. The bus drew up and we waited in line to step on board.

'Didn't feel the need to hang around,' I said. 'Glad it's all over to be honest.'

'It wasn't that bad at school,' she smiled. She hopped up on to the bus steps. 'Was it?'

'The last few weeks haven't been the best,' I said.

'Oh,' she shrugged, sliding into a seat. She had loosened her tie and untucked her shirt so it flapped in the breeze from the door, revealing her belly. I slid down next to her. 'I bet you're glad it's the summer then?'

'Couldn't be happier.'

'You didn't want to cycle today?'

'Nah, too hot this morning.'

'I thought the same,' she said. 'Shall we get off the bus before the ridge and cut across the lane to get our bikes from home? Then go to the canal together?'

'Okay,' I said, slightly confused the atmosphere of the last few weeks had vanished. But I didn't say no. She rang the stop bell, and I followed her out of the bus.

We remained in mutual silence as we brushed Minty, scoured his field for fresh dung to barrow over to the muck heap, and then tidied everything away back into the boat. Dexter and Will failed to show, so we both agreed it was time to head back home before dinner.

'See you around over the summer?' Liberty asked. We climbed down off the boat and walked over to our bikes, tangled in a heap.

'Possibly,' I replied. 'I'll be around after the exams. Not much before.'

'Same here. Will and Dexter said they'll be in charge for the next couple weeks.'

I pulled my bike up from the ground, 'Well, good luck with the exams, Liberty.'

'Thanks,' she smiled. 'You, too.'

'Bye,' I mounted my bike. 'I'd better dash on ahead. Dad said to come straight home from school. I managed to grab the bike without them noticing. They'd probably forgotten school finished early for us anyway.'

'Oh shit,' Liberty exclaimed. She was glaring down at the front wheel of her bike, her eyebrows furrowed.

'What?' I asked.

'Fucking puncture,' she swore. 'Fucking hell. What the hell am I going to do?'

'Do you have a puncture kit?' I asked.

'Yeah, I carry one everywhere,' she patted down her tight top and shorts then rolled her eyes. She kicked at the flat front wheel with her trainer. 'Of course I don't. Do you?'

'At home,' I replied. 'Not with me, sorry. Should, really, with all the cycling we do.'

'I'm going to be late,' she shook her head crossly. 'It'll take ages. Bloody bike.'

'What are you going to do?' I asked.

'Have to walk the bike back, won't I?'

'Why don't you leave it here and get a lift back with me?'

'On your bike?' she looked dubious.

'Yeah. You can sit on the handlebars.'

'I'd prefer a backy.'

'Frontie is the new backy apparently,' I grinned. 'Come on, hop on.'

'Is it safe?' she asked.

'I'll go slow,' I promised. 'Chuck your bike in the boat. We'll take the puncture kit down tomorrow.'

'Wilbur can help me with the puncture.'

'Okay,' I replied, shrugging at her instant dismissal of my help. 'Come on then, get on.'

'How do I get on?'

'Hold onto the side of the boat and lower yourself down?'

'Okay.' She clung to the side and I positioned my bike under her and she lowered herself onto the bike handlebars.

'Feel okay?' I asked her.

'No,' she replied, shifting her bottom on the bars. 'Just cycle.'

I pushed off from the boat and wobbled along the path, tilting my head to see beyond her as I cycled. The bike felt top-heavy and cumbersome. I navigated the brambles carefully to avoid her bare legs and tried to avoid looking directly at her bottom. That was hard. I think I should earn a medal for averting my eyes. An Oscar maybe. She held tightly onto the handles, fingers turning white, as her feet stuck out over the wheel.

My god, my legs hurt trying to pedal her up the towpath onto the bridge. I paused at the top looking back along the canal, holding onto the brick side with my hand.

'Alright?' I asked her.

'Yeah,' she replied.

'Ready for the slope down?'

'Ready as ever,' she replied, turning to grin at me. Her black hair had loosened from the band and dangled down onto her shoulders. Her face was flushed. 'Go on then.' I felt her fingers grip as I pushed off from the bridge.

'Hold on,' I cried, as the bike picked up speed. 'Hold on!' The bike picked up the pace as we plunged down the slope. I smiled as my hair was whipped back in the wind. She loosened her grip on the bars and spread her hands out, shakily at first and then far and wide.

'Yeeeeeee,' she cried, her arms and legs, spread wide. 'Amazing.'

It totally was.

Chapter Thirty-nine

On the day the last exams finished, Mum and Dad gave me an evening of freedom. A welcomed relief after over a week of being chained to my study desk, then bored to death in the exam hall.

Exams aren't my thing, I've come to the conclusion. I think my studying had paid off. The questions didn't seem totally alien. But we all have to wait until the end of summer for the official results. Hopefully, would scrape enough grade points to do the courses I wanted at college.

For now, weeks of freedom stretched before us.

I had been staying clear of the canal whenever Will and Liberty were down there, but after Liberty's change of heart last week, I went down in the evening knowing they'd be there, too, and looking forward to seeing them. Nigel had mentioned an end-of-school party at Rudy's, but I wasn't interested. School was over. The politics done and dusted. It already felt in the past.

I think many others felt the same way.

'You won't catch anything in there,' I laughed, spying Will perched on the edge of the boat with a white line hanging down into the water. A little orange float bobbed around on the water's surface.

'Why not?' he looked up at me and grinned a lopsided welcome.

'Look at the colour of it,' I peered into the swirly green. 'Don't reckon anything can live in there.'

'Course it can,' he replied, his eyes peeled on the floating plastic, twitching on the water. He pulled the line up on its wooden stick and peered at the empty hook. 'It's water, isn't it? Something must live in there.'

'Manmade water,' I replied. 'Don't think they added fish to canals.'

'That doesn't mean there won't be any.'

'Suit yourself,' I smiled, and sunk down to sit next to him. I glanced up the hill at Liberty, astride Minty, being led in circles around the field by Dexter, who stood in the middle holding a long rope. I peeled my socks off and dipped my toes into the cool water. Despite the murkiness, the water had a soothing feeling. 'Did you make that yourself?' I nodded towards the stick and line.

'Yeah,' he replied. 'A bit basic, isn't it?'

'Should do the job,' I said, and added, 'If there's anything living in there, of course.'

'You wait,' he grinned. 'I'll catch us one big enough for dinner.'

'One what?'

'A fish.'

'Bet you a fiver you won't.'

'You're on,' he leant over to shake my hand. 'You'll be putting your money where your mouth is.'

'Doubtful,' I laughed.

'You'll see.'

'Think we've got a rod and line someone in the garage if you want me to look?'

'Really?' Will's eyes lit up.

'Yeah, it's a half-size one, think Dad got it for me when he was trying to make an effort to bond. Don't think he ever got around to taking me out with it though. There's a box, too, with all the bits that go with it. Weights, hooks, and such. I'll bring it down if you want. Don't know how to use the rod, but I'm sure we'll figure it out.'

'Amazing, thanks, Raff,' said Will. 'That'll be brilliant.' He drew up the line on the end of the stick and tried to cast it as far out as he could into the canal. The line, without a weight, didn't go far before it glided down into the water. 'This is hopeless.'

'I look forward to your fiver.'

'No way,' laughed Will. He pulled the line out of the water and wound it up over his hand. Pushing off his shoes, and placing his glasses carefully on the side, he reached over onto the deck and grabbed a net on a long metal pole. 'I'll try another method.'

'You're mad,' I replied, as he held his nose and jumped off the side into the water, taking the net with him. He rose to the surface and took a long breath. Wet, brown hair plastered his forehead.

'If they won't come to me,' he said, treading water and flashing a smile. 'I'll come to them.' He took another breath and disappeared under the water, net and all.

'Good luck with that,' I muttered, shaking my head. 'Madness.'

I watched him squirming around in the water like an otter. Rising for gasps of breath, before disappearing under the brown/green surface again. Sweat trickled down my forehead and I felt tempted to join him. I glanced behind me. Liberty and Dexter climbed over the stile, carrying various ropes and equipment.

'Good ride?' I called.

'She's getting better,' said Dexter.

'What?' Liberty's eyes flashed. She heaved herself onto the boat and chucked the ropes into the cabin. 'I was already good.'

'Always room for improvement,' he said and winked over at me before descending down the steps into the cabin.

'The ride was good,' she said, ignoring Dexter's comment. 'I'm beginning to get used to no saddle. Still slippery, though. Minty is always very patient and careful. Where's Will?'

'In there,' I nodded over toward the ripples on the water. 'He's fishing for our supper.'

'Supper?' she screwed up her face.

'Yeah. Unless you'd prefer the food we brought.'

'I'll see what he catches first.'

'Maybe an eel or two if he's lucky.'

'Yuck!' she laughed.

'I'll stick to the picnic.'

'He loves it in there,' she said. 'Never really enjoyed swimming lessons but give him a dirty brown canal and he's at home.'

'Feel like joining him?' I asked. 'I'm melting in this heat.'

'I didn't bring my swim stuff,' she replied.

'So?' I said. 'That didn't stop Will.'

'He's a boy. He doesn't care about swimming in his pants.'

'Don't be a prude,' I laughed, ripping off my T-shirt and pulling down my shorts. 'At least you'll have dry clothes to put on after.'

'What about your pants?' she smiled up at me. 'They'll still get wet.'

'I'll take them off too,' I raised my eyebrows. 'Nothing stopping me doing that.'

'Good. Then I will too,' she said. 'No one likes soggy pants.'

'Go on then.' We both stood staring at each other, willing the other to go first and yet not brave enough. 'You first.'

'You're the gentleman. You go first.'

'I'm clearly not a gentleman,' I grinned. I stood in my pants on the deck, waiting. Liberty had slipped off her dress and stood, trying to hide behind her hands, in her knickers and bra.

'Please,' she asked. 'Then look the other way when I jump in.'

'Fine,' I said. 'Can you turn the other way first?'

'Just do it.'

'You do it, then.'

'You two are total wimps,' laughed Dexter, coming out from the shadows of the cabin. 'Have you never been skinny dipping before?'

'No,' we both replied.

'I'd envisaged blue water and a sandy beach for my first skinny dipping experience,' Liberty said, her eyes looking skywards. 'With cocktails at midnight and a tall, handsome man.'

'I'm not sure I envisaged that,' I said. 'The cocktails sound nice, though. Think we've only beer tonight. And…hey, wait, you've got the tall, handsome man.'

'Dexter isn't tall,' she frowned.

'I meant me.'

'I know,' she grinned.

'Stop your time wasting, girls,' laughed Dexter. He stripped off his top and stepped out of his jeans, throwing them behind him.

Underneath the clothes, he only looked about twelve with his skinny arms and legs sticking out of a ribby torso. I barely got a glimpse at the faded, yellowing marks around his shoulders before he thundered past us and jumped high. I caught an unwelcome flash of white, bare arse as he tucked up into a ball and disappeared in a spray of murky water. He laughed as he surfaced and beckoned us in.

'Close your eyes,' I said to Liberty.

'Why?' she asked.

'Just do it,' I said, and she obeyed. I whipped my stripy pants off and threw them to the deck. 'Your turn,' I told her, clutching my privates as Dexter and Will looked on, laughing. 'My eyes are closed, promise. Don't open yours.'

I heard her hopping around on the deck, one foot to the other, before she said, 'Okay, ready,' and reached over to grab my hand. We opened our eyes and kept them locked on each other as we climbed up the side of the boat.

'Ready?' she asked.

'Three … two … one,' I shouted, before, still holding hands, we leapt after Dexter.

Skinny dipping is awesome.

Chapter Forty

'Can you help me?' Dexter asked.

I shrugged, unwilling to leave my sun spot on the boat, but tore myself away reluctantly. I followed him over the stile into the field. He led me up the windy path to the top end of the field, where the land flattened out slightly around the corner. Minty stood, head down, munching on a bale of hay. A lead rope hung from his head.

'What you up to?' I asked.

'Here,' he said, 'grab the other end of this.' He motioned over to a pile of long logs. 'Can you help me shift them?'

'Where?'

'On the tyres.'

'Tyres?'

'Yeah, those ones,' Dexter pointed to pairs of car tyres he'd set out in the field. The tyres were a couple of metres apart from each other. 'I need a log balanced on each pair of tyres.'

'What on earth are you making?'

'Jumps,' Dexter grinned.

'You're mad,' I laughed. 'You can't jump Minty.'

'Why not?'

'Do you know how to jump?'

'Might do,' he shrugged, picking up one end of a log and pointing at the other. I rolled my eyes but picked the other end up. God knows how he'd managed to get the logs up to the corner of the field, they weighed a ton.

'And what about Minty?'

'He's a racehorse, isn't he?'

'I thought we agreed that he wasn't?'

'But we all know that he is.'

'Do racehorses jump?'

'They do in the Grand National,' Dexter winked, balancing his end on top of one end of the tyre. I raised my side up to the other end. 'I'm not sure if he ever raced over jumps. He can learn otherwise. He launched himself over that huge hedge when we first found him. I think he'll be fine.'

'Is it safe?' I asked. 'I always see the horses falling over.'

'My jumps are only a few inches off the ground,' Dexter laughed. 'I'm sure we'll be fine. I'm more worried about whether his legs and back can take it.'

'His back?'

'Yeah, some racehorses get injuries from racing so jumping could be painful. I don't want to hurt him. I'll see how he does today and take it slow. I'll keep him safe, promise.'

'What about you? You've got no saddle to hold on.'

'I've got balance.'

'Or a bridle?'

'I don't need one.'

'How does he know which way to turn?'

'He's clever,' smiled Dexter. 'He knows by the pressure of my foot on his side and the head collar on his nose. Then he turns that way. Jockeys normally perch on top so he has had to learn from scratch about what my leg signals mean. It's taken him a while to get the hang of, but he's good now.'

'Impressive,' I replied. I wouldn't have even known where to start but Dexter clearly had done his research.

'How do you know all of this?' I asked. 'Google?'

'Something like that,' he grinned. 'But I've no internet, so just good old fashioned books.'

We finished placing the last logs on top of the tyres and stood back to admire our jumping course. Six sets of jumps set out in different places around the field; some on a slight slope and others on the flattened ground. Minty eyed us from the middle of the course, his jaw chewing the hay relentlessly. His ears flattened as I approached and then pricked back up when Dexter stroked his neck.

'Come on, boy, we've work to do.'

'Good luck!'

'Help me up?' he asked. 'I can usually do it, but we're on a slope. He's finally stopped dancing about when we mount.' He leant against Minty's side and I squatted down so he could use me to pull himself up. He settled on to his back and grinned down. 'Here goes.'

'Wait.' I snapped a short branch from a tree and handed it up to Dexter.

'What's that?' he asked.

'A whip,' I said, 'like they have in the races.'

Dexter shook his head and threw the stick to the ground. 'Minty doesn't need a whip.'

'But don't the jockey's all use one to get the horses to go faster?'

'Yeah but it's not meant only for that reason. It's meant to be used for guidance and safety. I don't need to go fast anyway. This isn't a race.'

'Oh okay,' I said, feeling stupid. I picked up the stick and tossed it into the bushes. 'You're all set to go then. I'll leave you to it. I need to get back home.'

'No, don't go,' Dexter said, before flashing a grin. 'I might need you.'

'Need me?' I asked, my heart dropped a little. 'I'm not having a go at jumping.'

'No, not you,' he laughed, pointing over to a stack of unused tyres. 'I need your manual labour.'

'Not more jumps?' I whined.

'No,' he grinned. 'Higher jumps.'

'Let's see how you do with these ones first.'

211

'Agreed,' he beamed, before setting Minty off into a trot around the edge of the field. Dexter's legs relaxed around Minty's tummy, knees tight against his side as they smoothly glided around towards the first jump. Minty's ears pricked forwards as they approached and I could hear Dexter's voice encouraging the horse. Just as the horse gathered his legs ready to jump, he skidded to a stop, nearly flying Dexter over his head.

'What happened?' I asked, walking over to them.

'Not sure,' replied Dexter, shaking his head. Minty snorted and tossed his mane around. 'Maybe he was never a jumping horse after all.'

'Try again?' I suggested.

'Of course,' Dexter grinned. He swung Minty around and approached the first jump with more speed, the horse's legs pounding in rhythm. A canter, I think. Horse and rider as one. This time Dexter would fly over the horse's head if he stopped. But Minty didn't, he flew over the small jump with ease, Dexter clinging onto his mane tightly, and headed towards the next, and the next, until the course was complete.

'Okay,' smiled Dexter, leaning forward to hug the horse's sweaty neck. 'Come on, course designer. Make us more. And higher this time.'

'I'd better be off,' I told Dexter, after he had slid down from the horse and was patting him enthusiastically. I'd had enough of building more jumps.

'Oh. Already?' he asked.

'Yeah, sorry. Dad will be cross if I'm late back.'

'Why?'

'He's always cross.'

'At you? Your lateness, or in general?'

'Mostly at me,' I smiled. 'Well, it seems that way anyway. I think he's just a cross person all round.'

'Has he always been like that?'

'Suppose so,' I replied, avoiding Minty's head, outstretched to nip my leg. 'Since I can remember anyway. I probably had a bit of an attitude when my mum first met him. A big attitude.'

'You were a kid.'

'Yeah, but not a very friendly one.'

'He's the adult; surely he can forgive a young kid's bad attitude when a new man comes on the scene with his mum?'

'You'd think, but he's never liked me since then. Don't think he liked the fact Mum came with baggage. So, yeah, he's always been like that.'

'Doesn't your mum mind?'

'Don't think so. She's not said anything,' I said. 'She's used to him.'

'Doesn't sound fun,' he said, rubbing Minty's neck as he pulled the head collar off.

'Guess not,' I frowned. 'What about your parents, don't they mind that you're always here all the time?'

'Don't be silly, they love it,' he grinned. 'Out of the way and all. I dunno why your dad doesn't think the same. Why does he care? If you're such a pain in the arse, why does he always want you around?'

'I'm not a pain in the arse,' I reached over to swat him, but he dodged out of the way.

'You must be,' he laughed. 'I can see how you'd be a complete pain to have as a son.'

'I'm not,' I cried, launching at him. Giggling, Dexter hid behind Minty, who in comradeship, flattened his ears at me. I raced around to the other side of the horse, but Dexter had already torn away down the hill towards the path.

Despite my training with basketball, Dexter was fit and he streaked away ahead down the path. I'd only just caught up as he threw himself over the stile and lay in the grass panting back up at me. His chest heaved and he flung his arms out wide.

'Okay, you win,' he winked up at me.

'So, I'm not a pain?'

'Oh, no, you're still a pain. You're just faster at running than me.'

Chapter Forty-one

It hadn't been a particularly unusual or special day when Dexter brought it up; the thing lingering in the air never to be mentioned. We, all four of us, were sitting by the canal on the edge of the boat, dipping our toes over into the murky green water. It had been a good day.

Nothing significant.

Busy denying the fact that the peak of summer had been and gone, and time was now slipping down towards the end.

We were spending more and more time by the canal whilst we had the chance. Riding Minty and generally lying about in the sunshine doing as teenagers do.

Not much.

When Dexter started the conversation, we were lazing about and chatting before the bike ride home. The air hung heavy in the sky, as if a thunderstorm may finally shatter the weeks of blue sky. Despite the colour, the water lapped refreshingly onto our hot feet.

I tried to touch Liberty's bare toes under the water, but she looked irritated, so I stopped. She'd stiffened up again since the skinny dipping. Her ever-changing mood was back to ice queen status. I didn't have the energy to worry or even care why.

'I think we should give him back,' Dexter said casually, whilst sucking through a hollow straw like a cigarette. He looked far too comfortable.

'Who?' Will asked, confused. 'Give who back?'

'Minty, of course.'

'What? Why?' Liberty's response came fast and urgent as she turned on him. I sat between her and Dexter and could feel the venom radiate from her. Dexter sighed, oblivious to her rage, and continued swinging his bare legs, trousers rolled up, back and forth in the water.

'We can't look after him properly.'

'We can,' exclaimed Will. He'd been lying back on the deck on his elbows and scrambled upwards to sit.

'Of course we can,' agreed Liberty. 'What more can he need? He has water, grass, plenty of company, you name it, he's got it. You brush him a ridiculous amount until you can admire your reflection in his coat. He gleams. He's happy. He doesn't need anything else.'

'He needs a farrier.'

'A what?' I asked, frowning.

'Like a blacksmith,' Liberty rolled her eyes, looking scornfully at me. 'You know, to put the metal horseshoes on and stuff.'

'But he doesn't have horseshoes on.'

'Why hasn't he got shoes on?' asked Will, frowning. 'Don't racehorses wear them?'

'He's not a racehorse,' snapped Liberty.

'Just saying,' stuttered Will. 'Isn't it odd he wasn't wearing shoes?'

'I don't know,' Liberty said, breathing crossly. 'Maybe he's never had any on in the first place.'

'He has,' said Dexter.

'How do you know?' I asked.

'He had nail holes in his hooves.'

'That doesn't mean he's a racehorse,' said Liberty.

'No, it doesn't,' agreed Will. 'It doesn't mean anything, just once upon a time, not too long ago, he had horseshoes on.'

'Either way, his feet need looking at,' continued Dexter. 'The hooves are getting long and I noticed the other day there are some nasty-looking cracks in the hind ones. Big fuck-off cracks, splitting the hoof up.'

'Horses in the wild don't have shoes on or a farr... whatever that is,' I said. 'They cope. Can't Minty do the same?'

'Yeah but wild horses walk miles every day,' replied Dexter, simply.

'So? What does that do?'

'It kind of sands them down, I think,' he shrugged. 'Like a nail file. Anyway, horses in the wild don't need a farrier but Minty does. He's not in the wild. His field is big, but not enough by far to wear his feet down. The grass is too soft anyway.'

'Do we need to get shoes for him?' I asked. 'What's the point of them?'

'To stop his feet wearing down or getting sore.'

'But they're not.'

'Sometimes for grip or protection if they're doing a lot of work.'

'But he's not.'

'Exactly, so we probably don't need shoes. We only ride him on the towpath or around the field and it's grass. His feet aren't getting sore or anything, just not worn down enough. He needs them trimmed down every so often.'

'We'll have to find someone then,' Liberty's voice was determined. 'A farrier from out of the area. One who doesn't know we don't own him and won't ask us any questions. Or ride him out more so his feet wear down naturally.'

'It's not just his feet, he will need his teeth checking, rasping whatever that is, and vaccinations. Worming tablets. Supplements. It's all expensive. Grandad always used to moan about the costs of keeping his horses. It really does cost a fortune.'

'We'll work it out I'm sure, Sis,' Will said, patting Liberty not so convincingly.

'We need a lot of money.'

'Where is a group of high school kids going to get money from?' asked Will.

'College kids,' Liberty said at the same time as me. I smiled at her, but she looked away. I don't understand her moods.

'Yeah well, some of us are still at school,' said Will. 'And we've all stopped or given up part of our paper rounds so we can come here. All the other money is going on hay, apples and carrots, and treats. There's nothing left.'

'Write a list down,' Liberty addressed Dexter, 'write it all down and I'll sort it.'

'How?'

'I just will,' she snapped.

'We need to talk about these things,' shrugged Dexter. 'What happens if he ever needs the vet?'

'He might never need one.'

'But what happens if he does? What would we do then?'

'We can't live by 'what ifs', can we?'

Dexter sighed loudly and stood to his feet, leaving wet footprints in the wood on the deck. 'We can't keep him forever, you know.'

'Why not?'

'You two are off to college soon. Things change.'

'No, they won't. We will keep him forever, Dexter. Promise.'

'Forever is a long time.'

'I want to keep him forever,' mumbled Liberty, not backing down.

'And so do I,' agreed Dexter, slumping back down next to us. 'But nothing fucking good lasts forever.'

We all remained silent, the soft splashing of the water on our legs, as the weight of his words hung over us.

And so it was forgotten, well, pushed aside for a while at least, and life continued peacefully in the hazy summer heat.

But as Dexter said, nothing good lasts forever.

He was right.

Chapter Forty-two

'So…I got the paper horse,' Tallie said.

'You did?' I asked, clenching my teeth together and screwing my eyes up — waiting. I'd waited long enough for her to phone. She'd made me sweat it for a good week or so. The other end of the phone went silent for the longest few seconds ever, before she replied.

'I did,' she said. She really didn't make anything easy for me.

'So?' I asked. 'What did you think?'

'Cryptic,' she said.

'Did you understand?'

'I think so,' she said, slowly. 'And yet I'm still confused.'

'What are you confused about?'

'I'm confused as to exactly the message you were trying to tell me,' she began. 'Do you know something about the missing horse, or are you yourself involved?'

'I'm involved,' I said. I wanted to give her total honesty now I had opened the box.

Nothing to hide.

'Is this something that's going to get you into trouble?'

'I don't think so,' I replied. 'Not anytime soon. We've been very careful and no one else knows.'

'We?' she asked.

'Liberty and her brother Will.'

'It's starting to make sense now,' she said.

'And Dexter.'

'So that's how you all link together. The relationship among you four didn't seem to fit in any way. Now it does. Did you steal the horse?'

'More like acquired him. We didn't do anything deliberately wrong. And we don't know for certain if it's the racehorse from the paper.'

'But more than likely he is?' she asked.

'Possibly,' I said. 'But we are all in denial.'

'Why did you tell me?' she asked.

'Because I didn't want to keep anything from you anymore,' I said.

'Why?'

'I suppose, if we meant anything to each other, we shouldn't keep secrets. Should we? I'd like to be at least friends again, if possible.'

'Okay,' she said.

'Okay? Okay as in I'm forgiven?'

'Okay, we shouldn't keep secrets.'

'You don't sound very convinced,' I frowned. Her voice sounded quiet and distant. Talking about secrets seemed so childish, considering we were both now college students. 'Are you okay?'

'It's the sharing of secrets thing.'

'I can't apologise enough, Tallie,' I said. 'I'd made a promise to the group and I didn't want to break it and then I let you down and broke your promise. I didn't think. I know I need to grow up more.'

'No, it's not that,' she said.

'What then?' I asked. 'I know I let you down badly.'

'Can I trust you now?'

'Of course,' I said. I hoped she could, but keeping anything to myself isn't a strong point of mine.

'Then I have some more secrets to tell.'

'Huh?' I said. 'What secrets?'

'Shit, we sound like a couple of kids,' she laughed. I could picture her in her bedroom, twisting her red hair tassels between her fingers. I relaxed, glad the tension was broken.

'We do,' I agreed, smiling. 'Not kids for much longer though. Go on then, Miss Phillips, tell me.'

'Mum was quizzing me earlier tonight.'

'Quizzing you?'

'Yeah, asking me odd questions.'

'What about?'

'Well, she started talking about college and the friends I used to have a Rhynside High. Asking who they were and what they were up to.'

'Were you mixed up with the wrong crowd?'

'No, not at all,' she said. 'I had boring, nondescript friends at school. Like I said before, school wasn't a great time for me. Kids aren't nice. Managed to branch out a little at college, away from the high school groups, and find people with my interests, but, back then, there was no one that stood out.'

'Then, why was she asking?'

'She asked about you and Liberty.'

'Us?' I groaned. 'She thinks I'm a bad influence doesn't she?'

'Let me finish,' she said. I could hear the smile in her voice. 'Yes, she probably thinks you're a bad influence. But it wasn't that. She wanted to know who I hung around with and who your friends were.'

'Why?'

'She wasn't doing a great job of being subtle, so I asked her.'

'What did she say?'

'Well,' Tallie began. 'Mum wanted to know about Dexter. She didn't want to accuse me of anything after the file incident, but she wanted to know if I knew any of his friends. If you two were linked in any way.'

'How would she know?' I said, the panic rising in my voice. 'Has someone seen us? Does she know about the horse?'

'No, nothing like that,' Tallie hushed me. 'She was asking questions because of the case she's working on. You see, Dexter has been missing on and off for a while.'

'Missing?' I asked.

'Yeah. Seems like he was going to be placed into foster care after his Grandad died, and now he's done a runner. Hasn't been seen at school for a while either.'

'But I saw him earlier.'

'Where?'

'At Minty's field.'

'Minty's the horse?'

'Yeah, he's always there...' my voice trailed off. 'You can't tell your Mum.'

'I know,' she said. 'But you need to talk to Dexter.'

'I doubt he'll listen.'

'He's still a kid,' she said.

'He's also a friend,' I replied. 'No, no one can know where he is until we've spoken to him. If he doesn't want to talk about it, there's not much we can do.'

'Mum will get into trouble at work if she doesn't say anything.'

'Don't tell her you know where he is,' I said.

'Back to keeping secrets?'

'Afraid so,' I said solemnly. 'For a while. For me, please.'

'Okay,' she said. 'But you owe me big time.'

'Of course,' I grinned.

'Dinner?'

'Cooked by me? Really?' I clenched my teeth again and sucked in air noisily. 'Please don't say I need to cook, Tallie. Anything but that.'

'Dinner out somewhere? As friends? We could get the bus into town?'

'That I can do,' I laughed. 'Tonight? Pick you up at half 7?'

'You're on,' she said. 'But don't come near the house yet, Mum is still on the warpath with the shaking Holly incident.'

'Ah,' I said, wincing at my behaviour. 'I forgot about that. I'll climb up to your window like a knight in shining armour.'

'Sounds amazing,' she said. 'Just watch out for the rose thorns on your way up.'

'My armour will protect me,' I grinned. 'On another thought, maybe I'll text you when I'm coming up the road.'

'Doesn't have the same romancing effect as the knight but you're on. See you at half 7.'

I hung up the phone smiling, then looked at my watch.

Four pm.

I had three and a half hours to get to the canal and find Dexter.

Chapter Forty-three

'Now watch,' said Liberty. She was leaning over a tall green plant with gardening gloves on. The plant had an abundance of little yellow flowers and some stripy orange and black caterpillars firmly attached to them. Her hair was scraped up into a band and, like me, she wore just shorts and a T-shirt.

'Watching,' I said.

'Do exactly as I do.'

'Okay.'

'Take hold of the base of the plant, right down the bottom near the roots and give a good pull. Hold tight.' Liberty leant her body right over the plant. I admiringly watched her tugging. She gave a loud grunt before she swung back up, scattering soil around us. She held the plant up, roots and all, looking satisfied. Then she frowned at my expression. 'Were you even watching?'

'I was watching. Promise,' I told her grinning. I didn't mention what I was watching, but I was definitely watching her. Minty looked up from where he was grazing on the hill near his half-finished temporary pallet fence divide. He pawed at the ground in boredom and then strolled off away from us.

'Okay,' she said, throwing her plant into the wheelbarrow next to us. 'Your turn next.'

I bent down over another plant, grasped it firmly as instructed, then pulled as hard as I could. I felt a grunt inside ready to escape, too, but bit my lip. The plant was firmly wedged in the soil. Caterpillars shook off the plant, falling to the ground and wriggling around in the soil.

'Lower,' shouted Liberty.

'What?' I asked before the plant snapped in two and I stumbled back on to the ground.

'Useless,' she said. 'You needed to hold the plant lower. You've left the roots in the ground.'

'So?' I said. 'I got most of it out.'

'That's not good enough with Ragwort.'

'Why?'

'Because they are devil plants,' she said. 'One little bit left and they'll grow again.'

'Devil plants?' I laughed.

'Yeah, pure evil.'

'Why can't they be in the field?' I asked. 'They're only plants. I don't see us pulling out the thistles or nettles. Unless we have to do that as well?' I hoped not. I'd barely been listening on the walk up from the stile to the top of the hill as she'd gone on and on about the weeding job.

'Don't you ever listen,' she shook her head. Oh. She knows me too well. 'They're toxic to horses, and other animals. That's why. Liver failure or something.'

'Well, if Minty's stupid enough to eat them that's his fault.'

'Nice,' said Liberty.

'Just kidding,' I grinned. 'Couldn't let that happen to Minty. Come on then, there's tons to do.'

'Okay,' she nodded, looking around the field at the mass of yellow plants dotting the expanse. 'You take the bit around the corner and I'll work back towards the gate.

I looked at my watch, 'Let's give it an hour and then meet at the canal for a break. We should, hopefully, be done by then.'

'Where are we going to empty your wheelbarrow?' asked Liberty.

'Won't our muck heap do?'

'No,' she said. 'When the seeds dry out they'll blow back round the field and make more plants.'

'Then what?'

'We need to bury or burn them.'

'Burn them then?' I shrugged, running my fingers through my cropped hair. Paranoid about wiggly caterpillars. 'Let's heap them down by the stile path. We could make another bonfire and burn them one evening again with the others. Make an evening of it. Beers and BBQ.'

'Sounds a plan,' she said and smiled up at me. 'We could camp over again.'

I could see in her eyes what she was thinking. I thought the same. Although now I was confused about Tallie. I know Tallie and I were only friends at the moment, but I did hope for more. But then there's Liberty. Oh, why did life have to be so hard?

'Okay,' I said, breaking the thoughts and picking up my barrow. 'Back to work.'

I reached over to a huge plant, taller than myself and grasped it firmly by the roots. The plant held. I twisted the roots around, walking in circles around the plant until I could hear the tear of tiny strands beneath the surface. Liberty stood and watched, amused.

'Come on bloody thing,' I said, my face flushing as I strained against the plant. The roots finally gave way and the plant tore from the ground, taking me by surprise. I yelled as I crashed back down to the ground again, the tiny caterpillars spraying all over me. 'Urgh,' I cried. I rolled over to shake them off but instead squashed several of them onto me. 'These are devil plants.'

Minty ambled over through the rickety fence we badly needed to finish, and sniffed at me lying on the ground. Satisfied I was without mints, he snorted and nibbled at the corner of my T-shirt.

'Here,' Liberty laughed, reaching a hand down to heave me up. She pulled me up with more force than I thought she'd be capable of, until we stood chest to chest. I stumbled and she caught me around the waist.

Then reaching up on her tiptoes, she kissed me.

Chapter Forty-four

Finally our movie moment.

I let my mouth kiss her back, soft and warm. Her tongue poked at mine hungrily trying to explore my mouth. I resisted. Something felt wrong. Someone else entered my head.

Tallie.

I pulled back.

'I can't do this,' I told her.

'What?' she replied. Her eyes glared as her smooth forehead furrowed. She gave a little smile, tilt of her head, and pulled me in again.

Believe me, this was the hardest thing I've ever had to say no for. Imagine kissing your life-long idol. That's how it felt. But then imagine suddenly realising your idol is actually human and sometimes not a particularly nice person. The bubble burst once and for all. But the internal torment let the kiss linger longer than it should before I pushed her back.

'No,' I said firmly, holding her at arm's length. 'I'm not doing this with you. I'm with Tallie.' Well sort of, but I wasn't going to explain myself to Liberty.

'The ginger freak?'

'Pardon?' I said. My eyes grew round as I stared at her in astonishment. 'What did you say?'

'You heard.'

'You don't know the first thing about Tallie.'

Liberty shrugged. 'Don't need to. I can tell.'

'You're incredible.'

'Thanks,' she winked, moving back in towards me.

'No,' I said, stepping back and holding my hand out. 'You're unbelievable. I don't know what I ever saw in you. Without the pretty black, shiny hair, smooth skin and legs up to your arse, well, you're actually the biggest bitch going.'

'What did you call me?' her eyes blazed.

'You heard,' I laughed. 'I pity poor Will and I pity your friends but do you know who I pity most of all, Liberty?'

'Who?' she asked, pulling off her gloves and inspecting her nails for splits with exaggerated boredom.

'I pity you.'

Liberty's eyes flashed up at me. She threw the gloves to the ground.

'Don't you dare pity me,' she spat. 'You're the one that should be pitied. Do you know how pathetic you've been? Practically drooling over me at school. Always with a hard-on around me. Gross. We all think it.'

She wrinkled her nose. I looked down at my shorts, embarrassed, then frowned back at her. I think she was joking. Hope so. I'm usually better at hiding my teenage dilemmas.

'Everybody's been laughing at you,' she carried on. 'Your ridiculous blackboard stunt and that stupid song I told everyone about. You've humiliated me. Yeah, you might be tall and nice-ish-looking but we all think you're a true loser Rafferty Lincoln. No girl will touch you after this. I'll make sure of that.'

'In a few weeks we'll be starting college,' I said.

'So,' she replied. 'Your point?'

'No one cares about this high school shit at college. No one. And no one will care about you and your status in high school. Everyone's an equal. Thank fuck.'

'Some more equal than others.'

I laughed, bitterly. 'You've a lot to learn, Liberty Ashburn. I'm not sure college will be easy on you.'

'What are you talking about?'

'You'll see,' I grinned.

'Well, you'll see, too. Two can play that game.'

'That doesn't make sense,' I told her.

'Maybe I know something you don't.'

'About what?'

'Something I did,' she smirked. 'You'll see.'

'What did you do?'

'Wait and see.' She was practically giddy. I became nervous. I wasn't sure what she was talking about but she looked very smug. My mind racked through recent conversations but came up with nothing, apart from the recent kiss.

'Leave Tallie alone, will you. She's done nothing wrong. She doesn't need to know about any of this.'

'She's a big girl.'

'Please,' I said.

Liberty came up close and planted a kiss on my nose. I could feel her minty breath on my face. 'What she doesn't know won't hurt her.'

'There is nothing between me and you, Liberty.'

'I know,' she smirked. 'But I can have a little fun, can't I?'

'Whatever,' I replied, and turned away from her. I dumped the last pile of weeds in my wheelbarrow and headed down the hill.

'Where are you going?' she called after me.

'Home,' I replied. 'I'm done.'

Chapter Forty-five

🧲

'This is Minty,' I said, patting the horse's neck enthusiastically. Minty eyed me with suspicion. 'Minty, meet Tallie.'

Minty's neck felt damp and glistened with sweat. He smelt sweet; like clover and leather. I pushed his long wavy, black mane over to one side hoping it would help the air waft around him on the sticky evening.

'Hi, Minty,' Tallie rubbed his nose and offered him a carrot. He lifted his head and looked at her solemnly, whilst crunching. Carrot spittle spraying from his mouth. He blinked his long lashes at her in appreciation. 'Do you like him, Holly?'

'Love him,' Holly replied, with a grin. She patted his shoulder. 'He's totally amazing.'

'You can ride him one day. When Dexter's about. He's the expert,' I told her.

Dexter failed to make an appearance that evening, or to think of it, failed to appear any day recently. Since my warning of his hiding place, his eyes had widened, before he laughed and shrugged it off.

Then he'd disappeared.

'That would be amazing, wouldn't it, Holly?'

'Yeah,' mumbled Holly, distracted, her eyes resting on the horse as she gently rubbed her hand down his neck.

Tallie nudged her, 'It's nice of Raff to offer isn't it?'

'Guess so,' she muttered. 'Can Abby and me go and play in the field?'

'Okay,' agreed Tallie, sighing. 'But stay within our sight. Just in the field.'

The girls left us and walked up the path towards the highest point, at the top of the field. We watched them go before turning back to Minty.

'She still hates me, doesn't she?'

'She'll come round,' said Tallie. 'I think you scared her a bit. A lot. With the shaking and everything.'

'Sorry,' I groaned. 'I don't know what came over me.'

'You still haven't explained exactly what happened.'

'It's too embarrassing, believe me,' I told her. 'One day I will.'

'I'll make sure of that,' she smiled. 'So this is the famous horse? He's not what I expected.'

'What did you expect?'

'Something a bit more glamorous, maybe. He's just a horse.'

'He is a horse!'

'Yeah, but I expected something, I dunno, something more…' she waved her hand, 'showier.'

'Poor Minty,' I said, laughing and tickling Minty behind his ears. 'Don't listen to her, Mint. You're a beautiful horse.'

'He is kind of beautiful,' she agreed. 'His coat feels so silky and soft. Lovely colour, too, almost scarlet. I guess racehorses look different all dolled up on the telly.'

'We still don't know if he's the actual horse though.'

'The missing racehorse?'

'Yeah.'

'What happens if he's not and some poor girl is broken-hearted because her beloved horse, Pickles, went missing?'

'Pickles?' I laughed.

'That's a great name for a horse,' she said seriously. 'Mr Pickles. And he misses the little girl who used to brush his hair till he gleamed.'

'Don't say that,' I said. I grimaced and sucked noisily at my lip. 'If he belonged to anyone else and went missing, don't you think someone would have said something by now? It would have been in the news. Local papers or something?'

'Suppose so,' she shrugged her shoulders and looked at me. 'Then, he is the racehorse, isn't he?'

'I'm not sure,' I said, shaking my head. 'There are still tons of unanswered questions. Like, how did he get in Petersfield lane? Why wasn't he wearing anything like the other horses were wearing travelling? Leg bandages and stuff. He had no head collar on; one of the horses was strangled because of the rope tying it up. Something doesn't add up.'

'Don't you feel guilty?'

'For keeping him?'

'Yeah.'

'A little. Sometimes more than others,' I blew out a puff of breath, my lip vibrating. 'But Dexter would kill me if we had to give him back. So would Liberty. We all promised. You can't tell anyone either or Holly. Please.'

Tallie nodded. She glanced up the hill at the girls, who were trying to roll down the steepest grassy part on their sides. Over and over like a Swiss roll, until they bumped together.

'Any sign of Dexter?' she asked.

'None,' I replied. 'Think he's keeping a low profile. He doesn't like questions. We all don't. Please, Tallie, this is important for more than one reason.'

'Okay,' she agreed, nodding quietly. 'We promise. Holly loves horses, she'll be desperate to ride him, if Dexter allows, so that'll definitely buy her silence. I'll make sure of it.'

'Thanks,' I said, gratefully.

'Maybe she'll warm a little to you, too.'

'I hope so,' I grinned. 'I'm not scary at all, promise.'

'Not to me anyway,' she smiled and reached up on tiptoes to kiss my nose. 'Right, Mr Noisy Breather, we'd best get the girls home before suspicion arises.'

'You're right,' I agreed, grinning. She'd kissed me! Surely that meant I'd progressed from friend-zone relegation. I cupped my hands and called, 'ABBY!' as loudly as I could muster. Tallie covered her ears.

The girls came pounding down the hill behind us as we turned and made our way slowly through the overgrown path to the stile.

A couple of bikes lay strewn in the grass beside ours.

'Who's are those?' Tallie lay a warning hand on my arm looking concerned.

'Oh, the bikes? Will's and Liberty's. Dexter usually pulls his bike up onto the boat if he's staying a while, in case anyone walks by if he's out riding.'

'Will she mind if I'm here?' she asked.

'Soon find out,' I nodded towards Liberty on the deck of the boat. 'I'm sure she'll be fine,' I reassured, seeing Tallie's worried face.

Inside, my heart crushed slightly as I wished Liberty hadn't arrived. I breathed out and remained light and happy on the surface. Liberty turned at the sound of us approaching on the rubble towpath. I pulled myself up onto the boat first, and Tallie held back with the girls, slightly out of view.

'Who have you brought here?' Liberty said, her eyes blazing. She curled her lip up, her pretty face twisted into something else. 'I saw all the bikes. Who have you told about this place?'

'I brought some friends. I'm allowed to have friends.'

'What?' Her voice rose to almost shouting.

'Calm down, Libby, they won't tell.'

'Since when do you ever called me Libby?' Her blue eyes were almost black with rage.

'Since never.'

'We all promised. We had a pact.'

'Yeah, but this was necessary.'

'How? Tell me one good reason why other people needed to know?'

'Because I'm not good at secrets, *Liberty*. I needed to tell someone. I need someone to share this with. And you lot aren't my friends out of this place. Not you, not Will or Dexter. Tallie is.'

'Tallie,' Liberty roared. 'Why on earth have you brought her here? There's no way she won't say something. We all heard how good she was at keeping her Mum's secrets confidential. She'll tell for sure.'

'No, she won't.'

'Yes, she will.'

'No, I won't,' Tallie pulled herself up onto the boat next to us. 'Stay there, girls.' She motioned for Holly and Abby to stay on the towpath. She approached, looking up at Liberty, a whole head higher than her, despite being a year younger. 'Liberty. I don't know you, but I know Rafferty and we've become good friends. He trusts me and I trust him. I promise I will keep your pact. I've no reason to tell anyone else.'

'What about them two down there?' Liberty spat, staring down at the girls. Holly's eyes grew round. 'They're bloody kids. You can't trust kids. Who knows who they'll tell.'

'We've already sorted it out,' I told Liberty. 'Both the girls love horses. I'm sure Dexter wouldn't mind giving them a few rides to keep them sweet. They won't tell anyone.'

'We'll help out,' piped up Abby, stepping forward to the side of the boat. 'I don't mind mucking out the field and helping. We'd both love to,' she nodded at the frozen Holly, who copied the nodding blindly.

'Fucking kids,' Liberty glared back at me. 'You did this to spite me after the other day, didn't you? You've ruined everything, again, Rafferty Lincoln. And for once Dexter will agree with this one.'

'He might. He might not. But he's not here. Where is he anyway?'

'Dunno. Haven't seen him for days. But he'll be fuming when he comes back. Fucking fuming. Do you hear me? Fuming.'

'I hear you, Liberty. We all hear you loud and clear. But what's done is done. There's no need to be rude. Let's get on with it.'

'No,' she said, shaking her head. 'No way.' She looked around for Will, and caught a glimpse of his brown mop of curly hair bobbing in the canal. 'WILL. Swim's over,' she called to him. 'Get your stuff, we're going.'

Hearing the shouts, Will swum back over to the boat and used the rope pulled himself aboard. He lay panting on the deck and grinned up at us.

'That was amazing.' He spotted Tallie and looked confused. 'I didn't know we had guests. Who are they?'

'We don't have guests,' replied Liberty. 'They're not welcome.'

'Come on, Liberty,' I said. 'I thought we were over this.'

'You stay,' Tallie soothed, holding up her hand. 'We need to get the girls home anyway. It's nearly their tea. Come on, Raff, let's leave them to their swim. Bye, Will, lovely to meet you.'

'I don't want to see you here again,' said Liberty, folding her arms as Tallie slid past her and jumped down from the boat.

'But I want a ride,' Holly whined, as Tallie pushed the girls towards their bikes.

'Not now,' said Tallie. 'Possibly one day. We need to check with Dexter first, don't we?'

'Over my fucking dead body,' Liberty called after us.

Pushing off, we headed up the towpath. We rode in pairs, the girls in front, with Tallie and me behind. If the path narrowed too much, we had to go single file and shout.

'Well that went well,' I grinned at Tallie.

'Yeah brilliantly,' she laughed. 'I can see we're all going to be best pals.'

'She wasn't nice,' said Holly, wobbling on her bike as she turned to shout at us.

'I agree with you, Holly,' I smiled. She smiled back at me shyly, before turning her eyes to the towpath. 'She's a bitch.'

If completely losing Liberty's trust meant winning over Holly, it was job completely fucking well done.

Chapter Forty-six

Would the next events have happened if Liberty hadn't reacted how she did? Or did she somehow predict the girls' betrayal before it happened?

Who knows.

Whether Liberty was right or caused the following to happen, I'll never know for sure. Whatever the reasons, I know visiting the boat that day with Tallie and the girls, then seeing Liberty, sparked a chain of events that truly changed everything.

But for a couple of hours after leaving the boat, nothing changed. I cycled the girls back and waved them inside, both staying for tea at the Phillips' household, with a possible sleepover if Dad agreed.

Tallie and I chatted for a while by the gate before I kissed her goodbye, softly on the lips. She grinned, waved bye and blew a kiss, before running up the driveway. I turned for home and cycled slowly, a smile spreading across my face. Life couldn't be better. School was over, exams finished. Despite the days quickly slipping by, the summer still stretched ahead as far as I could see. Minty was happy. Dexter and Will were more relaxed and carefree, and Liberty, well, she'd never change and for once I didn't care.

I dumped my bike into the garage and headed indoors. Dad was waiting by the door, his face tight and solemn.

'Tallie's mum has been ringing the house. For you.'

'Oh?'

'Did she try your mobile?'

'I didn't take it with me.'

'What have you done this time? I thought you weren't meant to be anywhere near that family.'

'I haven't done anything. Maybe Abby wants picking up already?'

'Then why did she want to speak to you?'

'I don't know,' I replied, crossly. I didn't want Dad to spoil my happy bubble. 'Didn't you ask her?'

'I did. She said it was private. Why does a grown woman want to have a private conversation with you? What have you been up to?'

'I don't know,' I shrugged my shoulders and tried to duck around him towards the stairs.

'No you don't,' he said. He grasped my shoulders tightly and turned me towards the lounge. His pudgy grip dug in around my neck as he reached up. I scrunched up my shoulders and winced, leaning forward against the pain. Mum was sitting bolt upright in a chair, looking stiff and frightened.

'Let go,' I squirmed, struggling beneath his grip.

'Sit,' he boomed. 'Now.' He threw me forward onto an armchair. I grabbed the arms to stop from stumbling, then turned and sunk into the chair.

'Mum?' I asked, slumping back and resting my head. 'What's going on?'

'Listen to Dad,' she said. Her voice was tight, hard to read.

'Mum?' I asked again. She averted her eyes away from mine. Lines grooved around her eyes. Saggy, tired skin. Age had crept up on her without me noticing.

'Here's the phone. Go on.' He handed over the home phone to me and waited. I looked down at the phone, confused. 'Phone her.'

'Who?'

'Who do you god damn think, Son, the Queen? Ring Mrs Phillips back. Now.'

'I'll do it upstairs, thanks.'

'You'll do it now,' Dad said, and thumped the table next to him. Mum jumped in her chair but remained silent.

'No,' I replied. My palms were starting to sweat. 'If it's okay with you, I'd rather do it in private.'

'It's not okay. Phone her now.'

'Please, Rafferty,' pleaded Mum. 'Phone her back. Do as your Dad says.'

'Why?' I asked. 'I'm a grown man.'

'Grown man,' Dad snorted. 'You don't know the first thing about being a man yet. Now phone her or do I have to make you?'

This time I snorted, 'Make me how, Dad?'

'Like this,' he said, raising his eyebrows. He grabbed the phone back and punched recall. He held the phone to his ear smirking. 'Hello? Mrs Phillips. Yes, it's Rafferty's Dad phoning back. I have Rafferty here. Yes, sitting right here with me. I'll pass you over.' He smiled and handed me the phone. I scowled but took it.

'Hello? Mrs Phillips?'

'Hello, Rafferty. Thanks for ringing me back.'

'That's okay. How can I help?' I stood and made my way towards the door. Dad blocked my way. I raised my eyebrows angrily at Mum, but she looked away. Her hands fiddled with her reading glasses. I went back towards the chair.

'I heard you had a nice time with the girls this afternoon.'

'I'm sorry…' I started, but she cut in.

'No, Rafferty, I'm not here to tell you off. I'm glad you've made things up with Tallie. She's so much happier to be around. Thank goodness. None of those dark moods and dramatic charcoal paintings. No, this is a different matter. A more complicated matter.'

241

Oh no. Minty. There couldn't possibly be anything else Tallie's mum would want to talk to me about. I remained silent, trying to keep any clues away from Dad. He'd begun to pace the room, frustrated about being kept in the dark with my silence.

'I need your discretion, please, Rafferty. This is about Dexter Forrest.'

'Dexter?' I said and clapped my hand across my mouth. Dad frowned and shrugged at Mum. She looked down at the floor, her fingers now pulling at the threads on the throw.

'Yes. Dexter. Holly came home this afternoon in a bit of a muddle. She was all animated about someone called Liberty who had shouted at her? Then mentioned something about a boy called Dexter offering her a riding lesson. This Liberty girl had been mean and had said no. Do you know anything about this? Tallie clammed up when she came in and made a swift disappearing act. Your sister also seemed to be holding back something and kept nudging Holly to be quiet. Do you know anything? This is important.'

'Mmmm,' I nodded, unsure of any words I could say without rousing suspicion.

'Anyway,' she continued, 'Holly's now clamped a hand across her mouth and won't talk to me again; nothing that makes sense anyway. She wants to see this horse again but is afraid she can't if she tells. A secret or something. She's distraught about this horse… and about Liberty.'

'Ah,' I replied.

'Yes. I'm very confused, too. But you see, I have been working with Dexter and I've been rather concerned about his whereabouts. Holly, before her vow of silence, mentioned you've become close friends with him?'

'Just acquaintances.'

'So you might know where he is? This is important, Rafferty. I don't want to make some very serious phone calls without knowing there is some truth in what the girls are saying. Have you any idea where this horse is? Or Dexter? Does he go to stables to ride or anything? Please, I need to know any information.'

'Uh huh.'

'So, what I'm asking Rafferty, is can you help me?'

'Maybe…' I said. 'Maybe it would be best if I come around to explain.'

'Really?' she asked. 'I don't mind chatting on the phone.'

'Okay, no problem. I could come tomorrow to talk when I pick Abby up.'

'I need some information tonight, if possible.'

'I'll see what I can do,' I said. Dad tapped me on the shoulder and held out his hand for the phone. I shook my head at him. His eyes opened wide and he lurched for the phone.

'Mrs Phillips. Yes? No, I won't let Rafferty out. Dinner is ready. No. What is this in regards? Yes. Okay. I'll drive him over. Okay. No, I'm afraid I will have to stay with him. I can be confidential. He's my son, I have a right. I will see you soon.'

I tried to catch Mum's eye but she refused to look my way. I made a low growl at her and her eyes flashed quickly at me then away. A single tear ran down her face. That tear told me more than I would ever need to know. I bit my lip and sucked in air, trying to think. Dad hung up and turned towards me, jangling his keys.

'Car,' he said. 'Whilst you're in my house, it's my rules.'

'What about Mum's rules?'

'Her rules are my rules. We are a team. The car. Now.'

'I thought dinner was ready.'

'It can wait. Car,' he nodded towards the door.

I knew in that second what I had to do. How close everything was to total collapse. I couldn't see any way to save Dexter and Minty. It had to be one or the other, not both. I lowered my head and followed Dad meekly out of the door. He blocked the doorway, tugging his jacket on. He held up mine, frowning at my shorts and T-shirt.

'No, thanks,' I said. 'It's so muggy out.'

'Suit yourself.' He nudged my shoulder towards the door and practically marched me towards his car, parked on the drive in front of the open garage. 'In.' He lowered my head down and pushed me inside, like a cop with his felon.

I complied.

As he slammed me inside, I gripped my fingers around the door handle and waited. I edged the handle open, his crunching footsteps on the gravel drowning out the light pop of the door. Just as he reached his door and swung himself heavily into the seat, I threw my door open.

I scrambled out and behind the car to the garage. My bike rested up against the wall. He was quick. Quicker than I thought possible. His hand ripped the bottom of my T-shirt clean off. I swung up onto the bike and thrust forwards. The bike tyre sprayed a scattering of pebbles across the front lawn as I made the road. Heavy panting and cursing directly behind.

Once on the tarmac, he was no match for the bike and finally I gained ground.

'You little fucker!' I heard him shout. 'Get the fuck back here.'

His voice drowned out as I made for the country lanes.

I was in shit.

Chapter Forty-seven

'So that's it,' Dexter put his hands to his face, and slumped back down onto a hay bale at the back of the boat. 'It's all over.'

'Not necessarily.'

'How the fuck are we going to get out of this?'

'I don't know,' I said, miserably. I stood in the entrance to the boat, awkwardly. 'I'm sorry, I didn't think it would turn out like this.'

'That's the problem. None of you think, do you? Not you. Not Liberty, and not even Will.'

'Will's done nothing wrong.'

'Really?' his nostrils flared, and he rose up from the bale. I remembered the strangling incident and put my hands up in surrender. 'None of you realise the consequences of your gossiping. Not one of you.'

He took a step towards me, his little, scuffed fists clenched tightly. As he stepped out from the shadows, I got a proper glance at him. I resisted the urge to gasp. One eye bulged from his face, puffy and closed. The stretched skin had a white sheen, like a corpse, and wept oozy, pinkish-yellow liquid, streaking down his dirty face. The other side was splattered with flecks of fresh blood, sprayed down from a wound hidden in his long, messy hair. His arms were splattered, too. The blood was smeared, edges turning crusty brown, where he'd tried to wipe it off.

'What the hell happened?' I asked.

'Nothing,' he said. 'A result of all the gossiping.'

'We had nothing to do with that.'

'Not directly.'

'I don't understand. Who did this?'

'It doesn't matter.'

'Of course it matters,' I cried. I was horrified as to who would do this, and that Dexter would think we were somehow responsible.

'One problem at a time,' he grinned, teeth stained red with blood. A tooth missing. 'We've bigger problems than my face.'

'Have we?' I asked. 'I'm not sure anything I had to say remotely rivals what's happening with you.'

'Minty is more important.'

'He's a horse,' I said.

'Yeah, he's our horse.'

'Is he?'

Dexter glared. 'I thought we'd all agreed about this.'

'Yeah, yeah,' I held my arms out. 'But I think Minty is about to become public knowledge. I'm not sure others will think the same as us.'

'Do they know about the boat?'

'I don't think so,' I shrugged. 'All Holly said was about you and the horse. Not where he was kept.'

'Do you trust them not to tell?'

'I don't know,' I said, honestly. 'They're kids. They'll probably crack sooner or later if this gets serious. Tallie might, too.'

'Will her mum call the police?'

I shrugged, 'Dunno, sorry, Dex. I don't know how responsible Tallie's mum is, with her job and duty of care. She'll probably have to report you to her work. Whether that includes the police, I don't know. This isn't going to go away.'

'What should I do?'

'That depends on how much you want to protect Minty.'

'What do you mean?' he asked.

'Turn yourself in. They won't care about the random horse the girls mentioned. At the moment, no one is looking for a horse. They want you.'

Dexter slumped back onto the floor of the boat. 'I can't,' he said.

'Why not?'

He pointed at his face. 'This.'

'Social services aren't going to beat you up. Aren't they there to help you?'

Dexter shrugged back, 'You don't get it.'

'Then we have to give up Minty. If they're still looking for you, won't they eventually find the field? Then Minty. Game over.'

'There must be another way.'

'I can't think of one,' I said, apologetically.

'Can you give me some more time?'

'I don't know how,' I replied, shaking my head. 'Dad's gone mental. Tallie's mum knows I know where you are. I can't hold them off for much longer. The girls will probably crack sooner than I will anyway. They probably already have if Dad's gone round there.'

'Please,' he pleaded. 'Just a few hours so I can think. There must be somewhere we can move him to.'

'I'll try,' I promised. 'I'll get hold of Liberty and Will, and then get a message to Tallie. I know Liberty said phones are off limits but… this is an emergency, don't you think?'

'What if they're monitoring their phones?'

'They're not MI5,' I laughed. 'But, you're right, I wouldn't put anything past my Dad to try at the moment. I'll be as discrete as I can.'

'Thanks, Raff,' Dexter sighed heavily. 'This is all fucked up.'

'Tell me about it.'

Chapter Forty-eight

My house sat in silence, shrouded with darkness. I hesitated at the door before peering in and taking a quick look around. Even Mum had gone. I debated going to Tallie's house first but knew they must all be there, so headed to Liberty's instead. Her window light was on, but the stones I clicked against the pane went unanswered. Will's bedroom faced the other direction. I couldn't get near to try the same.

I gave up, texted her, and waited.

'What?' came her reply.

'Outside. Come down.'

'No. Why?'

'IMPORTANT.'

'Fine. Meet by back gate. NOT front door.'

I moved around to the side and waited. I heard a bolt slide across the gate a few minutes later. Liberty appeared through the back garden, looking flustered. She'd tied her hair up in a bun, strands of hair falling out, and wore a white T-shirt, no bra I noted, and black shorts. She appeared ready for bed, face scrubbed clean and glowing.

'What are you doing here?' she hissed, closing the gate softly behind her.

'It's Dexter.'

'What about him? He pissed at you, too?'

'Yeah, kind of,' I said. 'Game's over, Liberty. The girls told on us. Tallie's mum wants to know about the horse and Dexter.'

'I knew this would happen.'

'Might not have if you hadn't flipped out and scared the girls silly.'

'What have you said to her mum?' she asked, ignoring my comment.

'Nothing yet. I ran.'

She shook her head, 'Then what's to worry about?'

'Dad's gone around Tallie's. I think her mum will phone the police. Everyone's been looking for Dexter. He's only just fifteen. And obviously in some trouble. They have a responsibility.'

'What do you want me to do?'

'Ideas?' I asked.

'Go and see what's happening. Talk to everyone. Make up something.'

'Great help you've been.'

She shrugged. 'What do you expect me to do? Clean up your own mess. Just don't say anything about Minty. Or that we're involved. Leave me and Will out of this.'

'I thought you'd care,' I said.

'I don't,' she replied.

'But you've been okay again,' I said, confused. 'You've almost been normal. Well, that was before I took Tallie to the boat and you got mad. But I thought we were kind of friends again.'

She shrugged, 'Well things change. Go away, and don't mention us.'

'If they find Dexter, they'll find Minty.'

'Then make sure they don't find Minty. Say you don't know about the horse. Got it?'

I shook my head at her and got back on my bike. I didn't look back, just pedalled off leaving her standing there in the semi-darkness. I don't know why I'd bothered. The bike free-wheeled down the slope and up again before I pedalled furiously to make the top.

As I turned down Tallie's lane, I could see the blue flashing lights before I even saw the house. I knew the car was outside. I waited a few minutes, trying to think fast but getting nowhere. I got off the bike and pushed it slowly on the opposite side of the road. Dusk had arrived and I tried to merge with the shadowy trees lining the lane. I stopped directly outside, partly concealed by the parked cars. The lights were on in her house, but the police car was empty, blue lights switched off.

Everybody must be inside still.

'Where have you been?'

I jumped at the voice. Dad wound down his car window next to where I stood. He sat in the darkness, also watching the house.

'What are you doing?' I asked.

'It's getting heated inside. I've come out here for a break.'

'Where's Mum?'

'Comforting Abby. She's very upset. Gone to get her things. We're taking her home.'

'What's happened?'

'You'd best get inside and tell them. Tallie's mum has called the police. Off you go.'

'I can't,' I replied.

'You're not to see any of the Phillips family again.'

'You can't tell me what to do.'

'I just did,' he's eyes stayed peeled on the house. 'Look at the trouble you've caused. You and the bloody red-head.'

'We haven't done anything wrong.'

'I suppose one good thing will come from all of this,' he grinned, looking into my eyes. The whites of his eyes were tinged red. A light drizzle of rain began to speckle at the car's windows and a metallic iron smell filled my nostrils.

'What good thing?'

'The reward money of course,' he laughed, bitterly. He slumped in his seat. 'Your only use in life so far; getting us the horse reward money.'

'What money? What horse?' I asked.

'The one you took Abby and Holly to see. They've told the police everything. How you've all been hiding the horse for months. Since April. Since the car crash where an expensive racehorse went missing.'

'I don't know what you're talking about.'

'Of course you do. You've got to act all innocent, though; otherwise, they won't give us the reward. You're doing a good job of that already. Keep it up. Blame that Dexter boy for taking him. He's obviously got a screw loose anyway.'

'I seriously haven't got a clue, Dad, what you're on about.'

His hand darted out the window and gripped at me, twisting the T-shirt material into my neck. 'Don't fuck this up for us, Son. A few white lies and we'll be made for life. That kid doesn't give a shit about you. Blame him, got it?' He pulled me down close to his face, his breath stinking stale. I could smell beer and cigarettes. I wriggled against his grip.

'Let go, Dad.'

'They want you to take them to the horse.'

'I can't.'

'You can,' he commanded, twisting tighter. 'Think of the reward, Son.'

'You never cared,' I whispered.

'What are you talking about?'

'Not once. Not since you met me as a child.'

'Stop your blathering,' he hissed. 'Get inside and tell them.'

'I was just a child.'

'Bloody obnoxious child,' he said, face out the window pushed into mine with water trickling down his nose.

'You're not a child now. Pull yourself together and take them to the horse.'

The drizzle turned to hard rain, drops bouncing back up off the road. I twisted away from his grip and rubbed my sore neck. I wiped the water from my face.

'I can't. Sorry.' I backed away from the car, dragging my bike to the pavement. The front door had opened, voices muffled by the pounding droplets. Turning, I rode into the rain. I'd no idea what to do next. There wasn't any way out of it.

I turned the bike back towards the canal.

I had to warn him. Give them both a head start before it was too late.

Chapter Forty-nine

My cries were muffled by the downpour, soaking through my thin T-shirt. It clung damply to me. The hour was the weird time between the last strands of murky light and complete darkness. Last wisps of light bounced off the frothing water and just about reflected the towpath as I negotiated the overgrown pathway.

My bike hurtled towards the boat. Water-laden grass whipped against my legs, soaking my socks and trainers. Lashings of rain thrust ripple after ripple up the canal banks. The water seeped down onto my path.

I finally reached the boat, starting to bob around on the water, finally released from its muddy grip. Since we'd known the boat it had never moved, wedged fast in the sludge.

'Dexter!' I yelled again. My voice hoarse from all the shouting and swallowed by the downpour. My bike skidded to a stop, splattering mud up the sides of the boat. I threw it down and pulled myself on board. 'Dexter?'

I wiped my wet hair from my forehead and peered down the steps inside the dark cabin.

'Dexter? Are you here?'

'Shhh,' Dexter appeared at the doorway and put a finger to his lips. 'You'll scare him.'

'Who?' I asked, raising my voice slightly over the sound of the rain thudding on the wooden deck.

'Minty,' he mouthed back. Dexter was soaked through, too. The rain had washed the blood from his body, showing the full extent of his wounds. His eye remained closed and swollen, with a spreading purple bruise above his temple. Black shorts clung to his skinny, bruised legs and grazed knees.

'What?' I asked. 'He's on the boat?'

'Yeah.'

'Are you mad? What's he doing on here?'

He shrugged. 'To keep him dry. And hidden. It's his stable, isn't it? That was always the plan.'

He motioned me to follow him inside, out of the rain. Once through the entrance, he pulled across a board to block the door, entombing us inside. We had never finished the proper stable door. Rain thundered down onto the tin roof, echoing around. Hooves shuffled around in the darkness, muffled by a thick bed of hay strewn across the floor. The boat rocked gently. I moved to the side to lean against the swaying.

'It's moving,' I said.

'Yeah, all the water's released the bottom from the mud. It should settle when the rain stops. I've tied the ropes to those metal stakes on the towpath. We ain't going anywhere fast.'

'You need to leave. Now.'

'Why? What happened?'

'They know you're here.'

'Did you tell? You promised you'd give me time.'

'Sorry, Dexter. It was too late when I got there. They already knew.'

'Do they know about Minty?'

'Think so,' I said and sighed. 'The police were already there, Dex. I didn't go in. I doubt we've got long. You have to leave.'

'What about Minty?' His brow furrowed with concern.

'Can you take him somewhere?'

'Where?'

'I dunno,' I said. 'The farm you work on? Can the farmer take you both in? Why the hell did you bring him on here and how on earth did you get him on?'

'I made a ramp,' Dexter shrugged, simply. He looked defeated, broken. 'I just wanted to hide him. He followed a bucket of carrots and apples on without fuss. And no, the farmer is a good guy but he won't keep him. Or me.'

'Then it's game over, Dexter.'

'It can't be.'

'It is. He isn't our horse.'

'He is,' Dexter raised his voice. 'We can't give up on him now.' Minty gave a whiney and shuffled behind us in the cabin. Dexter spoke to him softly and he calmed and lowered his head back to the hay.

'Look at you, Dex.'

'What do you mean?'

'Look at you. You're living on a fucking boat. You're hiding a stolen racehorse and you're shit-scared about something or someone. You can't go on like this.'

'It's none of your business.'

'It is,' I cried, startling Minty, who skidded backwards in the cabin, his hooves sliding on the damp wood. The floor rocked and groaned. 'We all care about you. What the hell's going on?'

'Just leave me,' cried Dexter. 'Go.' He stood between me and the horse, scrawny and determined.

'No way,' I said. Minty paced back and forth behind Dexter, spinning on the spot as he turned in the tight space on the swaying boat. 'Not without you.'

'I'm not leaving Minty.'

'It's over, Dexter.' I stepped towards him, one hand outstretched towards him. Hoping he'd take it.

'Please,' said Dexter, shaking his head. His blonde hair flicked wet and dark around his forehead. He shrunk back away from me, backing into Minty's chest. The horse lowered his head protectively over Dexter. He reached behind with a hand to pat him. Minty's hooves danced nervously, scraping at the floor. 'I'm not leaving.'

I stood, arm outstretched, willing myself to say something to convince the determined boy to listen to reason.

But I failed.

I will always regret the moment I could have changed everything. 'If only' is a cruel thing. Had I possessed hindsight, everything would be different. But unfortunately that night, in the rain, on the boat, I had none.

I stepped forward again into the darkness.

To grab Dexter?

I'm not sure anymore. But as I reached forward, the boat gave a crack prising both our eyes wide open. Minty snorted, trying to rear in fright, but crashing his head into the roof. He lurched forward, knocking Dexter to the floor. I jumped sideways as he threw himself over the wooden panel, crushing it with his hooves. He disappeared up the steps out on the deck.

Dexter, scrambling to his feet, opened his mouth to give a cry. He stared straight at me, his mouth gaping before another snap of wood threw him towards the back of the boat into the blackness.

'Dex…' I reached my hand out to try and grab him. There was nothing but air. I felt around for him nearer the floor. There was water. Lots of water. Pools of cold water began swirling around my feet. I scrambled backwards, feet barely touching the wooden floor. 'Dexter,' I called. 'Where are you?'

The water rose fast, hay swirling around on the top of the murkiness. Stacked bales beginning to crash inwards. I backed up the steps and onto the deck. The boat sunk down towards the rear, with only the deck part sticking up out of the water.

I leapt off onto the towpath, rolling over onto the grass. I felt warm blood trickling down my forehead. I scrambled upwards and ran back towards the sunken rear.

'Dexter,' I yelled, looking out onto the water. Nothing but the constant torrent of rain answered me. My heart thudded in my chest; temples pounding around my hairline. I threw myself into the canal, by the sunken end, and fumbled around in the water, reaching for anything solid. My legs were numb, lead weights pulling me down. The rain continued relentlessly. I dragged myself back up onto the sodden bank and lay heaving, my chest tight and burning.

Had I not stepped forward in the boat to reach Dexter or even gone to the boat in the first place, would the outcome be different?

Counting to ten to summon the energy, I rolled over, grabbed my bike, and headed numbly in the rain towards the nearest house with lights.

My mind was blank. Everything was blank.

Dexter was gone.

Chapter Fifty

The rain soaked through her hair, clumping it together in black spirals, before trickling down into her top. Heavy drops pounded at the ground, as they had on the night, one week ago. The night I'll never forget.

I hadn't seen her since.

I hadn't seen anyone since, locked up in my room, pretending the world didn't exist.

'What do you want, Liberty?' I stood in the doorway, reluctant to let her past, to let anyone into the protective bubble I'd created around myself. Tallie understood. With a small nod and a look, she knew it was best to wait until I was ready. She kissed me gently on the doorstep after the police had returned me home, before turning back into the darkness. I'd yet to call her, but I knew I would, and she wouldn't even question why so much time had lapsed. Maybe she should. But she'd wait until the time was right and I'd go to her and apologise.

'Can I come in?' Liberty asked. The drips had spread a wet patch across her white top, highlighting the black bra underneath.

I looked away.

'No,' I replied. I fiddled with my hair, unbrushed and greasy. I couldn't remember the last time I had showered. I'd worn the same grey shorts and old footie T-shirt all week. I rubbed my tired eyes. 'There's nothing to say, is there?'

'There's plenty to say.' Her face was makeup free, scrubbed clean, making her look more like a child than the woman she tried to create. Her nails were unpainted and clipped short. I wondered where her long talons had gone. The illusion of perfection she'd created didn't seem so perfect anymore. 'Please, Rafferty. I need to talk to someone.'

'I don't want to talk about it.'

'But you should. It isn't healthy locking yourself away from the world.'

'How can I go on pretending nothing has happened?'

'I'm not pretending.'

'Didn't say you were,' I replied, crossly. 'I don't know what to say to anyone.'

'We don't blame you.'

I looked up at her, fighting the threatening tears. 'Someone's got to take the blame. It may as well be me. After all, I was there. I could have stopped it all.'

'Can I come in? Please?' her blue eyes, wide and solemn, stared into mine. I stepped aside, and she came out of the rain into the porch.

'You're soaked,' I commented. 'I'll find you something to put on. Come on.' I led her through the house and up the stairs towards my bedroom. I wondered what Dad would have said if he'd known. He'd never allow girls in the bedrooms. Or even friends. But he'd never know.

He's not there anymore.

Chapter Fifty-one

I told Liberty what had happened. From my perspective anyway. She'd already heard all the different versions. Once I started talking, I couldn't stop. It all came out in my quiet monotone voice, whilst I focused on the view out of my bedroom window trying not to cry. Liberty sat in silence, facing away from me, on the other side of the bed.

I pretended she wasn't there as I spoke.

A police car had picked me up from the stone thatched cottage to drive me home. It's amazing what details you remember and others that are completely lost. I can't even remember running up the driveway and screaming; banging on their lounge window until my fists bled. My muddied and bloodied hands smearing down the pane as I slid down to a heap on the gravelled driveway.

The strangers phoned and waited for the police before even opening their door; trying to shut me from their eyes and thoughts with thick curtains.

I sat numbly in the back of the car until we reached my house. Mum led me inside to the lounge and ushered the police officers into the kitchen, away from me. I didn't even notice Dad's absence at that point. She returned to talk to me, patting my knee to get my attention and wrapped a blanket around my wet shoulders. They needed to ask some questions.

Was I ready?

I nodded, but couldn't speak.

'Son?' she asked, turning my face to meet hers. Her eyes, the same shade as mine, brought me back home.

'Dexter?' I said. It was all I could mumble.

'Oh, love.'

'Where is he?'

'They're looking for him,' Mum said, squeezing my shoulders. 'They've found the boat from your descriptions. You're not to worry. You just need to concentrate on telling them what happened. Be honest. Try to remember everything.'

'Okay.'

She waved them in and pointed to the chair by the window. 'I'm going to sit over there, love. I'm here if you need me.' She sat and gave a nod for the officers to sit on the sofa beside me.

Their questions came thick and fast. Tears streamed freely down my face as I answered one after the other for what seemed like hours. I told them everything. Didn't hold back. From the very moment we all met on our paper round, back on that misty April morning to even the BBQ under the stars. A lifetime of memories happened in those few short months. The two officers didn't comment, everything was scratched down with black biros into their notebooks. The man stood up finally and smiled down at me.

'Thank you, Rafferty. We'll be in touch if we have any more questions.'

'Thanks,' I mumbled.

'We'll let ourselves out.'

'And Dexter?'

'As time passes, Rafferty, our concern does grow for his safety. The team are doing the best they can under the conditions down at the canal. Hopefully, we can let you know soon.'

'Is it still raining?' Mum asked, standing up to peer out of the window. Her voice trailed off as she cupped her hands onto the misty pane.

'The officers didn't tell me that the teams they talked about were divers,' I said, relieved the events had been told and Liberty had listened without interruption.

'Yeah, so? They probably needed the divers to go in the water to help. The boat was nearly completely submerged by then,' Liberty replied.

'For recovery, not rescue,' I said. 'Divers are for recovery. I still had hope at that point. Foolish hope. They should have told me they were looking for a body. Dexter was already dead.'

'You don't know that, Rafferty,' said Liberty, turning to face me. She reached out, as if to place a hand on my arm, but changed her mind. 'No one knew what had happened or where he was. Some of the canal banks were only accessible from the water. Dexter could have pulled himself up.'

'Well, he didn't.'

'The officers were there to get answers from you, they didn't know. They wouldn't speculate until they knew for certain.'

'Maybe,' I mumbled.

'Then what happened? Did the police come back to tell you the news?'

'No,' I said. 'Not that evening. I paced about in my room all night waiting, but they didn't come back. Another car arrived in the morning with the news.'

'Were your parents mad at you? All the lying about the horse, the sneaking out, and Dexter?'

'Didn't I say?' I frowned. 'No, I guess not. I haven't seen you…or anyone since then. Dad's left.'

'What? Why?'

'I dunno. I've not really asked. Mum said words were said between them after they'd left Tallie's house, and she asked him to go. She packed up all his stuff and took it outside. I haven't seen him since.'

'Really?' she said, her eyebrows furrowed. 'What about your sister?'

'She's been to see him a few times. He's in a flat in town apparently.'

'I didn't realise your parents weren't getting on. You didn't say anything.'

'I didn't really notice they weren't. Dad was always, well, he was always Dad. That's how he's been forever. I thought Mum liked him like that. Guess not. I never saw eye-to-eye with him anyway.'

'Your poor Mum.'

'Suppose,' I replied. 'She's better off without him. He's an idiot. All he saw were pound signs when he heard about Minty.' I felt bad. I'd not even talked to Mum about him. Wrapped up in my own problems, it hadn't even occurred to me she might be feeling awful, too. I changed the subject.

'What did you do with the box?'

'You knew?' she asked, her face turning crimson.

'Not at first. But then it made sense. You were so smug, but by the time I realised, it didn't matter anyway.'

'I didn't mean to hurt you,' she said. 'I felt rejected. You'd moved on with someone else.'

'But you didn't even want me. I did try. The song amongst other things.'

'I know. Sorry. Stupid, isn't it?'

'I don't understand,' I scrunched my eyes closed.

'I liked 'knowing' you liked me. I didn't want that to change.'

'You liked the attention?' I looked up at her bright eyes, searching for some truth. 'Just the attention and nothing else.'

'I guess so. Sorry,' she sighed and stood up abruptly. 'I've been very selfish, haven't I?'

I shrugged defeated by everything. I'd never given her my updated song. Probably for the best. 'Have you dried off yet?'

'Yeah,' she replied, hugging her arms around my hoodie, which swamped her. 'Thanks. Mind if I keep this on the way home? I'd best get going, told Mum I wouldn't be long.'

'No problem,' I replied. 'Keep it as long as you want.' She followed me back down the stairs to the front door, which I held open for her. She scooted around me.

'Don't be a stranger,' she said, backing down the step onto the drive.

'I know, I know,' I replied. 'Just haven't felt like facing the world yet. Sorry.'

'Have you got many summer plans?' she asked, looking towards the gate and back at me.

'None,' I replied. 'Not anymore.' The summer plans all but shattered that night.

'Will and I were thinking of going back down to the boat tomorrow afternoon. Did you want to come? Tallie, too, if you'd like,' she added.

'The boat?' I frowned and shuddered involuntarily. A wave of nausea flooded over me and goose bumps dotted my arms. Sweaty fingers gripped at the door.

'Yeah. I know the boat has gone, sunk and everything, but we just need to see… and say goodbye. And to Minty, we've lost him, too. It doesn't feel real for both of us until we actually see it again.'

'We're all invited to the memorial thing back at the school for Dexter in September.'

'Yeah, I know,' she said. 'But that's not the same. We weren't friends with him at school. The canal was 'our' place. We understand if you don't. Will wanted me to come and ask you.'

'I could,' I began and gulped. 'I'll check with Mum. It might be good for me to get out. I need to face everything again, I suppose.'

'So, see you there? Around 2?

'Yeah,' I replied. 'I'll be there.'

Chapter Fifty-two

'Night love,' Mum's soft voice called through my door, as she padded past in her slippers on the way to bed.

'Mum?' I called out to her. She opened the door and poked her head around.

'Yes, love?'

'Would it be okay if I went out for a few hours tomorrow afternoon?'

'Of course it would,' she beamed. 'I'm so glad you're beginning to feel better.' She perched on the end of my bed and fiddled with the ends of her dressing gown.

'To the boat?'

Her smile faltered. 'Is that such a good idea, Rafferty? Won't it bring back awful memories of that night? I'm not even sure you'll be allowed. Surely the place is cordoned off?'

'I need to,' I said, looking up into her eyes. 'I need to see it again.'

'Be careful,' she warned. 'I'd hate…' she began. She bit her lip before carrying on, 'I'd hate for you to stumble across something you shouldn't.'

'Don't be silly, Mum,' I shook my head and smiled at her. 'There is nothing to stumble across, the divers searched every inch of our stretch of canal.'

'He's got to be somewhere.'

'Yeah, I know. But, like they said, with the flash flooding that night and the water rising so fast, he could have gone anywhere.'

'They'll find him, Rafferty.'

'I know. They're working on the theory he went down towards the highway.'

'Ah yes, I remember,' she said, patting my leg and nodding. 'The lock gates to stop the water. Something like that wasn't it, Son?'

'Yeah,' I replied. 'They had to open the gates to stop the canal banks flooding. But then a bank broke miles further down and the water rushed out.'

'Flooding the fields,' Mum nodded.

'The police didn't know about Dexter at that point,' I tried to keep my voice even; not to break. 'If they'd known, they could've closed the gates. He wouldn't have gone so far.'

'They didn't know.'

'Would still have been too late to save him.'

'I know, love,' she reached over to hug me. I let myself sink into her, something I hadn't done since as long as I can remember. Probably since Dad arrived on the scene. I shouldn't call him Dad anymore. He was neither a Dad in the biological sense or in the sense of being there for me. I pulled back and looked up at her.

'Are you okay?' I asked her. 'About Dad and everything? I'm sorry I haven't asked.'

'Don't worry about me, Son,' she replied. 'It had been a long time coming between your Dad and me. I'm glad it's finally over. I'm surprised you didn't notice the wretched tension between us all the time.'

'I thought that was about me.'

'No, love. It was never about you. Or Abby.'

'I didn't know life with him was that bad for you. He was always like that towards me, so I presumed he was different with you.'

'We did have good times, love. I just can't remember them anymore. And I wasn't oblivious to how he was with you, Rafferty. I came to realise that night of the storm how much you and Abby mean to me, and he didn't give you the same thought. The final straw, you might say.'

'You shouldn't have ended it on our behalf.'

'I did it for myself. Don't you worry,' she smiled, her eyes bright. 'I always thought I needed a man around to be able to raise you. But I've realised I didn't. I couldn't take the controlling side from him anymore. I'm sure he'll be relieved a decision has finally been made. This was my house, you're my children. I can do this by myself and be happy.'

'I hope so, Mum. I'd like to see you happy.'

She squeezed me tight, 'Thank you, love. Now don't worry about me.'

Chapter Fifty-three

I sat on the canal bank opposite the stile, my toes dipping into the water. I arrived early. I wanted to see the place alone.

Just in case.

Apart from a gentle flap from torn strands of blue and white police tape, there was nothing to indicate what had happened. The horror of the night was impossible to imagine in the still, muggy heat. The boat had long gone. Not a trace remained, apart from scuffs across the down-trodden, sun-bleached grass where we'd stood to pull ourselves on board. The steep bank into the water had scars and tears slashed into the brown earth. They would disappear quickly as the undergrowth spread. It would be like it had never happened. I'm not sure I felt okay about that. How life resumes to normal too easily.

The water was still, barely a flicker across its shimmery brown surface. The meadow behind, stretching up high onto the hill, remained empty. No one had seen Minty since the night of the storm, his hoof tracks down the towpath washed away by the flooding.

As the bikes approached, the wheels churning up the stony path, I kept my eyes focused on the water. The whirring of wheels stopped and I waited before footsteps approached beside me. Will slid down next to me, Liberty the other side. They both peeled off their shoes and socks and dipped their toes in the water, too.

'Hey,' Will said, finally.

'Hey,' I replied.

'You're early,' noted Liberty. 'And you didn't bring Tallie either?'

'No,' I said. 'I needed it to be just us.'

'How have you been?' asked Will.

'I've been better,' I looked up at him and smiled. 'Have you been okay?'

'Yeah. Just about,' he replied. 'Been hard to take it all in.'

'Tell me about it.' I sighed and wiggled my toes, drawing circles in the water with my feet. 'Any news of Minty?'

'Haven't you heard?'

'No,' I replied. Withdrawing myself away from the world had its disadvantages. 'What's happened?'

'They think they've found him,' Liberty said, bitterly. She shook her head as if to wipe away the image.

'Who's found him?' I asked. My heart had sunk at this. I wasn't even close to the horse but it was if another part of us had slipped away.

'Well, when the police knew we probably had the missing racehorse, the owners were told,' said Will. 'They had everyone out looking for him around this area.'

'Ten miles away,' cried Liberty. 'They found him fucking ten miles away in Wales, grazing in some bloody farmer's field.'

'That's a long way,' I frowned. 'Are they sure it's him?'

'I thought the same,' said Will.

'I guess he followed the towpath and then veered off through farmland,' said Liberty. 'Dad knows someone over in the area and he heard about it. Bright bay horse with a star and snip, a dead ringer for Minty. Skittish as anything, apparently, when they approached him.'

I put my head in my hands and the last image of him flashed before me. 'He was terrified,' I said, looking back up at them. 'His eyes were massive and white.'

'He probably galloped all the way in panic,' said Liberty. 'Bolted; he's a racehorse after all.'

'Poor Minty,' I replied. 'At least he's been found, I suppose. But I'm surprised no one told me. The police have been round more than once this week and no one said anything about Minty.'

'It's not in the news yet,' said Will. 'I think they're formally identifying him through DNA, or microchip, or however it's done with horses before they announce he's been found.'

'So there's hope?' I asked.

'No,' said Liberty. 'I very much doubt that. We've got to accept the inevitable. Minty is no longer Minty. They have their racehorse back.'

'Are we in deep shit?' I asked, putting my head into my hands, before correcting myself. 'Am I?'

'I don't think you'll go to prison if that's what you're worried about,' she laughed. 'But don't expect the reward money either. I'm sure they're glad to have the horse back without parting with any money.'

'I think we should get the reward,' mumbled Will, adjusting his glasses. 'All that money.'

'For hiding a horse we knew was missing?' Liberty scoffed. 'Don't be silly. If we'd owned up maybe, but not since we got found out. We didn't voluntarily give him back, did we? I'd never have done that.'

'Nor me,' I agreed.

'Yeah, me as well,' nodded Will, scrambling to his feet and pulling his T-shirt over his head. 'Money isn't everything, is it?' He gave a lopsided grin before launching off the canal bank into the water.

'Going to join him in there?' asked Liberty, stretching back out beside me, before frowning. 'Makes me nervous thinking about the canal water. And what's in there.'

'Me, too,' I replied. 'Dipping my toes in is far as I'm going to do.' I sat awkwardly next to her, not knowing what else to say.

'So is this it then?'

'For what?'

'For everything,' she said. 'For us all meeting here. The friendship.'

'Life moves on,' I shrugged. 'We weren't all that close away from the canal, were we? There's nothing without Minty to keep us all together.'

'We weren't that close?'

'No,' I said. 'You didn't think we were? You made it perfectly clear what you thought about me.'

She frowned, 'I don't understand.'

'All the stuff that happened at school. The way you were with me.'

'I was angry, Raff. It's never okay to imply you had sex with someone when you didn't. It's never okay to do that. How did you think that made me feel?'

'I didn't think.'

'I thought we had something special that night. The night in the tent. I thought finally someone liked me for me, not the image I created for school. But no, all it was to you was an opportunity to brag you'd got laid by Liberty Ashburn.'

'I'm sorry, I didn't say that.'

'You didn't have to. You implied it, didn't you?'

'I didn't even imply it,' I said.

'But you did,' she cried. 'You did. By leaving it open for other people to imply that, that's the same thing. It's just as wrong. You could have squashed the rumours straight away, but you didn't. You let them spread around the school like a fire.'

'I know, I know.'

'I know I'm not perfect. Far from perfect, like taking your bloody box, I don't know why I did that. But having you spread the rumour around school about me, well, it wasn't okay, Raff. It made me feel about this big.' She held up her finger and thumb and narrowed them together. 'I've not even done it with anyone either. And now all of that's put me off. How can I trust anyone now? All boys are jerks.'

'Your punishment made me feel the same.'

'You deserved it.'

'I probably did, yes,' I nodded.

'I wanted you to see how things spread. How a small little rumour, not even that, how even a hint of a rumour can spread around the school. And how the rumour can change and develop. Rafferty Lincoln loves... well, everybody, it seems.'

'It did get ridiculous,' I grinned, pulling back on my socks.

'Yeah it did,' she laughed, wrapping her arms around herself, tucking her knees in, and rocking back and forth. 'Some of them were funny actually.'

''Rafferty Lincoln loves goats' was one of my favourites. Made me choke a little, even though I pretended not to. Most of the others were just unrepeatable.'

'They were,' she agreed.

'Abby asked me what blowjob meant.'

'Shit!' Liberty laughed.

'Yeah,' I said. 'I'm going to leave mum to explain that one. It's what parents are for.'

''Definitely.'

'Remind me to never have kids,' I grinned, winking one eye at her.

Liberty leant over and kissed me gently on my bristly cheek. Her fingers held the back of my neck. I shivered.

'Tallie,' I reminded.

'Yes, yes, I know,' she smiled, her hand dropping away. 'I just wanted you to know she's a lucky lady to have you. That's all. I'm sorry I tried to ruin it.'

I resisted the urge to stroke her soft, serious face. I pulled myself up to my feet and tugged my bike up out of the nettles. 'Will you be okay?'

'I've got Wilbur to keep me grounded. I'll be fine,' she replied.

'See you around college?'

'Maybe,' she smiled. 'Maybe you will.'

Chapter Fifty-four

The news we'd expected and were waiting anxiously for came only a couple of days later. I'd been waiting for this moment. Scanning the news feeds on my phone, waiting for the first mention. Keeping one look out on social media for the first share or like of the local news.

But I didn't find it first.

Mum placed the paper in front of me, tapped the article and patted my back, before leading Abby out of the room to get ready for her swimming lesson. She smiled softly as she went at the hand-picked wildflowers, tucked neatly in a vase, I'd given her from the canal bank.

It was all confirmed.

Minty vanished away with a blink of an eye. He was never really our Minty after all. Profits Red Ridge had been found safe and well in farmland to the west of the village, on the Welsh borders. DNA tests had confirmed his identity. There was no mention of the teenagers that kept him, nothing about the months of his disappearance. Just he'd been found in good health by a local farmer. Reunited with his owners, his training would resume after rehabilitation and recovery. There were concerns he'd never race again after his time away from the racecourse.

I put the paper back down on the table, and let out a sigh. I bit my lip and whistled. The paper rewrote the past as if the horse and Dexter never existed for us.

But they both had; clearly and vividly in my mind.

I reached for my mobile to text Liberty, but stopped myself and returned the phone to the table. She'd find out in her own time. I pushed backwards, my wooden chair scraping the floor as I rose. I went outside to get my bike.

I needed to see Tallie.

It was time to rebuild my life.

Chapter Fifty-five

The last two weeks before college began whisked by in a blur of swimming, walks with Tallie, and some occasional brooding in my bedroom. I threw myself into the task of keeping Abby occupied and her mind off the summer events. She had grown taller over the summer, and I was worried about how withdrawn she'd become.

I'd not seen Liberty or Wilbur since. So when I saw Will cycling down the road towards my house, just as dusk fell, an uneasy feeling spread over me. I watched from behind the curtain as he paused at the end of my drive before he propped up his bike against the fence and walked towards the front door. I counted down the seconds before I heard Mum's voice.

'Rafferty!' she yelled up the stairs.

'Yes, Mum?' I yelled back. I wanted to draw out the moment as long as possible. Unwilling to find out why he'd decided to approach the house.

'Visitor!'

I edged myself down the stairs towards Will, who fidgeted nervously in the doorway.

'Can I have a word, Raff?' he asked.

'Yeah, go on,' I sighed, waiting for whatever news he had that made my stomach flip and churn.

'Er,' he glanced up at my mum. 'In private if that's okay?'

'Mind if I go out?' I asked Mum. 'I won't be long.'

'Hmmm,' she pondered. 'Just don't be late, it's almost dark and your bike lights need fixing, don't they?'

'Yes, Mum.' I gave her a quick peck on the cheek before following Will out. I grabbed my bike and we walked side by side down the road.

'Raff,' he started. His hands shook and he twitched nervously. 'You won't believe it.'

'What?' I asked.

'He's back!' Will's eyes shone and he turned to stop me. 'He's back, Raff.'

'Who?' I asked, and for a brief moment Dexter slipped into my mind and crushed my heart all over again.

'Minty!' he cried. 'The horse is back, I tell you. He's back. Just grazing calmly alongside the canal on the towpath.'

'I don't understand,' I said. I frowned, unable to comprehend what he was saying.

'He's back!'

'How?' I asked. 'That's not possible. They've found him.'

'He's back,' repeated Will.

'Yeah, you've said, but honestly, Will, it's not possible. It's got to be some other horse or you're seeing things.'

'I'll show you,' he said and mounted his bike. 'Come on.'

'It's late, Will,' I frowned. 'Shouldn't you get home?'

'No, you've got to see him.'

Shaking my head, I followed him down the roads to the village edge, where we turned off down the narrow lanes towards the canal. It wasn't possible. By now Minty, aka Profits Red Ridge, was hundreds of miles away back at the stables where he came from. They'd proved it was him.

We rose up over the bridge and turned off down the towpath.

And there he was.

Grazing quietly next to the stile, as Will had said.

I blinked. Once. Twice. No, he was still there. Scrambling around in my jacket pocket, I retrieved a furry mint stuck to the bottom. I held it out and the horse lipped it gently with his hairy muzzle. I ran my hand down his neck, and he snorted, before trying to nip my leg.

'He's back,' I said.

'Told you.'

'I don't see how this is possible, but he's back.'

'Do we tell the police?'

I looked at Will and frowned. 'No. Let's wait it out. If the racehorse has disappeared again they'll be back around here before you know it. If he's really missing, we'll have to own up this time.'

'Maybe he was never that racehorse.'

'Where's he been for the last three weeks? I don't know anymore,' I scratched my head. 'Come on, let's walk him round the towpath and put him back in his field before the light goes.'

'Shall I tell Liberty?'

'Yes, you'd better,' I told him. 'I'm going to tell Tallie as well, I've had enough of secrets.'

'Just them though?' he asked.

'Just them,' I agreed.

And so it began.

After we had watched him trot off back into his field, we turned back in the dark and cycled carefully down the towpath towards home.

'I wish Dexter were here,' Will said.

'Yeah,' I agreed. 'Minty loved him most of all. If only he could waltz back here like Minty did. Appear on the towpath one day.'

'But he can't.'

'I know,' I shrugged, sadly. 'I know he's gone. It just leaves me with hope. If Minty can come back to us, maybe he can. Miracles can sometimes happen.'

Will looked over and smiled, 'You bet, Raff. You bet.'

279

Epilogue

Dear my friend, Dexter,

We let you down; we *all* let you down.

Every single one of us.

From the kids at school that turned the other way when they heard your whimpering pleas, to the bullies in the canteen pounding you until your nose split and bled red splashes all over the porcelain white tiles. The older kids cornering you after school, taking turns to practise their punch bag skills, and the friends that didn't dare to ask each time you had a new shiny black eye or purple mottled bruise. The classmates egging others on to hurt you and the kids joining in with the chants; its all a laugh right? The kids videoing the carnage on their phones and the others sharing and liking it online. Even the quiet kids in the corner stifling a snigger at the vicious, undeserved taunts you received. The teachers tutting when the class was disturbed — yet again — by the laughter at you, and the welfare officers rolling their eyes when you were brought in for another fight. There's nowhere to hide for us all.

We all let you down.

The system let you down. The one that was meant to protect you and keep you away from those that were hurting you the most, your parents. The people *you* loved with your whole being and were meant to protect you out of everybody. It breaks my heart to hear how they treated you and how you continued to defend them despite this. They let you down, Dexter, in the most horrific way. You became so lost in the system, you were unable to be protected. You couldn't even protect yourself. Going back time and time again to those you loved but who didn't love you back the way they should. You didn't know any better, why would you?

We are all to blame for this.

Everybody has excuses, reasons why they act like they did. Reasons why they turned away or didn't react when you were bleeding and sobbing on the cold school floor. Reasons why they joined in with the kicking and then went home trying to justify their actions to themselves. Beating themselves up at their own cruel deeds; continuing nonetheless at school, their conscience overruled.

Yes, children are incredibly brutal creatures. Thoughtless and careless with how they treat others. The bullies all have their own stories as to why they do what they do, but you, Dexter, you always remained yourself until the end. Despite the beatings, the bloodied face and broken bones, you never flinched, never retaliated or made excuses to use your own experiences to hurt others. You were better than that, Dexter.

And for that I admire you.

Maybe you should have stood up for yourself, I don't know. It might have made a difference at school. Others may have left you alone.

Respected you.

But that would have done you a disservice. You were yourself until the end. I only wish we, your friends, could have done that for you. Have fought for you. But we didn't, and we didn't even think to. Most shockingly of all, it didn't even cross our narrow, self-centred minds. I'm so sorry. They say teenagers are selfish creatures, I think we are worse. I can't describe how I feel about myself at the moment.

I let you down, Dexter. And for this, I apologise the most. I knew all along, from the moment I saw the dirty clothes and cutlery hidden in the depths of the boat, there was more to you than meets the eye. I guess I was wrapped up in my own troubles, unable to see or comprehend what was in front of me. Too wrapped up in my own pathetic romantic mess to care about what was happening with you. To care that you were all alone. Living alone, hungry and frightened on a boat, with only the horse as your friend. No wonder you clung so tightly to Minty, the horse that started all of this and brought us together.

He was all you had.

I don't ask for forgiveness. I expect none. We don't deserve your forgiveness. I hope from this lessons can be learnt.

It's all too late for lessons though, isn't it?

Over the last few months, I came to know you, not just as Dexter, the slightly odd, slightly smelly, quirky kid from school, but as Dexter, the incredibly funny, intelligent, loyal and kind kid that had an extraordinary way with horses. Words cannot express how I feel now about what happened. My mind is churning with 'what ifs'. I guess I will live with that legacy forever. But at least I live, whereas you do not, and for that, I am truly, truly devastated.

Life moves on. It already has. People are beginning to forget. The bullies have hidden their shame, pushed it back to the depths of their subconscious. Other kids are beginning to suffer the way you suffered. Wilbur sees it again at school. There are other Dexters out there. But the laughter isn't as loud. The punches aren't as hard. Frowns are deeper, mutters and sniggers quieter. The shares and likes on social media silenced. Phones put back into the depths of pockets, refusing to video the inhumanity. The kids are rattled. The seed in their mind has been sown.

It isn't right.

They are beginning to question, to stand up for their morals. And for this I am glad. Thankful.

There is a hope from all of this.

I will leave this letter to you on the memorial, engraved with your name, which I know you don't yet inhabit. Free as always, Dexter; as you should be.

Rest easy, my dear friend, Dexter Forrest. For I am, deservedly, not going to rest very well ever again.

I am your friend always,
Rafferty Lincoln

The End

There is no secret so close as that between a rider and his horse.
— Robert Smith Surtees, 1853

For you — by Rafferty Lincoln

For you, for you
This song I wrote for
you
The moment I saw you
My heart soared and
flew
The subtle art of hoping
For the art of loving
you
Our hearts and hands
entwine
And lovers' eyes subdue

For you, for you
This song I wrote for
you
Will you catch me
when I fall
Headlong into you?
The subtle art of hoping
For the art of loving
you
Our hearts and hands
entwine
And lovers' eyes subdue

For you, for you
This song I wrote for
you
The look that you gave
me
I knew my love taboo
The subtle art of hoping

For the art of loving
you
Our hearts and hands
entwine
And lovers' eyes subdue

For you, for you
This song I wrote for
you
I saw in your
perfection
An imperfection, too
The subtle art of hoping
For the art of loving
you
Our hearts and hands
entwine
And lovers' eyes subdue

For you, for you
This song I wrote for
you
My misguided love
withdrew
As my heart broke
loving you
The subtle art of hoping
For the art of loving
you
Our hearts and hands
entwine
And lovers' eyes subdue

Acknowledgements

This novel wouldn't have been possible without the support of friends and family during the writing process of my first novel *Letters to Eloise*. The support gave me such courage and inspiration to carry on writing. I am very grateful for the encouragement that the same people have given during the creation of this novel, Rafferty Lincoln loves....

Special mentions to Meggan for her help in turning my scribbles into a coherent and fantastic newspaper article. Thanks to Pip, Meggan, Daisy and Hayley for their valuable advice on the plot and character development. I took on board all the amazing advice given. A huge thank you to the fantastic Kristin @theedifyingword for her tireless efforts proofreading the novel.

Thank you to my friend Hanna for her advice and knowledge on the policing and social work aspects. A special mention to beautiful Bella, my American Quarter Horse, for allowing me to nab her 'proper' name Profits Red Ridge, and her grumpy personality, for the character of Minty.

Thank you to my fantastic readers for all your support. I love hearing your views on my stories so please leave a review on Amazon UK to let me know what you think.

Lastly a huge thank you to my lovely partner James and our two (soon to be three!) gorgeous, but mischievous, children. Without all your patience and endless support, this novel wouldn't have been possible.

27619953R00167

Printed in Great Britain
by Amazon